ANN —

STAY WARM

SPRING IS ON THE WAY . . .

ALL THE BEST —

ANDREW

# ALL LIES

Andrew Cunningham

ISBN-13: 978-1507801666
ISBN-10: 1507801661

Also author of

*Wisdom Spring*
*Eden Rising*
*Eden Lost*

Children's Mysteries
(as A.R. Cunningham)

*The Mysterious Stranger*
*The Ghost Car*
*The Creeping Sludge*
*Prisoner in the Sky*
*The Ride of Doom*

## ACKNOWLEDGMENTS

I couldn't do any of these books without the constant love and support from my wife, Charlotte. Thank you! Thank you as well, to my mother for her encouragement and enthusiasm after reading the early drafts of **All Lies**.

To my father, from whom I inherited my love of mysteries.

# Prologue

"I come from a long line of idiots..."

Those were his last words. I was tempted to have them inscribed on his headstone, because, in fact, he wasn't wrong. My family did have an abnormally high incidence of stupidity running through its genes. As far back as I could determine, my ancestors—the men, to be specific—were known for their questionable actions, actions that usually left them dead.

That worried me of course, as I was the next in line. An idiot-in-waiting, I suppose.

I would love to know what the rest of that sentence was going to be. Maybe "I come from a long line of idiots ... but thank God you're normal," or "... and it's up to you, son, to change the pattern." Sadly, it was probably more along the lines of "... and the future doesn't look any brighter."

It wasn't a lack of intelligence by any means. As far as I know, my ancestors all had the normal allotment of brains. There was a politician, a scientist, and even a minister mixed in somewhere down the line. My recently deceased father had been a university professor.

No, it had nothing to do with intelligence. Sometimes it was simply a wrong-place, wrong-time issue. More often though, it was a case of being confronted with an either/or decision and always making the wrong choice, usually out of greed.

Early examples of my boneheaded ancestors—all on my father's side of the family—included a relative in the mid-1800s in England who made a bet that he could sneak into Windsor Castle and meet Queen Victoria. Two things went wrong: 1) The queen wasn't there; and 2) Having accomplished the unlikely feat of scaling one of the castle walls, he tripped on some steps, fell, and landed on his head. He died a few hours later. I doubt if you will find any official mention of the incident in Windsor Castle logs of the time. Too humorous for the log books.

Another example was a relative in the British Army during the Zulu uprising in South Africa in 1879. He somehow got it into his head that he could make some money sneaking away from camp at night with rifles that he would sell to mercenaries who traded with the Zulus. That venture lasted one night. The Zulus got their rifles. He was never seen again.

Among the more recent examples was my great-grandfather, who lived in New York in the 1920s and '30s. Rumor had it that he worked for some local low-life mobster making deliveries of illegal booze, then went to South America for a while before getting kicked out. Who gets kicked out of a continent? Anyway, he somehow managed to survive those activities, despite some close calls with the police. However, in early 1935, some barrels came loose during a delivery and my great-grandfather was crushed to death. Ironically, since Prohibition had many ended months before, what had once been a dangerous smuggling operation had now become a legitimate and safe delivery job. Timing.

His son, my grandfather, was a bombardier on a B-24 during World War II. During a mission over Germany, a bomb came loose in the bomb bay, so he went to check on it. The story was that the navigator went with him. He turned his head for just a moment and my grandfather was gone. Nobody knows exactly what happened—a wrong step, a slip—but the bomb bay doors opened and my grandfather and the loose bomb became part of the German landscape.

And then there was my father. A still-desirable man of seventy when he died, he had risen through the ranks of academia to become the head of the history department at a small, prestigious college. Being handsome and influential, my father was inundated with female students (and I would imagine some males, as well) offering sex for passing grades. Once again a member of my family was faced with a decision. Once again the wrong choice was made. My mother caught wind of it many years ago and left with me—their only child—in tow. We didn't leave town though, and I was able to see my father on a semi-regular basis. In his later years he wasn't slowing down any and seemed to be leading a good life, despite his sleazy behavior. That is, until he compounded his bad decision with an even worse one. One of the students he slept with was married. Her outraged husband put three bullets into my father in the parking lot of the college as he was getting into his car.

He lasted a few days, drifting in and out of consciousness,

before finally succumbing. But not before reminding me that I came from a long-standing tradition of fine decision-making.

And it was altogether possible that I had just joined its hallowed ranks.

# Chapter 1

She wasn't my first online dating match, but she was certainly the strangest. And it wasn't like I hadn't had some weird ones. There was the exhibitionist. She could have been a lot of fun, but when she whipped off her shirt in the seats behind home plate at Fenway Park for everyone viewing the game on TV to see (with me sitting next to her), I decided that she might be a little over the top. Then there was the Voodoo priestess. Well, not really a priestess, but she *was* into Voodoo dolls and made sure to mention that she had a doll for each guy who dumped her. I called it quits after the first date, and then tried to convince myself that having to see my chiropractor three times a week for the next two months was simply a coincidence.

This one wasn't overtly odd. She just left me unsettled. She seemed to know things about me. She asked the "right" questions, almost as if she was searching for something. It was like she had part of a story and was trying to complete the picture—which, as I came to find out, was exactly the case. What made her different from the rest of my online disasters was that I couldn't just chalk her up to a "well, that was weird" kind of experience. No, this woman actually changed the course of my life. Because of her, I discovered that everything I thought I knew about my family was wrong. There was a whole history I was unaware of. And at times I wished it had stayed that way, because the multitude of sins of my ancestors had come home to roost—right on my shoulders.

*****

I suppose when you reach your late-thirties and you haven't been married, you start to panic a bit. After all, guys have biological clocks too. I wasn't into the bar scene and I had one of those jobs that didn't put me into contact with a lot of new people. I wasn't religious, so church get-togethers were completely foreign to me. Everyone always wants to give advice to single people. Usually it is some form of "You've got to get out more. Go to shows, or art exhibits. Meet people." Those comments are usually made by people already entrenched in a relationship. But in reality, it's just not that easy, and once you come to the conclusion that none of your friends are going to introduce you to someone, you begin to evaluate your options. Which usually leads to online dating.

There is nothing intrinsically wrong with online dating sites. You hear about the occasional tragedies, but those occurred from the old-style newspaper personal ads as well. If someone is sick, they will use whatever means are at their disposal. You also hear about the success stories of online dating, although not as much. They're not as newsworthy, so they usually show up in the ads for the site. But for most people online dating is just an endless series of unfulfilling matches. Always hopeful, they switch from one site to another, but the result is the same. Occasionally they will get tired and decide to give it up, and then another site will come along offering a new unique approach, guaranteed to help them find their soul-mate. The "three months for the price of one" deal is the clincher, and the cycle begins anew.

For me, it was *Wottacatch.com*. I had tried all of the sites that ask you a million questions and then email you someone "exactly" suited to you. *Wottacatch.com* was different. It was a throwback to the first dating sites, the ones that just showed your picture with some self-composed asinine bio that you considered funny or sexy, but really wasn't. I didn't want a computer making the match for me. I liked looking at all the pictures and imagining myself with some of the women. On the other hand, being a little balding—and self-conscious about it—made me question whether I wanted my picture out there for all to see. Other than my hair shortage though, I really wasn't all that bad looking: almost six feet tall and not overweight—not that I would be a poster boy for a gym ad though. My only distinguishing characteristic, I suppose, was a slightly crooked nose, the result of being on the wrong side of a door that was flung open when the lunch bell rang one day during high school. Part of my family tradition of being in the wrong place at the wrong time.

I know now that Izzy finding me wasn't an accident, but that was the impression she had to put out. She never wanted me to suspect that there was an ulterior motive. How she knew that I'd be on *Wottacatch.com* is beyond me. But I guess when you are a stalker, you have your ways. She wasn't really a stalker in the traditional sense though, because she had a very real reason for finding me. She thought I had answers. I had none.

Izzy—short for Isobel—contacted me through my mailbox on *Wottacatch.com*. I hadn't run across her in my searches, but that was because I limited my search for matches to within 50 miles of my apartment in Boston. Izzy was from Chicago. I'd had women contact me from afar before, but I always ignored those messages. I figured that someone making contact from hundreds or thousands of miles away was either really desperate or a little "off" in the head. Izzy's message, however, seemed logical. She was moving to Boston and would be in town scouting for apartments. She saw my profile and liked what she saw. What man is able to say no to that? We had a little correspondence after her initial contact, a few emails back and forth, and agreed to meet at Au Bon Pain in Copley Place on a Saturday.

I can't say that there was anything in our initial correspondence that took my breath away. Even the small picture in her profile didn't exactly wow me. She was not unattractive in any sense, just not my type. She had the sharp features of someone who had led a hard life. She looked to be a smoker, although her profile listed her as a non-smoker. She was a couple of years older than me—not a deal-breaker. I was willing to give it a try. If we clicked over croissant sandwiches, then we could make a more substantial date. It had to be Saturday or Sunday for me, as my job was very unforgiving when it came to taking time off during the week.

I was the customer service manager for a mail-order house based in Boston. The job was even less sexy than the title indicated. I worked an average of ten hours a day, Monday through Friday. Twelve hours wasn't out of the question. And I was on salary, so overtime pay was not an option. While I supposedly had an hour for lunch, that was a joke. Combine long hours with low pay and you get a pretty disgruntled worker. Depressed is more the word. I really had no time to job hunt, and even if I could find the time to scour career sites online, when would I interview? I couldn't quit and I couldn't look for a job. Basically, I was stuck, and they knew it. Perfect for them.

I arrived at Copley Place a few minutes early, but she was already waiting. We recognized each other from the pictures and introduced ourselves, giving the obligatory, but awkward initial hug of online acquaintances meeting for the first time. I had already pegged this as a one-time meet, and then we would both drift back into cyberspace to try someone else.

As we hugged, I caught a whiff of old cigarette smoke. Her first lie.

"Nice to finally meet you, Izzy," I said, not really knowing what else to say. I wasn't so sure that was even the truth.

"And nice to meet you, Del." We sat at the small table. I predicted five minutes of small-talk before going up to order. "I've already told you that Izzy is short for Isobel," she began. "What's Del short for?"

The part I hated. "Try Delmore."

She seemed to be trying hard not to laugh. It was all an act though. Little did I know at the time that she already knew my full name.

"Delmore Honeycutt. I have no idea how drunk my parents were when they named me. So how is the apartment hunting coming?"

"I just got into town last night, so I really haven't had a chance to look yet," she answered. "Boston sure is a confusing town, though."

"That it is. But you get used to it. Once you learn the 'T'—that's the subway—you're golden. Doesn't take long."

The five-minute mark had arrived.

"Should we go up and order something?" I asked.

We left our jackets on our seats and went up to place our orders. I let her go ahead of me—part politeness, partly so I could observe her more closely. I can't speak for the women who do online dating, but I think I have men like me pretty well pegged. No matter what we say in our online profiles, no matter how romantic we sound, it really all comes down to sex. Granted, most of us would give anything to be in a meaningful relationship, but the reality is that we can't wait to see our date naked. Maybe it's because we know that the likelihood of anything long-term resulting from online dating is slim at best, so we are willing to settle for a good roll in the sack. As such, our standards are pretty low. Sad, I know, but the truth.

And that's why this one was so confusing. She wasn't all that bad looking—nice body, and shoulder-length hazel hair that hadn't seen coloring too many times. I could even get beyond the hard facial features. With someone else, I could have probably put up with the hint of cigarette smoke. But the fact was, I had absolutely no interest in going to bed with her.

We sat back down at the table. I had a turkey and cheese on a croissant, and she had chosen some kind of tropical salad.

"So tell me about yourself," I said.

"Well, you know some of it already from my profile," she answered in between bites. "I'm an RN. I grew up in Chicago, went to school there, and was working at a hospital in the city. I was tired of it and needed a change. I applied to hospitals in different parts of the country, was made a few offers, and settled on Mass General here in Boston. My parents are deceased and I have a sister I haven't spoken to in almost ten years who lives in New York, I think. I had nothing to hold me back, so I figured, what the heck. What about you?"

One of the shorter life histories I had heard—by a good hour. I hadn't even made it halfway through my sandwich. So I started on my story—growing up in a small town in western Mass, no brothers or sisters, the sad demise of my father, and the fact that my mother still lived out there and whom I visited on a regular basis.

And this is where it took the weird turn. I started to talk about my hellish job, but I could see she wasn't paying attention. Granted, my job was boring, but I didn't usually lose them quite that fast. She interrupted me as I took a breath.

"No grandparents?" she asked.

"Uh, no. They'd be about a hundred years old now, at least."

"Tell me about them."

"Okay," I said slowly. I told her what I could remember about my mother's parents, which wasn't much. They weren't very interesting people. But that's not what she was waiting for.

"And your father's parents?"

"My grandmother died right after I was born. I don't really know much about her. My grandfather was a little more interesting." So I told her the story of him falling out of the plane.

"Wow, that's fascinating," she said, showing more enthusiasm than the story deserved. "What did your father say about him?

"Not much. He was less than two when his father died."

"Was he left any of your grandfather's personal effects or mementos?"

"I don't know. Maybe. I haven't gone through my father's stuff. I haven't cleaned out his house yet." Was she trying to decide if I was worth robbing? "Why are you so curious about my grandfather?"

She backed off a bit. "I guess because my grandparents all came from small Midwestern towns and never did anything with their lives. To be a flyer during World War II must have been exhilarating."

"Not so much for my grandfather, I would think."

"True. But haven't you ever been curious about him? Wasn't your father?"

"Not really. And if my father was, he never mentioned it. You have to understand, he never knew his father, so there was no one other than his mother to ask questions of. I'm sure she told him some things, but if you don't have the connection yourself, there's only so far you can go."

"But you have to know something. Everybody knows things about their grandparents. Think! There has to be something." She was becoming agitated. When I didn't respond, she calmed down.

"Sorry," she said. "It's just that family history is important to me. I think everyone should research their roots. What was your grandfather like as a kid? What were his parents like. What was it like living in New York at that time?"

She had slipped. I never said anything about where my family was from. I only ever mentioned Boston and western Mass. New York never came up. I decided not to call her on it.

I don't know if she knew she had slipped or whether she was just acknowledging to herself that I was a dead-end street, but the energy immediately went out of the conversation. I tried to make some suggestions about her apartment hunting, but she brushed them off. She said she had to go—she had an appointment to see a place—and she was gone. It was the shortest date in recorded history—forty-five minutes at best, and ten of those were spent waiting for our food.

Despite the disturbing feeling that she knew a lot more than she was telling me, I would have eventually blown it off and forgotten about it, except that the police showed up at my door early the next morning asking me if I knew an Isobel Worth. Her body had been recovered a few hours earlier.

She had been murdered.

# Chapter 2

In the movies, when the hero is questioned by the police, he always holds something back. Not me. Maybe that's why I never considered myself a hero. Nope, I spilled my guts. I would have given them my mother's secret recipe for carrot cake if they'd asked. Maybe it's because the police are a lot more intimidating in person than they are in the movies. They were polite, but I also knew that until I could prove otherwise, I was their primary suspect.

I buzzed them up to my apartment and offered them the couch. They preferred to stand. After they established that I was, in fact, Delmore Honeycutt, and explained why they were there, they started right in with the questions. I was nervous, but hopefully they were used to that and didn't think it suggested guilt on my part.

"How did you know Isobel Worth?"

"Well, until right now, I never knew her last name. We met on an online dating site initially and met in person for the first time yesterday at Au Bon Pain in Copley Place, but it was for less than an hour."

"Why so short?"

"Frankly, she was kind of weird." So I told them the whole story of her prying me for information about my grandfather, then becoming agitated and leaving. "I figured it would be the last I would ever see of her." I realized what I had just said and flushed. "I … I guess I was right. How was she murdered?"

"She was stabbed in an alley. Whoever did it made no attempt to make it look like a robbery. She still had her wallet. So why do you think she was so interested in your grandfather?"

"I have absolutely no idea. He died soon after my father was born. I can't say I've ever really given him any thought. He was just kind of a footnote in our family history. But she was definitely looking for some information. To be honest, I think she actually knew more about my grandfather than I did and was hoping I could fill in the blanks."

"The blanks for what?"

"Beats me."

"So what did you do after your meeting?"

"I finished my sandwich—that's how little time we were together—picked up a few things at Whole Foods, then went home. I just hung out for the rest of the day."

Then it finally dawned on me to ask the question. "How did you know that I knew her?"

"In her pocket was a paper with your name, address, phone number and email address. It also listed a one o'clock lunch with you."

"Wait a minute. It had my address and everything?"

The cop nodded.

"Did it have my full name?"

"It did."

"Then this is really weird."

"Why is that?"

"Because one of the first things she asked me was what Del was short for. Why would she ask me that if she already knew?" Then something else popped into my head. "Was she even from Chicago?"

"Was that what she told you?"

"Yeah. She was from Chicago, but was moving to Boston for a nursing job at Mass General."

"Her license gives an address in New York, but she did have a boarding pass from a plane originating in Chicago." He wrote something down. "We can check on the Mass General job."

My head was swimming and the interrogation ended soon after that. I think they realized I was harmless. They told me that someone else might be around to ask me questions, but for now they were done.

I tried to calm down, with little success. I thought about giving my mother a call, but wasn't really sure what I would say. I usually refrained from mentioning my father to her. I wandered aimlessly through my apartment for the next hour, and must have opened the fridge a half dozen times looking for who-knows-what. I had absolutely no idea what was going on and what to do. That dilemma was solved when my phone rang. It was the alarm company that serviced my father's house. I had kept the alarm in place until I had time to do something about the house. They told me that the burglar alarm had gone off and they had dispatched the police to the scene. I told them that I would get in my car now, but that I wouldn't be there for close to two hours, and asked them to give the police my number.

I grabbed my wallet, keys, and jacket, and headed out the door. If it turned out to be a break-in, it wasn't random. I knew it had something to do with Izzy. What the hell was going on here? Was it really related somehow to my grandfather? The man had been dead for seventy years. We were a couple of generations past that. What could possibly have come to light now? What did Izzy know that I didn't?

Being a Sunday, the traffic was light in the city, and I made good time getting to the Mass Pike. Usually I took Route 2 when I went to visit my mother—and previously my father—in Northampton. It was a more scenic route. But today speed was on my mind, and Route 2 was going to be a slow road. It was a sunny day in the middle of Columbus Day weekend, and the traffic would be crawling with all the leaf-peepers on the road. The colors were spectacular this year—not always the case—and people were feeling the oncoming winter. The perfect conditions for clogged back roads in New England.

The Northampton police called soon after I got on the highway to let me know that, in fact, someone had tried to break in, but was scared off by the piercing scream of the alarm. The police had done a quick walk-through to determine that the house was empty, and had stationed a car outside. When I arrived, an officer would go in with me and we could determine if anything was missing.

I felt totally unprepared for this. The truth was, I was 38 years old, but had never really lived. I had no passions—well, other than baseball, which can be a pretty solitary interest. I'd always been one of those invisible people. If I was a character in a movie, I'd be the first one eaten by the shark. I had worked at my current job for ten years and was good at my work. I handled the customers well and, as far as I could determine, my staff all liked me. I possessed a decent amount of common sense and problem-solving skills—a necessity of my job. But somehow, being confronted with this problem had left me feeling extremely inadequate.

Maybe it was time to search through my father's things and see if there was a clue to what this was about. I didn't even know if he had any of my grandfather's belongings. Where would I start?

I got to my father's house in record time and introduced myself to the officer, who escorted me through the rooms. I never ceased to be amazed at how sparse his home was. The image of college professors is one of clutter—piles of books and papers untouched for years—absent-minded scholars more interested in theory than real life. My father was the opposite. Not a thing out of place in the entire house. That often baffled me when I was younger, but he once told me that when he reached a certain stature in his job, he no longer brought work home with him, unless, of course, you count his grade-related trysts.

I could tell pretty quickly that nothing had been touched, so I thanked the officer for waiting around, and then called a friend from childhood who still lived in the area and was a carpenter. I could tell he wasn't happy about it, but he agreed to come over a bit later in the afternoon and fix the broken back door.

Now what? I wasn't overly close to my father, but I still felt his loss as I wandered through the house. Lack of closeness didn't mean lack of love. We had established our relationship and were comfortable with it.

I knew that I was going to have to clean out the house at some point and put it on the market, but I wasn't looking forward to it. It had nothing to do with sentiment. More like inertia. The house was paid for and selling it would bring me in a few hundred thousand dollars. With no siblings to share it with, I'd be in pretty good shape financially. I would offer to share it with my mother, but I knew she would turn me down. She wanted nothing to do with him even in death. Besides, shrewd investing of the alimony payments over the years had left her quite comfortable. I'd get to the cleaning out stage at some point.

In the meantime, I had a mission. I climbed the steps to the attic. As expected, it was immaculate. There were plenty of boxes, but each was clearly labeled, so I started my search. Clearly labeled or not, not one box had anything written on it that referred to my grandfather. My friend Steve showed up as I was finishing my search, and I set him to work on the back door. I went back up to the attic, took another quick look around and almost called it quits.

As I was about to head back downstairs, a thought entered my brain. What child doesn't have some remembrance of his parents? Some memento of his childhood? There had to be something there. So I set to work opening each box and pawing through it.

I was a third of the way through when Steve called from the bottom of the stairs. He had finished the job. I thanked him profusely and told him to make sure he added the weekend premium to the bill when he sent it to me. I had no doubt he would.

I went back to my boxes. I looked at my watch and saw that it was already three o'clock, so I called my mother and told her I would stop by for dinner. I just explained that I was going through some of dad's things. It was the truth. I just failed to tell her why.

I got back to work, and an hour later hit pay dirt. It was in a box labeled "old dishes," and there were, in fact, some dishes on top. I almost put it aside, then decided to give it a second look. Underneath three dishes was a rectangular package sealed in cardboard, with yellowed tape around the edges. It was so tightly sealed, despite its age, I decided not to open it right then. The real reason was that it had started to get dark and I was beginning to get a little spooked. All of a sudden I wanted to get out of there.

Remembering, however, that someone had tried to break in, maybe looking for this very package, I decided that they might also be watching the house. So I packed a few volumes of an old encyclopedia set under the top plates and brought the box downstairs. I left the house carrying the box labeled "Old Dishes." Between the box and my stomach though, was the taped package, with my jacket thrown over my arms, concealing the package.

To an observer, I was just carrying a box to my car. Once in the car, I set the box on top of the passenger seat and surreptitiously wedged the taped package under my seat. It was unseen and not easily pulled out. While I was at my mother's, if they chose to break into my car, the alarm would go off, scaring them. They would grab the box on the seat and take off. In some ways I wish I hadn't told my mother I was coming for dinner. On the other hand, I had a certain curiosity about the break-in at the house. Was it related to Izzy? If they tried to burglarize my car I would have my answer. I could live with a broken window to find out. I would have liked to have taken the book into the house with me, but if anyone was watching, it would be obvious that I was carrying something. No, I was taking a chance leaving it in the car, but I was pretty sure it was safe wedged under the seat.

This was all new territory for me, but there was something exciting about it. I had never been in danger before. Maybe I wasn't now, but it felt like it. The thought of going back in to my boring job the next day—yes, it was a holiday, just not for me—was suddenly distasteful.

I pulled up to my mother's house and she came out to meet me. My mother was a good-looking woman of sixty-eight. Full of energy, she devoted herself full-time to numerous charities as a volunteer. She always had a great outlook on life, and I could count on her to cheer me up when I was down.

"So what made you suddenly decide to go through your father's things?" she asked without a preamble and giving me a hug.

"Oh, have I got a story for you," I answered.

"Well, come inside," she said. "I made chicken." She stopped and looked at me. "Something's different," she said. She studied my face. "You're excited about something. You're never excited about anything. I like it. It's a good look for you." She smiled and took my arm as we went into the house.

Over dinner I told her the story, leaving nothing out.

"That's dreadful about the woman," she finally said.

"So did dad ever say anything about his father?"

"Not anything that you don't already know. And I can't believe he knew some secret about him that he didn't tell anyone."

As expected, my car alarm started screeching. I jumped up from the table and ran to the door.

"Be careful, Del. You don't know what these people are

capable of."

Actually, I did. But I wasn't listening. I ran out the door in time to see a man in a hooded sweatshirt jump into the passenger side of a late model pickup carrying the box from the front seat.

I flicked the alarm off from my key fob and approached the car. The passenger window was broken, as I figured it would be. I opened the door and pretended to brush away glass, quickly checking under the driver's seat. The package was still there.

It was real. My life and Izzy's life—and death—were intertwined. There was a deep dark secret in my family's past, and I wanted to find out what it was.

# Chapter 3

My mother suggested that I open the package with her, but as curious as I knew she was, I wanted to get it far away from her. It had probably been a mistake to involve my mother at all. She wasn't scared, but I could tell that she understood my reasons for heading home.

While I duct-taped some plastic over my broken window, she put together the leftovers for me, as she always did—even though I ate quite well, it was never good enough for her—and I hastily kissed her goodbye and was on my way home.

Again, I decided to take the Mass Pike, this time for safety sake. There were portions of Route 2 that could be a bit lonely, whereas the Mass Pike was a major highway with almost no chance that "they," whoever they were, could get to me. Once I got home it was going to be a different story. I lived in East Boston, not the safest place in the world to begin with. If Izzy knew where I lived, chances were that they did too. Would they be waiting for me?

The drive was uneventful, but I pulled up in front of my house warily scouting the street around me. Satisfied that I could safely make it to the front door, I grabbed the package from under my seat and the bag of food, locked my car—not that it would do much good with a missing window—opened my front door, and stepped into the safety of my house.

I lived on the third floor of an old triple-decker, in a neighborhood that seemed to be slowly getting its act together. Surveys indicated that crime had been declining there for a couple of years. All well and good, but if I was being targeted specifically, I think that fell outside the parameters of any surveys. I decided that I should warn my neighbors not to blindly buzz anyone in. Not that I had to worry. For completely different reasons, neither one of them would be likely to do so.

Mo—short for Molly—lived in the first floor apartment. I wasn't concerned about her. A radical lesbian in her mid-thirties, she was a third– or fourth-degree black belt something-or-other—in some martial art I had never heard of—who worked out constantly and could probably snap me in half in a millisecond. Rumor had it that she had suffered some traumatic abuse at the hands of a guy many years before. That didn't cause her to become a lesbian, just a radical one. For some reason though, she liked me—much to my relief.

Seymour lived on the second floor and was a recluse. He left his apartment as little as possible. He wasn't agoraphobic. He just didn't like people. He was six-foot-four and couldn't have weighed more than 160 pounds. He was older—probably hovering around fifty—and was a general sourpuss. But again, somehow I made it on his short-list of people he could tolerate. He ate pizza for almost every meal. No exaggeration. And he wasn't fussy. He switched off between deliveries and frozen pizza, and quite often made it from scratch. I would have hated to see what his insides looked like.

Seymour ran an eBay business from home. He had some sort of knack for buying items on eBay and then reselling them at an enormous profit. I once asked him how he did it, and he replied that it all had to do with the description. He looked for items that were described poorly, and as such, didn't sell for much. When he was done writing his own listing of the same item, it sounded like he was selling the Queen's jewels. He didn't write anything that was untrue or misleading, he just had a way with words. He would never indiscriminately unlock the front door if the buzzer went off, but since he was always getting deliveries from UPS, the mail carrier, or from countless pizza delivery guys, I would definitely have to warn him.

It was late, so I would call them both from work in the morning. I climbed the three flights and inspected the outside of my door before unlocking it. It looked fine. I also had a fire escape off my kitchen, but I really wasn't too worried since, as with my father's house, I had an alarm system in place. Since I hadn't heard from the alarm company, I could be reasonably sure everything was fine.

It was. I turned on my hall light, locked the door behind me, reset the alarm, and quickly went around the house shutting blinds and pulling curtains closed. Only then did I feel comfortable turning on other lights. I put the food in the fridge and took off my jacket, anxious to open the package.

I sat down at the kitchen table and inspected the package more closely. It was definitely old. Although originally well-sealed, the yellowed tape along the edges had come away from the cardboard and it looked as if it had been opened once or twice since the original sealing. I pulled back on the cardboard and found something rectangular wrapped in butcher paper, but not taped. Obviously a book, it was about twelve inches long, by eight inches wide. What struck me was its thickness—almost five inches.

Enough suspense. I took off the paper, only to reveal a plumber's manual. A 1933 updated edition, no less. To say I felt let down would be putting it mildly. I was expecting something other than that. Anything other than that. Something old and ornate, or something with obvious value.

Then I stopped. 1933. I had assumed all along, due mostly to Izzy's questions about my grandfather, that whatever was going on had to do with him. But my grandfather would have only been about thirteen in 1933. Could this have actually come from my great-grandfather?

I opened the book, more out of frustration than curiosity, and suddenly it all became clear. The book was hollowed out! In the hollow space was a yellowed letter-size envelope. It had once been sealed, but over the years most of the glue had disappeared. There were two small spots that had remained connected, but it looked as if someone had pulled them apart. Had someone else opened it? I carefully opened the envelope, dumping the meager contents on the table. There were a total of three paper items, two of which were so fragile I was afraid to unfold them. The third was a small postcard-sized paper from an art gallery in Fairfield, Iowa, called the Simpson Gallery, acknowledging receipt of a painting by Lando Ford on loan. It said it was loaned by a Bruce Honeycutt. My great-grandfather?

That made no sense at all. Fairfield, Iowa? Where the hell was Fairfield, Iowa, and why would my great-grandfather have gone there? And who was Lando Ford?

Next I unfolded a hand-written letter. *Robert, There were three of us involved…* I stopped.

Already I could tell that it was going to make as little sense as the other paper, so I put it down and unfolded the final piece of paper. It was actually two pages. A newspaper article from the *New York Times* from May 2, 1933:

> **Art Thieves Raid Brooklyn Museum ~ Ten Old Masters, Eight From Friedsam Collection, Taken During Week-End ~ World Alarm Is Sent Out ~ Dangling Rope Is Left By The Invaders ~ Fingerprints Of Two Found On Window**
>
> *A daring week-end theft of paintings from the Brooklyn Museum was revealed yesterday by Dr. William H. Fox, director of that institution, who asked the police to broadcast an international alarm for the thieves and their loot.*
>
> *Ten paintings, eight of them from the valuable collection of the late Colonel Michael Friedsam, were taken from the fifth floor galleries. They were valued at about $35,000 and were not insured.*
>
> *A sixty-foot length of rope, knotted fast to a newel post on the fourth floor of the building at the Washington Avenue end and extending to the ground, gave a hint of the manner in which the thieves escaped. Fingerprints on the window sill indicated that two men committed the crime, the most sensational of its kind in years.*

The article went on to describe the paintings that were taken, including one each by Rubens and Van Dyck. I had never heard of any of the others—and had barely heard of those two. The article also mentioned that the thieves probably snuck in while the museum was open and hid behind statues or in dark corners. They were able to avoid the eight security guards on duty that night. Rather than being cut from the frames and rolled, the wood panels had been pried whole from their frames and the pictures carried out on their "stretchers." Since most of the paintings were reasonably small, the thieves were able to escape with them pretty easily.

I opened my laptop and Googled the art heist. There wasn't a lot about it, but the little bit I found indicated that it was still considered an unsolved mystery. Of the ten paintings, four were later recovered—supposedly a botched ransom demand. The other six were never found, and the thieves were never identified.

I went back to the letter and began reading it again. I assumed Robert was his son, my grandfather:

*Robert, There were three of us involved, not two. Tony, Mikey, and me. Four if you count John. I helped plan it, but I didn't do the actual heist. And there were eleven paintings stolen, not ten. It was the eleventh one we were after. The special one. They were only supposed to get that one, but I guess they got greedy. Too bad. It got Mikey killed. That painting is dangerous. There's a fortune down there, but I don't know exactly where John hid it. And now he's probably dead too. You need to get the painting first. It'll help you find where the treasure is hidden. If you want to try for the treasure, you can, but be warned: A lot of people have died because of it. The slip shows where the painting is. There are eggs, too. They might be the most valuable of all. You'll understand when you see them. Maybe by the time you read this people will have forgotten about it. Good luck but be careful.*

Treasure? Fortune? Eggs? I knew without a shadow of a

doubt that this is what Izzy was looking for. It also meant that the people who killed Izzy were also looking for it.

This wasn't just any painting.

# Chapter 4

I had nothing but questions. It had been over eighty years since the heist. Why now? Had some new information come to light? Why did the official report state that ten paintings had been stolen, when in fact it was eleven? Was something being covered up? If my great-grandfather was so anxious to get rid of it, why leave a note for his son to find later? Why not just be done with it?

It suddenly dawned on me that I had to go to work in the morning. I made a copy of the article and put the original back in the envelope inside the book. The gallery receipt and letter I kept. Then I carefully wrapped the book and put it back in the cardboard, then set it on my bookshelf. My thinking was that if someone broke in, they were going to ransack the place looking for it. But if they found it with little trouble, they might leave without doing too much damage. By putting the original article back in, they might think that was all there was. It was worth a try.

I got to work the next morning at my usual time of 7:00, and was immediately overwhelmed by a feeling of stagnation. I hadn't liked my job for many years, but I had never had this sensation. I suddenly had thoughts of quitting, this time without the accompanying fear of the unknown. Really, how much worse off could I be? I'd have the freedom to look for something interesting. I had always been frugal, and had accumulated enough in my savings to keep me going for a while. And now, with my father's house, I could either sell it or take out a mortgage on it and use the cash to live on. No matter how I looked at it, there were no downsides to quitting. I would just have to find the right time to quit, and then would give my notice.

The right time came at 9:30 when I got a call from my alarm company that the burglar alarm in my apartment had just gone off. I told them I was on my way. Upon leaving the office, I found myself grabbing a few of my personal belongings. This *was* my notice. I was never coming back. How easy was that?

I got to the T station with a mixture of elation and fear. The fear part had more to do with how much damage I'd find in my apartment. I didn't keep any cash in there—not that that was what they'd be looking for—and my gun safe was in a secure place, so it was more a question of how quickly they would find the package and leave. Luckily, with the alarm screeching at them, they wouldn't be long. And God help them if Mo was home. She and Seymour each had a key to my apartment, and the last person in the world I would want to see bursting through a door and coming at me would be Mo.

I arrived at the Orient Heights T station near my apartment and ran all the way to my building. There was a police car out front and one of the cops was talking to Seymour, who looked bullshit to have to be out of his apartment. He barely said anything to me as I approached. He probably figured it was my fault that he had to be questioned.

I identified myself and was led up the stairs by the cop. Seymour was right behind us and veered off into his apartment without a word, slamming the door behind him.

"Pleasant guy," said the cop.

"You should see him when he's unhappy," I answered.

"The woman downstairs," he looked at his notes, "a Molly Peters, is up in your apartment with my partner. She says she's not leaving until you get home. Said she's part of some neighborhood watch and it's her job to remain until you arrive."

I smiled. Her idea of the neighborhood was our building.

"She says the perpetrator was already gone by the time she got there."

"Lucky for him," I said.

We reached the third floor landing and were greeted by the cop's partner.

"It's all yours," he said sullenly, brushing past us. "I'll be in the car."

The cop with me looked at his partner's back as he headed down the stairs.

"What's with him?" he muttered.

I knew immediately what it was. He had tried to hit on Mo and she put him in his place. Mo got that a lot. She was quite attractive: average height, jet black long hair—I never knew whether it was natural or dyed—and a great body. She had massive muscles, but not the bodybuilder type, and I could easily see how she appealed to a certain kind of guy, like a cop. The funny thing was that her lover was a petite thing with curly blonde hair. She reminded me of Little Bo Peep.

"Hey, Mo, thanks for watching the place."

"My pleasure. This is the first burglary we've had around here in a while. I'm surprised. I can't see that anything was taken though."

I looked over at the bookshelf. The package was gone. The cop was on his radio, so I whispered to Mo, "I know what's going on. I'll tell you later."

She raised her eyebrows, nodded, and headed out the door.

I quickly looked around the apartment and checked my gun safe in the bedroom. Everything seemed fine. The only thing missing was the package. No real damage had been done to the place, except for the broken door leading out to the fire escape. Time to call another carpenter.

"Anything missing that you can see?" asked the cop.

I lied. "No. Doesn't look like they got anything."

Interesting how things had changed. Just the day before I was ready to spill my guts and give my life story if they wanted it. Now, I was realizing that this wasn't a police matter. It was something in a completely different realm. Maybe I wasn't as intimidated as I thought.

The police quickly lost interest and were gone within minutes. I looked around my now quiet apartment and took a deep breath. In twenty-four hours, my life had completely changed. It wasn't so much the specific events, although they certainly jump-started the whole thing. It was more that for almost the first time, something exciting had happened in my life and I was embracing it. I just wasn't quite sure what to do with it all.

My cell phone buzzed. A text, and I knew who it was from without looking. It would be my boss asking when I was coming back in. Sure enough, it was. *How about this, asshole, never.* That's what I would have liked to respond. However, I had a little more class than that. Obviously not enough to actually give notice, though.

I responded, "*A major personal situation has just come up that*

*I have to take care of, and I'm afraid I have to make today my last day on the job. Sorry for the inconvenience.*"

The predicted obscenity-laden response appeared two minutes later. I'd have to remember to contact the HR department about payment for my vast amount of unused vacation time. I took a minute to send a group text to all of the employees under me—a more personal version of the text I sent my boss. I also let them know that I would contact them individually when time permitted. Somehow though, I knew I wouldn't. As of about 9:30 that morning, the job, and everything—and everyone—connected to it ceased to exist for me.

Mo knocked on my door and let herself in. I offered her a beer and we sat at my kitchen table, where I told her the whole story, leaving nothing out. I always found Mo easy to talk to, despite me being a little intimidated by her attractiveness and—more so—by her ability to break me in two. The funny thing about Mo was her job. One would think by looking at her that she ran a gym or a security agency. No, she was a second-grade teacher in the Boston Public School system. And, from what I heard, a pretty awesome teacher at that. I was glad that today was a holiday and she was home for me to talk to. I needed to bounce this off someone, and I didn't want to involve my mother any more than I already had.

"Shit," was her response to it all. "The good thing to come out of this is that you quit that fucking job. How long have I been telling you just to quit?"

"Well, you moved in six years ago. So, six years."

"You bet your ass."

"Do you talk like that in front of your second-graders?"

"Absolutely. It's a new plan I instituted. 'Swear word a day.' I've had great success with it. In truth, I'm so sweet there, if anyone—including the other teachers—heard me swear, I think they'd have a stroke."

"So you save it all for me."

"Hey, that's what friends are for. So, what's your plan?"

"I don't know," I answered. "I guess I'll start looking for another job."

"No, I mean about all this shit."

"I don't know. What can I do? I figured that when they stole the book, it'd be pretty much over."

"And that's it? You're not going to pursue it?"

"I'm certainly curious, but I wouldn't know where to start."

"Oh, c'mon Del. I always thought you were smarter than that. Do what Izzy wanted you to do. Research your great-grandfather. Research your grandfather. Research that old gallery in Fair-fucking-field, Iowa. Research Izzy. Find out where she was really from. Try to find out why she would know something about your family. There are all kinds of things you can do. You've got your freedom. You said you have money in the bank. You have your dad's house to fall back on. For the first time since I've known you, you've got some life to you."

"Why does everyone say that?"

"Because it's true. Let's face it, Del. Your life kinda sucked. All you had was your work, and that was a real prize. Your life has been going nowhere. And now you've been handed something exciting. Follow it up. This could turn out to be quite the adventure."

With that rationale in place, the decision was easy. "Okay,

I'll do it."

I thought back to my father's final comment. Like my relatives before me, I had now made a choice. The question was, would I be continuing the Honeycutt curse or breaking it?

# Chapter 5

Mo was gone and I was still sitting at my table, feeling like a deer-in-the-headlights. She was right. I had taken back my freedom, and if I couldn't do anything with it, then I was a real sad case. I should be jumping at the chance to solve this mystery. She was also right that Izzy was on track about one thing: I should know something about my lineage. Granted, my situation was a bit different from some. My father never knew his father, and my grandfather was a young teenager when his father died. There wasn't a lot of information that was passed down, so I couldn't really blame my father for not talking about it.

It was time to get started. I made a list of all the angles that I needed to cover. I realized that there were a few people to research, so subscribing to Ancestry.com would be my second order of business. My first would be to go back to my father's house and spend some more time in the attic. There had to be something else up there.

However, that first order of business turned out to be something entirely different. My door buzzer went off and I jumped out of my chair, banging my knee on the table. After the robberies, it seems I had become a little nervous. I limped over to the window and looked down. Whoever was at the door was under the overhang, but I didn't see anyone who looked suspicious hanging back from the door. I pressed the intercom.

"Hello?"

A woman's voice. "I'm sorry to bother you. Is this Delmore Honeycutt?"

"Um, yeah. Can I help you?"

"My name is Sabrina Spencer. I think you knew my sister, Izzy. I'm wondering if I could talk to you."

Oh great, there was another one.

"Uh, sure. Give me a minute and I'll come down."

I made my way into my bedroom and opened my gun safe. I pulled out my Sig Sauer .40 and stuck it in my belt behind my back. She might be alone, but she might not be.

A word about my gun. When I moved to East Boston, everyone I knew who lived in the city told me to take a gun course and get my firearm concealed-carry permit, then go out and buy a gun. If I was going to live in East Boston, I was going to need one. At first I thought they were joking, but after my first month there, and suddenly realizing that I didn't even notice the police sirens anymore, I decided to take it seriously. I took the course, got my permit, and bought a gun. I was told that for home protection, a revolver was my best choice, but I thought the semi-auto looked cooler, and hey, I had my license, so I could buy what I wanted. I had been to the gun range a half a dozen times over the past ten years, and I had renewed my license when it came due, but in reality, I was a terrible shot. Carrying it with me to meet Izzy's sister gave me a little confidence though, so it was worth it.

I got to the bottom of the stairs and could see through the opaque glass that she was alone. I still opened the door cautiously, just to be safe.

I almost fell over. She was stunning! She wasn't fashion model beautiful, but my kind of beautiful. She had a natural look about her, with little or no makeup. Wavy auburn hair flowed to her shoulder blades, the red tint gleaming in the sun. She was about 5'5" with a body to kill for—an expression that had more meaning of late. She smiled, revealing an ever-so-slightly crooked front tooth that somehow just enhanced her beauty.

"Um..." My mind had gone blank.

"Delmore?" she asked.

"Uh..." *C'mon, get it together.* "Del. You can call me Del." Was she used to this kind of reaction? If she was, she didn't show it. She had a combination of innocence and strength about her. She probably knew how beautiful she was, but it was almost like she didn't care.

Amazing, I gleaned all that in about five seconds.

She also looked nothing like her sister. There wasn't a hard edge to her. I also picked up a faint scent of strawberries. Much nicer than her sister's old cigarette odor. She was also younger than Izzy by a few years. Thirty-four, maybe?

"Hi, I'm Sabrina. Do you mind if we talk for a few minutes?"

Uh..." *I've gotta stop that.* "Not at all. Would you like to come up?"

"Thank you." She started up, hesitated for a moment, then continued.

I let her go ahead of me, mainly because I didn't want her to see the gun in my belt.

As we made our way up the stairs I said, "You don't look anything like your sister."

"Half-sister, actually," she replied, looking back at me. Her eyes had clouded over slightly, almost a little fearful. "Same mother, different father."

We walked into my apartment and I motioned her to the couch. I retreated to the kitchen, asking her if she'd like a bottle of water.

"Yes, please."

I opened the refrigerator, took out two bottles of water and put my gun in the cheese drawer. I carried the water into the living room and sat down on my recliner opposite her.

"Nice apartment," she said.

Actually, it was. The building was old, but the apartments had been re-done. Mine had two bedrooms, a living room, kitchen, and bathroom, all fairly new. I had a lot of "stuff," but I tried to keep it clean. It was a bright apartment, mostly due to an extra-large kitchen window.

"Thank you. I'm so sorry about your sister. I have to admit that I didn't really know her, though."

"That's okay, she knew enough about you."

"Yeah, I kind of got that feeling."

"Izzy and I weren't close ... at all. We really hadn't seen each other in a lot of years."

"That's what she told me," I said.

"Well, at least she was truthful there. A rare occurrence for her."

"I sort of picked up on that too."

"But we had been in touch lately. We talked on the phone a few times over the last couple of months. She was excited about something. It had to do with you, with my grandfather, and an old art heist. I really wasn't very interested, and in fact, wasn't quite sure why she had contacted me. Then I realized that she was pumping me for information about our grandfather—

information I didn't really have. She stopped calling when she realized I couldn't help her. I would have let it go, but when I got the call about her death, I started to wonder. Since I'm her only relative, I had to come up to claim her body."

"Did the police give you my address?"

"No, Izzy mentioned your name. It was an ... uh ... unusual name, so I remembered it. I thought I'd come and meet you to see what this was all about, so I looked you up online."

Was she being honest with me? Was she actually in league with her late sister? My gut feeling was no. But that could have been an area a bit lower than my gut talking. I took a chance.

"I've got to be honest with you, and please don't take offense, but how do I know that you two weren't working together on this? You have to understand that in the past two days, someone I met was murdered and my father's house, my car, and this apartment have all been broken into. When I came down to meet you, I had a gun behind my back. That's how much this has shaken me."

"Yes, I saw the gun."

"How?"

"You twisted slightly at one point and I saw it before we went up the stairs. I'll be honest with *you* now. When I saw it, I almost turned around and walked away. That scared me a little. But I guess I can understand now why you had it."

"On that subject, do mind if I take it out of my refrigerator? I'm not sure the cold is good for it."

She chuckled. "Not at all. But can you leave it in the kitchen?"

She continued as I got up. "I'm not sure how I can convince you that I'm not—wasn't—working with my sister. All I can tell you is that I didn't like her. I'm not sure I ever liked her. She was dishonest and she was a liar. I couldn't trust her when we were young and I was relieved when she left home. I saw her from time to time after that, the last time at our mother's funeral eight or nine years ago."

She took a breath. I came back and sat down. She said, "As for what she was into when she contacted you, you probably know more than I do. It seemed to be consuming her, though. She kept talking about this lost painting, and she wanted to know how much mom had told me about our grandfather—technically Izzy's grandfather. Our father—my adopted father—died about twenty years ago. His father had died a couple of years before that. I don't know anything secret about either of them. Del," she added. "I'm very different from my sister. I'm here simply out of curiosity. What was she into and why did it get her killed?"

I was beginning to believe her. I looked down at her hand and saw that she didn't have a ring. That made me *really* want to believe her.

"Did she tell you anything about the painting?" I asked.

"Kind of. She kept referring to it as being extremely valuable, but I don't think she meant from an art point of view. In one conversation, she mentioned that it contained valuable information, but I'm convinced she had no idea what that information was."

So how much should I tell her? Not everything yet. I figured I'd dish it out slowly and see how I felt about her.

"Did she tell you anything about the heist itself?"

"She really didn't tell me anything about anything. What I told you was everything I know."

I stood up and walked over to where my jacket was hanging and unzipped an inside pocket. From an envelope I took out the copy I made of the newspaper article. I put the envelope back in the pocket and zipped it closed.

"I found an old package in my father's attic after the police informed me about Izzy. It was a hollowed out book that included an article, which I made a copy of. I put the original back in the book. It was stolen this morning when the person broke into my apartment." I handed it to her.

She was quiet while she read it. She pored over it slowly, then looked up and said, "1933?"

I nodded. "I think it goes beyond our grandfathers. My guess is we're talking great-grandfathers, or at least my great-grandfather."

"Do you have any guess about the painting? What it means and what might have happened to it?"

"I have no knowledge of the painting. I do know what happened to it. It was loaned to a small-town art gallery. What happened after that, I have no idea."

I could tell that Sabrina knew I was holding back some information, but she was obviously smart enough to know that until I trusted her, I couldn't show all my cards.

"I have some time on my hands," I said, "so I thought I'd look into it. I'll be happy to let you know what I find."

She was quiet for a minute, then said, "I have a proposition for you. I'm here for another two days, and I could easily extend it. How about if I help?" she asked.

I cocked my head to the side in a "why would you want to" gesture.

She hesitated. "This is going to sound kind of egotistical,

and I really don't mean it to, but you've never heard of me, have you?"

"Uh..." *I did it again.*

"I didn't think so. It's kind of refreshing, actually. It's the other reason I couldn't possibly be working with Izzy on this, and one of the many reasons I steered as clear from her as I could. I have a reputation to think of. I'm a bestselling mystery writer. My fans wouldn't appreciate it if I was involved in something shady."

Sabrina Spencer! It just showed how discombobulated I was.

"I'm sorry. Yes, I have heard of you. I'm sorry to say that I haven't read any of your books though, but I will remedy that immediately."

She flashed a very genuine smile.

"No, I'm sorry. I sound so full of myself when I say something like that, but it was important for you to know that, because I don't just write mysteries, I live for mysteries. This one hits close to home because I have an actual connection to it. Del, we're both involved in this. You've already dealt with three burglaries and I lost my sister, regardless of how I felt about her. Beyond that though, our families seem to be involved with each other going back two or three generations. How much more mysterious could this get?"

She was quickly selling me on the idea, but I had to note, "Technically, it was Izzy's family. You didn't have the same father."

"You're right. It's not my family by blood, but that differentiation was never made when I was a kid—except by Izzy when she was being especially mean. My adopted father accepted me as one of his own. That makes it my family and my business. How about it? Another hand, or another pair of eyes, might make a difference."

My radar had turned off.

"Okay, you have a deal."

# Chapter 6

Sabrina walked into her room at the Westin, sat in a chair overlooking Copley Square, and dialed the number of her agent. She had become a hot commodity of late, so getting through to Peter Sheppard was no longer a "he'll call you back as soon as he can" deal. He picked up immediately.

"Hey Sabrina. What's cooking? How'd it go with your sister's stuff?"

"Okay. I guess these things are never pleasant. Listen, I know everything is about to heat up with all the pre-release hoopla of my new book, but I've got to take a few days off to deal with all of this."

"Yeah, that's fine. Not to be insensitive, but is it all of her arrangements, or the 'other thing'?"

"Mostly the other thing. I met the guy she came up here to talk to. Turns out he has some information that can fill in a lot of blanks. He seems nice, and as confused about all this as I am. He's agreed to let me be a part of it."

"And what do you get out of it?"

"Closure? Excitement? Peter, this is turning out to be a real mystery, not something made up."

"Fodder for a new book?"

"You never know. But I really want to sink my teeth into this."

"So, does this guy know who you are?"

"He knows that I'm Sabrina Spencer, the mystery author."

"You know that wasn't my question."

"Does he know my past? No. Only you and Ellen"—Ellen was her editor—"know about that."

"And you're not going to tell him?"

"There's no reason he has to know. Besides the fact that I want to keep my past as private as I can for as long as I can—and who knows who he would tell—there's another reason. Just being Izzy's sister was enough to make him suspicious of me. If I gave him this information, there is no way he'd want me in on this. And Peter, I really want to be in on it."

# Chapter 7

Sabrina Spencer was the real deal. She had five books to her credit—all mysteries. Her first one was put out by a small publisher, and it received the expected amount of attention—none. Her second wasn't much more successful, but it did catch the fancy of an editor at a major New York publishing house, who signed her to a two-book contract. Her third, now with the right publicity behind her, made the New York Times Bestseller List for a couple of weeks, and her fourth took off and made her a big name in the mystery world. Suddenly, all of her books started selling, and the big publisher bought the rights to her first two, making the small publisher a lot of money in the process. Her fifth was due to be published around Christmas, and was expected to hit the bestseller lists its first week in print.

But what impressed me more than her accomplishments was her sincerity. I picked up on it as quickly as I had picked up on her sister's insincerity. In so many ways she was he exact opposite of her sister. I was looking forward to working with her.

She had to take care of a few things, seeing as how she was going to take some time off from her writing and publicity planning, so we agreed to meet the next day at her hotel. Funny, she didn't seem all that comfortable in East Boston. Who can figure? However, an excuse to meet at the Westin was okay with me.

I looked at my watch. I couldn't believe it was only 2:30. So much had happened in a few short hours. I was anxious to check out my father's attic again to see if there was something else—anything else—related to my grandfather or great-grandfather.

I called Mo and explained that I had to drive to my father's house, and did she know anyone who could fix my door. Turns out she belonged to a whole network of professionals—all female—in different fields. She told me not to worry, that she'd get someone over there to fix it.

So once again I took off for my father's house, my gun in the pocket of my jacket. I felt extremely uncomfortable carrying it. I called my mother and gave her an abbreviated update, but explained that I probably wouldn't have time to stop by.

The two-hour trip was a perfect time for reflection. I could have worked through all the details I knew about everything that had happened up to that point. Or, I could have thought about what I would do next for employment. I did neither. It was just all a little too overwhelming. So, I thought about Sabrina and how attracted I was to her. That took up the whole trip.

I arrived at my father's house close to five, having stopped for some take-out along the way. The house was dark and felt very empty—empty of life, that is. Once inside, I reset the alarm and turned on just about every light in the place. I could never understand in the movies people who ventured into dark houses. Hey, if there is a light, I'll switch it on.

Before making my way to the attic, I decided to check my father's office, hoping I would find something to preclude my having to deal with the attic. But there was nothing there. I turned on his laptop, but like the rest of the house, it was pretty Spartan, with the expected business and household files, as well as a file containing notes for a nonfiction book about South America that he had been working on for almost ten years. I don't think he had ever gotten beyond the note-taking stage for it. But I knew all this. I had checked his laptop right after his death—at that time looking for copies of a will, as well as bank account and investments information. I had found a simple will leaving everything to me, but other than the equity in the house, my father really didn't have much. He spent his money with abandon, going on vacations all over the world and buying expensive gifts for his many girlfriends. There was also no evidence of a hidden safe-deposit box filled with secret files that would explain all the craziness of the past few days.

No, like it or not—not—it was off to the attic for me.

Luckily, I had been through almost half of the boxes already. I had stopped when I found the package. My goal now was to go through the rest of them, even if I discovered something early on. I didn't ever want to find out later that if I had kept looking, I would have found something vital. I started up where I had left off.

As I worked my way through the boxes, I couldn't help wondering why my father had hidden the package the way he did. But the fact that he had hidden it in a box labeled "kitchen stuff" was enough to convince me that he knew that it was worth hiding. If he knew that much, why hadn't he pursued it? And if he did pursue it, had he run into a dead end?

The truth was, my father wasn't very motivated when it came to work—and this would have entailed work. He was motivated by two things: sex and fun (the first also falling into the second category). He didn't bring work home for the simple reason that he no longer really cared. It's probably why his book never got beyond the compilation stage. Early in his career he must have had some drive—he wouldn't have achieved the position he held if he hadn't. He had even written a few dozen papers that had been published in scholarly journals and had cowritten some textbooks. But I had a feeling that laziness was with him most of his career. Definitely in the last ten years, the emphasis was solely on having fun.

Why he hadn't done anything with the package was a question for another day. For now, the mystery was in my lap, and I was determined to solve it.

I found what I was looking for about an hour into my search. By that time I had been through about eighty percent of the boxes. It was in a box labeled "curtains." I suspected something when I picked up the box. It seemed too heavy for curtains, considering the size of the box. My heart was pounding as I slit the tape and opened the box. I was greeted with—surprise—curtains. But I expected that. I pulled them out and was left with a small canvas bag, like an old satchel.

I removed it from the box and opened the latch to the bag. The bag and its contents smelled heavily of mildew. I removed a stack of papers, which filled most of the bag, and quickly flipped through them. It was my grandfather's wartime papers. He was with the 392$^{nd}$ bomb group, part of the 8$^{th}$ Air Force, stationed at Wendling, England. Already, that was more information about him than I had known before. I put the stack back in the bag, and the bag back in the box. I replaced the curtains and folded the corners of the box to close it. That was something to look through later.

I continued my search, but found nothing more of interest. I looked at my watch. It was almost eight. Time to head home. I carried the box downstairs, turned off all the lights, locked the door, and set the alarm. I carried the box back to my car, gun in hand.

But I wasn't accosted, and was back in my apartment by ten.

I was exhausted. It had been a long, strange day. I was due to meet Sabrina at ten the next morning, so I decided to get to bed early. If I woke up early enough, I could look through some of the material in the satchel before meeting with her. I had already decided to be totally forthcoming with her. If I wanted her help, I needed to be.

I set my alarm and noticed that my door to the fire escape had been fixed. A nice job, too. A better job than my friend Steve had done on my father's door. There was a note on the table from Mo: *I had Amy replace your shit lock. And your deadbolt? What a joke! So she replaced that too. She put in the best of the best. Hope your father left you a lot of money! Lol. Here are the keys. Hey, who was the gorgeous babe leaving your house today? Whoa, I'd do her in a second!*

I smiled. Nothing subtle about Mo.

*****

I couldn't sleep. Whether it was adrenaline, a little fear, curiosity about the contents of my grandfather's belongings, or the anticipation of seeing Sabrina again, whatever the reason, I was wide awake at 1:30. I made a cup of coffee and took a quick shower to clear my head, then sat at the kitchen table and emptied the contents of the satchel in front of me.

In addition to the papers I had seen a few hours before,

was a collection of medals, the usual Army Air Corps items: wings, lieutenant bars, and a couple of patches, so I moved on to the papers.

It took me a couple of hours to read over all of the material to fully understand the timeline of my grandfather's military career. The short of it was that his B-24 crew was part of the 392nd Bomb Group. They arrived in Wendling, England in the fall of 1943. Their plane was the *Lonesome Cowgirl.* My grandfather died in March of 1944 on his 19th mission. Included in the papers was a copy of the telegram my grandmother got from the Army telling her of the death of her husband. It gave no details, only that he had died bravely in combat over Germany.

There was a lot missing, so I Googled the 392nd Bomb Group and discovered a website devoted to it. I found the whole thing fascinating, and felt myself getting a little sad that I had known none of this growing up. But again, I really couldn't blame my father. I wondered how much of his father's material he had even looked at himself.

The website featured all of the missions, as well as pictures. I could click onto my grandfather's name and it brought up any pictures associated with him. One of them showed the crew of his plane. I studied it for a moment to get a feel for what my grandfather looked like. I could see a family resemblance between him and my father. I think I looked more like my mother than my father, so I couldn't see too much of him in me. I then looked at his crewmates and felt my jaw drop. Standing next to my grandfather was a man who bore an uncanny resemblance to Izzy!

I quickly looked at the names printed below the picture.

The man next to my grandfather was Ray Worth, the navigator. Izzy's grandfather was the man with my grandfather when he fell through the bomb bay doors!

# Chapter 8

"I found our families' connection," I blurted out upon entering Sabrina's room at the Westin.

I was only a few minutes late, but it wasn't an attempt on my part to be fashionable. My goal was to get to the hotel before ten, but the thought of seeing her had me so excited I kept forgetting things—like four times. Twice, I didn't remember until I was halfway down the block on my way to the T station. The fourth time, I was passing Seymour's apartment on my way back down when he opened the door and yelled, "Stop!" I stopped.

"Think," he said. "Stop and think for a minute. 'Have I remembered everything this time? Can I avoid clomping up the steps for a fifth time, assuring that Seymour, who was up until two doing business online, can maybe attempt to get back to the sleep from which he was so rudely interrupted?'"

"Sorry, Seymour. I'm going to be late for an appointment, and the things I'm forgetting are important. I really didn't mean to wake you up."

"Well, if you *did* mean to wake me up, then we'd have some issues. " He looked me over. "If you're going to a job interview—yes I heard—or on a date—yes, I saw her—you might want to change your clothes." I was wearing jeans and a Disney World long-sleeve shirt, along with my jacket.

"No to both of those, but yes, I'm meeting her. But we're working on something. I'll tell you about it later."

"No need. Molly already told me." He was the only one

who called Mo, Molly. The two of them had a weird relationship. They couldn't be at further corners of the world, opinion-wise, and yet, you couldn't tell something to one of them without the other knowing soon after. The funny thing was, I never saw them together. Never. Very strange.

I got to Sabrina's room at about 10:15. She greeted me wearing jeans and a Red Sox t-shirt. She was barefoot. I was in love! And how in the world could her hair shine like that in a hotel room on a cloudy day? I was beginning to think she wasn't human. Goddess, maybe?

After my outburst, she ushered me to a seat, as anxious to hear the story as I was to tell it.

I gave her the lowdown on my grandfather, ending with the picture, which I showed her on my iPad.

"That's him," she said. "I've seen pictures of him before. I met him when I was young, but he died when I was nine or ten. Lung cancer, I think. He was a heavy smoker."

"Weren't they all in that generation?"

"So does that clear anything up or just make it murkier?" she asked.

"Probably a little of both," I answered. "I have a couple other things that I didn't show you yesterday. I didn't want to reveal everything until I could be sure you weren't working with Izzy."

"I knew that."

So I showed her my great-grandfather's letter. She had already read the article about the art heist. I carefully unfolded the letter and held it out to her. She read it slowly.

"Treasure?" Sabrina asked, laying the paper on the table. "A treasure hunt? Oh, that's never good. That never ends well for anybody."

I think she was being facetious, but I couldn't tell for sure.

"He also refers to 'down there'," she said. "Down where?"

"Funny, I didn't pick up on that," I answered. "I picked up on the treasure part of it." I shook my head. "Don't know about the 'down'."

"And what's with the eggs?"

"Couldn't tell you."

I showed her the slip from the Simpson Gallery, the town, and the artist's name.

"Fairfield, Iowa?"

"Ever been there?" I asked.

"I probably flew over it."

I liked her sense of humor.

She was typing something into her laptop.

"There is no record of an artist by the name of Lando Ford," she said.

"So the painting—whatever it is of—might have been painted with a purpose. Ford might really be the artist, or it was a made-up name."

"It probably isn't too bad," Sabrina said, "or a gallery wouldn't take it."

"Maybe my great-grandfather—I'm assuming his name is Bruce from the slip, but I suppose I should spend some time and research my family—maybe he knew the gallery owner. I mean why Fairfield, Iowa? You don't just stop off in a random town and lend your painting to a gallery then drive off, do you?"

She was typing again. Wow, she was fast. Does being able to type fast make you a better writer?

"As I would have expected," she said, "that gallery no longer exists. So, the question is, when did it close and what happened to its collection? Want to go to Iowa?"

She said it as if we were going out for pizza. I only had one thought. More time alone with her. Well, that was a no-brainer.

"It's never been at the top of my vacation destinations, but sure. I'd like to go, but is this information we could get online just as easily?"

"Maybe," she answered. "But what I've learned from … well, from my own books, I guess," she rolled her eyes at the comment, "is that actual legwork sometimes uncovers things you'd never find online. Hey, it works for my detective anyway."

"I can understand that theory," I said. "You never know who or what you're going to run into. Here's the thing, though. I pick up the tab for everything. It seems that my relative started this, so it should be up to me to pay for the investigation."

"We split it," said Sabrina. "We'll take turns paying for things. My family was involved too. We just don't know to what extent. Besides, depending how this goes, I might be able to turn it into a book. So I can claim it as research expenses."

So the money was settled. "Something we have to think about," I said, "are the people who killed Izzy. I know there are at least two because the person who broke into my car jumped into a car driven by someone else. Why? How do they figure into all of this?"

"Maybe Izzy employed them to help her find whatever aspect of this she was looking for. Maybe they turned on her."

"And how did Izzy get involved in the first place?" I asked.

"Her involvement was fairly recent. What spurred her on?"

We had oodles of questions. An answer might be nice.

Sabrina's phone rang. Actually, her phone had rung a few times while I was there. Each time she looked at the caller ID and ignored it. After the third one, she apologized. "It's the publicity person from the publisher. He's really annoying. My new book is coming out just before Christmas and they are trying to line up the publicity campaign. I asked him to contact me by email, because I really hate the phone, but he doesn't seem to get it. Now that he's tried three times, he'll email me in frustration."

So when the phone rang a fourth time, she actually looked surprised, like it had blown her theory. But this time she picked up. "I think it's that detective I was talking to yesterday."

She listened without talking, then asked a couple of questions. From what I could gather, the call had something to do with Izzy's living situation before she died. She got a notepad from her briefcase and copied down some information, then said, "Thank you so much for all your help. Could you do me one more favor? Could you call them back and let them know that I'm on my way, and to keep the room rented? I'll settle the bill when I get there." She listened, then ended with, "Thank you detective. I appreciate it."

"Well, that was interesting," she said, turning to me. "It seems that Izzy was renting a room at a Residence Inn outside of Chicago. She was only paid up through yesterday, so they called her cell phone to find out what she was doing. Of course, it's in police custody, so they answered. The detective called the Chicago police, who inspected her room, but didn't find anything of significance. So he called me and asked me what I wanted the hotel to do with her stuff. I guess we're going to Fairfield by way of Chicago."

"I didn't know they had her cell phone. Did they find anything in the call log?"

"He mentioned that. Nothing of any significance."

We wrapped it up. Sabrina was going to reserve the tickets for the next morning, and I was going home to pack. I was happy that I had an ally, and that we had recovered some information, but there was still too much we didn't know.

I approached my house deep in thought, wishing that something would happen that would break the case apart.

The bullets missed my head by inches and I heard three loud pops. I dropped to the sidewalk. Three bullets had embedded themselves in the side of the house. I heard a car speed off, squealing its tires. Slowly I got up. My right hand was bleeding from scraping it on the sidewalk, and I could see a small blood spot appearing in the knee of my pants.

Seymour opened his window and peered down. "You okay?" He said it with genuine concern.

"Yeah, I think so. I didn't get hit. Just scraped myself when I fell." I could hear a police siren.

"What the hell did you get yourself involved in?" asked Seymour.

"I wish I knew."

I may not have known what it was all about, but there was no question about that message. I was meant to join Izzy in death.

# Chapter 9

I called Sabrina before the police arrived and let her know what happened. I suggested she call her detective. I didn't want to have to explain everything to the cops who showed up, since it was obviously related to Izzy's murder.

For the next few hours, my street was a crime scene, crowds behind the yellow tape taking pictures with their cell phones. I think in general though, they were pretty disappointed by the lack of blood. I could show them my knee if they really wanted to see blood. I already had a Band-Aid on it though.

Sabrina's detective, Detective Marsh, arrived on the scene about fifteen minutes after the first cops showed up. I didn't hold anything back—but I didn't go into great detail either—and let him know whatever I could. Unfortunately, that wasn't much. We were pretty much flying blind. Until we had a few more answers, we still had no idea who these people were.

Mo showed up in the middle of it all, gave me a hug, and asked if I was okay. I heard nothing else from Seymour, but that was expected now that there were throngs of people about.

I kept Sabrina updated by phone and warned her not to venture out alone. She informed me that we were booked on the 8:30 a.m. flight from Logan to O'Hare. We'd meet at the airport. Mo offered to drive me in the morning before she went to work.

I slept that night with my gun next to the bed.

*****

I didn't sleep well and got to the airport dragging. Sabrina, as expected, looked wonderful. She was signing an autograph for a fan who recognized her. As the fan walked away, Sabrina came over and hugged me, letting me know how relieved she was that I was okay. Again I smelled the strawberries. Sigh.

I was wild about this woman. Obviously I hadn't said anything to her—after all, we had only known each other for two days—but there was something about her that just captivated me. And it wasn’t only her beauty. She was smart, she had a good sense of humor, and she was humble. In short, she was perfect. But being perfect wasn't so good for me. After all, it was obvious: like Gomer Pyle meeting a princess. I could tell that she liked me and felt comfortable around me, but would it go any further than that? I could only dream.

The plane was on time and by 9:00 we were in the air. Sabrina asked me what it felt like to be shot at. She might have been subconsciously compiling information for future books, but I also knew that her questions were coming from a genuine place. It was hard to answer her. I didn't really feel anything when the shots came. Maybe I wasn't really sure what was going on. I just knew that I felt compelled to duck. The emotional reaction didn't come until later, long after I had gotten into bed. I started shaking and began to think about how close those bullets came. Another few inches and any one of the three could have killed me. I was lucky. Very lucky.

About an hour into the flight, a fan—who probably had been working up the courage to approach Sabrina since we boarded—finally got up and hesitatingly came over and asked for an autograph. Sabrina was in the window seat, so the fan had to lean over me to talk to her. She had on so much perfume, it was going to take hours for my nostrils to clear. I could tell that the odor affected Sabrina as well, but she was gracious and talked to her for a minute. Well, that started a steady stream of autograph seekers. The funny thing was, I don't think most of them knew whose autograph they were getting, but if there was someone famous on the plane, it's best to get the autograph and then try to figure out who she was later. It got a bit much after the seventh one, so the flight attendant offered to keep people away—for the price of an autograph, of course. Sabrina was visibly uncomfortable throughout the whole ordeal, and was almost shaking by the end of it. She kept apologizing to me, saying that it was actually rare for people to notice her.

We had decided to rent a car in Chicago and drive down to Fairfield after we checked out Izzy's hotel. Where we went from there would hinge on what—if anything—we found in Fairfield. The Residence Inn was out in the suburbs, but we found it without too much trouble. When we got up to the check-in desk, Sabrina asked to see the manager, who was prepared for her visit. The manager explained that everything was all set and that no one had been to the room after the police, including housekeeping.

"When did she check in?" asked Sabrina.

The manager checked the computer. "Last Thursday."

We decided to stay for the night and I offered—like a perfect gentleman—to take another room, hoping, of course, that she would say "no need." She did, but only because she knew that her sister had rented a two-bedroom suite. I could have the other bedroom. I had to keep reminding myself of the purpose of this visit.

We let ourselves into the room and looked around. It was pretty devoid of Izzy's things; a single carry-on suitcase, a pair of shoes and a jacket in the closet, and a few toiletries. I kept looking at Sabrina, trying to get a sense as to her mood. Was she sad seeing her sister's belongings? But I saw no signs of sentimentality. It was clear there had been no love lost between the sisters.

"This looks like a bust," I said.

"Anything in the safe?" asked Sabrina.

"I'll see, but I'm sure the police would have checked that." In fact, the safe was open and empty. I shook my head and asked, "What now?"

"She was obviously intending to come back," she replied. "And quickly. She only had the room through Sunday, so I'm thinking that she set up the meet with you for Saturday and had a ticket to come back the next day. She wanted to get the information and leave."

"Hmm," I said.

"Hmm what?" she asked.

"Oh nothing." I hesitated for a minute. "I'm sure you've never had to do online dating, but I think for most people, the first thing they do when they meet their date is to do a quick evaluation of their chances to eventually sleep with them." I was blushing. I could feel the blood rushing to my head.

"That's not limited to online dates," she said. "That happens with regular dates too."

"I guess you're right. It's been so long since I had a date not initiated online, I kind of forgot. Anyway, my first thought about Izzy was that I had no interest in ever sleeping with her.

Turns out, she had no interest in me. Kind of a blow to the ego."

"Have you evaluated me?"

I swallowed. I suddenly was very dry.

"You don't need to answer that." She turned away with a little smile on her face. Was she flirting with me? "And to answer your assumption about me and online dating, no, I've never done it, but don't for a minute think that just because I'm a little famous—I hate using that word—that I have men hovering all around me. I suppose I do to a certain extent, but it's not sincere, and it doesn't mean I'm interested in any of them. You saw it on the plane. People have a fascination with famous people. But you begin to question everyone's intent. I love being successful with my writing, but I don't particularly like the fame that comes with it."

"I hadn't thought about that," I said.

"Here I am complaining about being famous. I have no right to. I have so many good things in my life." She switched subjects. "I'll go through her clothes if you want to check her suitcase and drawers. Then we can go through her toiletries."

My search was quick and revealed nothing. Sabrina, though, had better luck.

"Del, look at this. I found it in a pair of jeans."

It was a keycard. I looked at her expectantly.

She said, "I'll bet the police had the same reaction you did, and I'll bet nobody looked at it carefully."

I took another look. And then I saw it. It wasn't for the Residence Inn, it was for a Hyatt in downtown Chicago.

"Do you think she stayed there before coming here?" I asked. "Or maybe she had a 'friend'," I made quotations marks in the air, "who was staying there."

"Both of those are possible, although if she had a friend at the Hyatt, why didn't they just stay in the same hotel? Here's another theory. What if she had two rooms? Did she know someone was on her trail. What if she booked a second room to try to throw them off? It's an idea."

"Possible," I said, but I know I had a doubting look on my face. "It was here that she was staying, so if the other was a diversion, it's probably empty."

"Not necessarily," Sabrina replied. "What's odd about this room?"

I guess this was why she was the mystery author and not me. Nothing popped out at me. "I don't know. What's odd?"

"You can probably be forgiven," she said, "because you're not a woman. Men don't think along those lines. It's her lack of clothes. Look, she has a small carry-on with very few items in it. I count one pair of jeans, one piece of underwear, one pair of socks, a long-sleeve shirt, and in the closet, a jacket and a pair of shoes—which don't go with the jeans and sweater, by the way. For toiletries, she has the bare minimum. She checked in almost a week ago! No woman—and I bet no man either—would check in for four or five days with only a carry-on. She was only going to be in Boston for one night and only took another carry-on. I saw it. It was as empty as this. So where is all her stuff? There has to be a suitcase somewhere."

"You make a compelling argument."

"Want to take a ride over to the Hyatt?"

We took the Hyatt keycard and headed out to the parking lot, always on the lookout for suspicious people. On the drive over, I was mulling things over in my head when I heard in the background, "Earth to Del." Sabrina was looking at me.

"You were deep in thought," she said. "Care to share?"

"I was thinking about the guys who killed Izzy and tried to kill me. When did they come into the picture? I'd bet anything that Izzy knew them. So were they friends or hires who double-crossed her, like you suggested? There had to be a connection between them."

"And if so, did she meet them in Chicago? Maybe the Hyatt room will shed some light."

"How are we going to find out which room she has, assuming this isn't an old reservation?" I asked. "They won't just give it to us."

"I'm going to be honest," she replied.

A unique approach.

We arrived a few minutes later and parked in the check-in area. Once inside, she asked for the manager on duty.

"Hi, my name is Sabrina Spencer…"

"Are you the mystery author?" interrupted the clerk standing next to the manager. She had a really annoying squeaky voice.

"I am," replied Sabrina, giving the woman a warm smile, but subtly motioning the manager aside.

Now realizing he was dealing with someone important, the manager was more than happy to oblige and took us into his office. When we were seated, he asked, "What can I help you with?"

"I believe my sister, Isobel Worth, had a room here. She was killed in Boston on Saturday, and I'm trying to clean up loose ends. I found a keycard for your hotel in her belongings. If she was still registered here, I'd like to gather her things and pay her bill."

"Oh, I'm so sorry for your loss. Let me see if she was registered." He typed into his computer. "Yes, she was … is … currently registered."

"Would you mind telling me what room?"

He shifted uncomfortably. "Well, this is where it gets a little problematic. I can't just give you access to her room. Please understand, I believe you, but since you are not registered, I'll need to speak to the authorities about it."

Sabrina pulled something from her wallet. "This is the business card for the detective who is handling the case in Boston. He can vouch for me."

She started to hand him the card, but let go just before he touched it. The card fluttered to the floor.

"I'm so sorry," she said.

"Not a problem," he answered, and they both reached down at once. As he picked it up, she now had a clear view of his computer screen and glanced over at it. The manager picked up the card and everyone settled back.

We waited while the manager called Detective Marsh. He said "okay" and "yes" about a dozen times before he finally hung up.

"Well, I'm afraid there is going to be a delay," he said apologetically. "The detective said that since it is still an open case, he needs to contact the Chicago PD to come by and go through the room first. I'm very sorry."

"That's not a problem at all," said Sabrina. "We'll wait out in the lobby for them. Thank you so much for your help."

We quickly excused ourselves and made our way back out to the main lobby. Out of sight of the manager Sabrina handed me the keycard.

"Room 1798. I don't want the police going through it first. I should stay here and meet them, since she was my sister. Plus, I've always treated the police well in my books, so I might be able to stall them by letting them know who I am—the one time I want to use my fame—giving you a few minutes up there. I'll text you when they are on their way up."

"Gotcha. I'll look as quickly as I can." I went through the side stairs exit, up to the next floor, and caught the elevator to the seventeenth floor. Time was not on my side. I didn't know how fast the Chicago cops would be. I figured I had a few minutes, but not many more than that.

I found the room and used the keycard to get in. I pulled a handkerchief from my pocket and used it to open the door. I turned on the lights the same way. I figured just to be safe I shouldn't leave any fingerprints. I looked around. This was definitely where she was staying. A large suitcase still full of Izzy's stuff sat over by the window. Like me, Izzy was not one to make use of hotel room drawers. I went over to the suitcase and carefully pawed through it. Nothing of interest. Next, I checked the closet. There I found a thin leather briefcase full of papers—mostly notes on legal-size paper that she had probably made. There really wasn't much else to look through, so I grabbed the briefcase and was about to leave when I thought of the safe.

It was closed. She had something in it. But how could I open it? I didn't know her well enough to come up with any passwords, so I tried some simple ones: 1,2,3,4; the year in which I assumed she was born, as well as a couple near that, just in case; the numeric value for Izzy; and a few more. Nothing worked.

My phone pinged. It was Sabrina. The police were on their way up. Time to leave. Just for kicks, I tried one more code: 1933, the date of the art heist. The safe opened!

I looked inside. There was some money, which I ignored. There was also a thin book—an old log book of some sort. On the cover was a name: Ray Worth. The log of the last man to see my grandfather alive!

# Chapter 10

I closed the safe and got out of there quickly. I found the stairs and went down one flight and caught the elevator on the 16th floor. If I had been waiting for the elevator on the 17th and the door opened revealing a car full of cops, I probably would have peed my pants.

I met Sabrina in the lobby, trying to conceal my excitement. We retreated to a remote corner, where I told her what I had found. As anxious as we both were to go through everything, we knew we had to wait. After they did their search, the police would be calling us up to the room, and I wanted to ditch the briefcase before then. I gave the log book to Sabrina, who put it in her purse, then I took the briefcase out and locked it in the trunk of the car. Then we waited.

An hour later, the lead detective sent for us and we made our way to the room. In the elevator I found myself a little nervous. Suppose they looked at security tapes and saw me go in. I mentioned it to Sabrina.

"I don't think so," she said. "She wasn't killed here, so I don't think they'd have any reason to. Even if they did," she added, "they would do it for the nights she was here, not for an hour ago."

That made me feel marginally better.

The meeting with the cops was quick and painless. They explained that they found nothing that would explain her death in Boston. Luckily, they didn't ask us if we had gone in before them. So they cleared out of the room—leaving the safe open so we could gather Izzy's belongings—and suddenly we were alone.

"I don't think we should go back to the Residence Inn. If this hotel was her secret hide-out," said Sabrina, after giving the room a once-over, "It should probably be ours too. We are probably safer here."

"I agree. Besides, I don't know about you, but I'm starving. It's dinner time and it looks like they have a decent restaurant here."

"I'll go down and reserve a room for the night." She hesitated. "I'd rather not stay in this room."

"I understand." Did I hear her say "reserve a room," and not "rooms?"

"I'll deal with this stuff later," she said. "Do you want to go move the car and bring in our things? I'll meet you in the lobby."

"Will do."

"And Del?" She had a look of concern. "Be careful."

A feeling of warmth spread through me. "I will. I'll let them valet the car. That'll keep me in public view the whole time."

I had the bellman take our bags—all except Izzy's briefcase—and I met up with Sabrina in the lobby.

"I hope you don't mind," she said, with a touch of color in her face, "I only got one room. We're probably going to be up late going through Izzy's stuff, and, to be honest, I'd feel more comfortable sharing the room."

"I think I can live with that," I said, trying hard not to smile too widely.

*****

We had a relaxing dinner, despite the fact that the log book was burning a hole in Sabrina's bag. We knew we had plenty of time to go through it, and after the events of the last few days, we needed the break.

We filled each other in on our lives. I first regaled her with the stories of some of my less fortunate ancestors, then got a bit more serious when I told her about my childhood, living with my mother and visiting my father far less frequently than I would have liked, despite him living only a mile away. He loved me in his own way, but he wasn't a father type. He was way too self-absorbed—and he knew it—to be an effective parent. A little effort on his part would have meant everything to me. My mother had confessed to me a few years earlier that she often pleaded with my father to show me some attention. He would give it a try for a few weeks, then lapse back into his old ways.

Sabrina asked me if I had ever married.

"Not even close," I answered.

I also explained that when I was in my mid-twenties my mother was diagnosed with leukemia, and I moved in with her to help her out. During those years I came to hate my father for abandoning my mother like that—although she later convinced me get rid of the hate and try to keep some sort of relationship with him. I spent three years living with her. My mother always felt that because of her my prime dating years had gone to waste, and she always felt guilty about it. I didn't though. As hard as it was, I felt I owed her at least that much. And to be perfectly frank, I wasn't sure if any years were my "prime" dating years.

Her cancer went into remission—and had never returned—and I got the job in Boston, a job that left little time for developing a real relationship with anyone.

"So there's been no one special?"

"No. I had a few relationships that lasted a number of months, but when it's not the right person, it's not the right person. You can fool yourself only so long. How about you?"

"I was married for five years back in my early twenties. It seemed like the real thing. I thought it was a storybook marriage. After a couple of years we tried to get pregnant, but couldn't. That's when I noticed a change in Kevin. Sex lost its enjoyment and instead became a mission, a mission to have a baby. The more obsessed he got about it, the less I wanted to have a child with him—or even sex, for that matter. Finally, the doctors determined that I couldn't bear children. That sent him over the edge. Our last year of marriage was a nightmare, and when I finally took out a restraining order on him, he left. I promptly filed for divorce. We were living in a small town in Pennsylvania, near where he grew up. I moved to New York, got a job as an editorial assistant with a small publisher, and shared an apartment with two other women who were also struggling to survive. After my experience with Kevin, I vowed I'd never get married again. Like you, I date, but nothing serious has ever resulted."

"And Kevin?"

"Never heard from him again and never want to."

She didn't seem to want to say any more on the subject, so I changed it.

"Do you like life as a successful author?"

She perked up. "I love it! Writing is my passion. As I said, the fame that has greeted me over the last year or so can be a little overwhelming—even embarrassing—but I love my life. I love traveling for research, and I love writing. I also can't complain about the money that has suddenly started to enter my life over the last year, but I would do this even if I was just scraping by."

"You said you like traveling for research. How about for author signings?"

"They can be good sometimes." There was no further explanation, so I decided to move on. I noticed that here seemed to be certain subjects that bothered her. A couple of times she had glossed over the subject of book signings. I was curious, but said nothing.

"Why mysteries?"

"I think it's because I have an adventurous side to me that I've never been able to act upon. Deep down I'm Indiana Jones. Writing mysteries allows me to act on some of that, in an armchair sort of way. It's also why I wanted to join you in your search. It's a real adventure, one that I can actually live. Even if it turns out to be a dead end, it will have been worth it."

It was after eight, so we headed back to the room. We took turns showering, washing off the day of airports, rental cars, and Izzy's rooms. Sabrina had asked for two double beds, which was okay with me. I was still crazy about her and was hoping something could develop, but over dinner I had formed a different kind of bond with her—something of a deeper nature. I was willing to let our relationship—whatever it turned out to be—take its own course. Not that it wouldn't be difficult sleeping knowing that she wasn't much more than six feet away.

I was also happy to see that Ms. World-Famous Writer seemed a little unsure of what to do. I sensed some very real sexual tension in the air, but there was something refreshing about not acting on it. And I think she thought so too.

We were both exhausted. It suddenly occurred to me that I had had practically no sleep the night before—or the night before that, for that matter—so we decided to table the log book and papers until the morning, when we would be fresh. Our weariness had dampened the urgency to go through everything. I think we were both asleep in minutes.

*****

I heard Sabrina stirring at about seven, as she got up to use the bathroom and take a shower. While she was in the bathroom, I checked emails on my phone. I had two from my former boss letting me know—in his usual unsubtle, obscenity-laden way—that the way I left was unprofessional. No argument there. It was. However, as I read his threats of blackballing me from ever working in that industry again, I had to smile. First, I had no intention of ever joining that industry again, and second, he was a jerk and an idiot. I had no regrets.

I also had a short email from Mo, wishing me well on my search, and telling me to be careful. I sent my mother an email just to let her know that I was out of town and that things were going well, and that I was staying safe.

Sabrina emerged from the bathroom a half hour later, hair back in a ponytail, and once again taking my breath away. If she kept doing that, I was going to suffocate. She apologized for taking so long, and I made some stupid comment about the result being worth it, which made us both blush a bit. Then I took my turn in there, spending only a fraction of the time Sabrina did. Of course, the results were nowhere near as successful, either.

We ordered room service and Sabrina finally pulled out the diary.

"I can't believe we had the willpower to resist looking at this last night," she said.

"I'm glad we waited," I responded. "We are both much more awake today."

We sat next to each other at the table by the window and started to read. At first we were a little disappointed, as it seemed to be only a log of his missions during the war. But the more we read, the more we were hooked. The first entry was dated December 14, 1943, the target Bremen, and it was a fairly dry account of his first mission:

*We took off at 0830. Left the coast at 12,000 and climbed on course. Our bombing altitude was 22,000, so we had to use oxygen. Our course took us over the North Sea. We made a 90º turn to the South and attacked the target from a Northerly direction. There was a 10/10 cloud coverage, going and coming. We didn't meet any enemy fighters due to the fact that the cloud cover was so low. It prevented them from taking off. It didn't prevent the flak from coming up however. The flak was extremely heavy and very accurate, and although we didn't lose any planes from our group, most of us came home with damaged planes. Some of the other groups weren't as fortunate.*

*Honeycutt's oxygen mask was leaking and he passed out a couple of times. I had to wake him up just two minutes from "bombs away."*

It went on like that for another page, describing their

return home and some of the damage they received. Frankly, I found it fascinating, and was almost a little jealous. I had thought about joining the service when I graduated high school, but since my father worked at the college, I was able to go at no cost, so there was no way I could turn that down. But I envied the camaraderie that people like my grandfather experienced during the war. Obviously it was dangerous, but that made it even more exciting.

I could tell that Sabrina was finding it interesting as well. I only wish that my grandfather's log had been in with his things.

The next few entries were similar to the first, with each one corresponding to a mission. The entry for the fifth mission took on a different feel, however. While the account of the mission itself remained fairly straightforward, he started adding more conversational tidbits, such as *Honeycutt offered me $10 to clean his gun. He said he could make more than that spending the time playing poker.* Sounded like something a relative of mine would do.

By the tenth mission, the descriptions had shortened considerably. After a while they must have become old hat. It meant his entries were becoming shorter as well, but more space was given to funny happenings and everyday events. But the tenth was also where we found our first clue to Ray's involvement. It was just a throwaway line at the end: *Honeycutt was talking about his father today. Interesting story. I need to learn more.*

We looked at each other, eyebrows raised.

"Did you say you met your grandfather?" I asked.

"I did. I was young, but I sort of remember him."

"What was he like?"

"He was always sitting and drinking beer. I don't have any memory of him without a beer can in his hand. He was quite fat. He also wore those sleeveless t-shirts. I remember he had hairy arms and shoulders."

"Not to be insulting, but sort of a white trash kind of guy?"

"Exactly a white trash kind of guy. But I also think he was smart. You can sort of tell by the way these are written. After he died, I don't remember my parents ever talking about him."

Our breakfast came, so we put everything on hold while we ate. We tried to eat slowly, but failed. Both of us were too anxious to get back to the log book.

From that point on in the entries, my grandfather was mentioned numerous times.

The eleventh mission: *Honeycutt's dad made booze runs for the mob back in the late twenties and early thirties. I would have liked that guy.*

The twelfth mission: *I think Honeycutt's dad committed some sort of heist. He might have hidden the loot. Maybe I can get Honeycutt to spill some more about it.*

The thirteenth mission: *This is getting interesting. I pumped Honeycutt for more information. He swore me to secrecy. He figured since we are friends, he could tell me. His dad was involved in some big art heist in New York. They stole 11 paintings, but there is something special about one of them. He doesn't know what happened to the other 10 paintings, but the other two guys are dead. Tony Guidry and Mikey Flynn. I asked him what happened to the eleventh painting, and he said that his father hid it. He wouldn't tell me where it was, though. I think he's sensing that I'm a little too interested.*

"Why do you think your grandfather put all this stuff in his log?" I asked. "Who's he writing to?"

"I was just thinking about that. My best guess? Probably with all these guys it started out as just a log of their missions. But they didn't know from one day to the next—or one mission to the next—if they were going to live. Maybe they just wanted to leave a little of themselves behind. I'd bet they all did that. Besides, maybe it also served as notes that he could refer back to if he needed to."

Made sense to me, so we continued on.

The next three entries didn't mention my grandfather, but the seventeenth entry did: *It's all about some kind of treasure. And it's fucking big! That eleventh painting holds a clue. He said that when things got hot, his father left the painting with a guy he knows in Iowa. His father died before he could go back and get it.*

The eighteenth was more ominous: *Honeycutt shut down. I know it was a small town in Iowa. He gave me the name of the town. And the painter's name is Lando Ford. I got that much before he stopped talking. Could I find the painting? If I live through this war, maybe I should try. I think I know as much about the painting as Honeycutt does now. Maybe I will go after it.*

The nineteenth was the clincher: *I told Honeycutt I might try going for it after the war and said I'd split it with him. He got really angry and said it was none of my business. During the mission, a bomb got stuck in the bomb bay. Honeycutt went to look at it and I went to give him a hand. He tripped and fell through. We'll all miss him. Guess I know where I'm going after the war.*

"Wow," exclaimed Sabrina.

"The story I always heard was that the navigator turned his head and my grandfather was gone. Here he said he tripped."

"Are you thinking what I'm thinking?" she asked.

"Yeah, that your grandfather killed my grandfather."

She thought for a moment, then said, "Oops. Sorry about that."

I looked at her and started to laugh. She joined right in, and we laughed so hard that tears came to our eyes. It wasn't funny, and yet, it was.

We finally calmed down.

"Well," I said. "We know now how our families got involved with each other. The question is: Did your grandfather ever pursue it?"

# Chapter 11

The rest of the log book went back to being all about the missions. They became shorter and eventually petered out. My grandfather wasn't mentioned again. We had lost interest anyway. Finding out that Ray was a murderer had taken away all of our historical fascination for the log. So we pulled out the briefcase and emptied it on the table. There wasn't as much in there as we had hoped, but enough to know that Izzy was on the right track.

She had done quite a bit of research on the three crooks, which is where she had come up with my name. In fact, the thieves took up the bulk of her notes. Since her grandfather didn't mention Fairfield in his log, and probably never knew the name of the gallery, she was missing a big chunk of information, so she had concentrated on the perpetrators of the heist. It was also why she was so frustrated by our meeting at Au Bon Pain. She was disappointed that I was such a loser and didn't even know my family history.

But her loss was our gain, as we were able to put some pieces to the puzzle together. Although there was no explanation of how, it seems that Tony Guidry, Mikey Flynn, and my great-grandfather, Bruce Honeycutt, were friends—probably all from the same neighborhood. Izzy hadn't been able to determine how they knew about the eleventh painting, although Sabrina and I were able to put together a theory.

After the heist, Bruce took the eleventh painting—as we knew from his letter—and it seemed that Mikey took the other ten for safe-keeping. It was Mikey who tried to ransom some of the paintings, and it got him killed.

Izzy had talked to Mikey's grandson, and although he was reluctant to talk about it, she eventually got his take on it all. It was all family legend, but supposedly Mikey was told to lay low. When he tried to ransom the paintings, Tony killed him. At least it was assumed that Tony was responsible. No one ever found Mikey's body. Although they had no proof of Mikey's death, they didn't seem interested in pursuing it, or even talking to Izzy about it. "Scared of something?" wrote Izzy in her notes. Mikey's grandson was convinced that Tony was the ringleader, and that he was a member of the mob.

"Izzy didn't make the connection in her notes," I said, "but my guess is that the eleventh painting was some sort of mob deal. Maybe they had it shipped to the museum and let Tony—who was probably trying to prove his worth—get it for them. Using old friends Mikey and Bruce to help him, Tony did the heist."

"And for whatever reason, they stole more than they went in for," added Sabrina, "which probably created a lot more publicity than the one alone would have. So Tony's reputation was on the line. As long as Mikey laid low with the other ten paintings, everything was fine. But the minute he tried to ransom them, Tony had to shut him up."

"And then Bruce took off with the one they really wanted," I said. "The question is, why wasn't it turned over to the mob right after the heist? Did they need to give it some time for the hubbub to die down?"

"Hubbub?"

"Yeah. You know. Confusion. Uproar."

"I know what it means," she said with a laugh. "I'm just not sure if anyone has used that word in sixty years. You're really getting into this time period, aren't you?"

"Yeah, well, anyway," I said, "assuming that's why Bruce had the painting, he threw a monkey wrench…"

"Wow, you are really coming up with the oldies today. Monkey wrench?"

"Hey, people still use that expression."

"Okay, continue," she said, still laughing.

"He screwed up—better?"—she nodded her approval—"their plans by hiding the painting."

"I wonder if he decided that after Mikey was killed," suggested Sabrina. "He was probably really scared that he would be next."

"And maybe he felt that if he hid it, it would be his insurance policy. As long as he was the only one who knew where it was, they wouldn't kill him."

"Stupid," said Sabrina.

"Hey, he was a Honeycutt. What can I say?"

"Which brings up the question: you said he was crushed by some beer barrels that fell off a truck. Do you think it was an accident?"

"Not anymore. What do you want to bet Tony killed him and made it look like an accident?"

"I think that's exactly what happened." She looked through some more notes. "It says Tony died a few years later, but it doesn't say how."

"Well," I offered, "He was in a dangerous business. It could have happened any number of ways."

"There's another name," I said. "In the letter I found in the book, he mentions a John. Where does he fit in?"

There was no answer to that one, so we continued looking through the material.

"You know," said Sabrina, "We're making a lot of assumptions here based on sketchy information. You realize we could be totally wrong."

"I wouldn't be surprised, but I suppose we have to start somewhere."

Sabrina nodded. "So our cast of characters includes your great-grandfather Bruce, and his cohorts Tony, Mikey, and maybe some guy named John. Then the next generation includes your grandfather and mine. Then it kind of skips a generation, other than your father being the keeper of the book. Which leads us to our generation: You and me—two of the most clueless individuals I've ever seen, I must say—Izzy, and Mikey's great-grandson, who sounds like he wants nothing to do with this. Who else?"

She continued reading, then tapped the journal in dramatic fashion. "Mario."

"Who?"

"Mario Guidry. Tony's great-grandson. And I think he may have been the one who killed Izzy and is after us," she said.

I raised my eyebrows.

"After she talked to the Flynns, Izzy tried to find Tony's ancestors. She found one living here in Chicago..."

"And now we know why she was here," I interrupted.

"Here's what she wrote in her notes: *'Found Tony's great-grandson. Mario is his name. Creepy! I may have made a mistake looking him up. He knows about the treasure, but I could tell he didn't know where it was. He asked me about some eggs. It must be slang for something, but I didn't want to ask him. I didn't give him much of the story, but it was still too much. He knows that I don't have the answers, but I told him about Ray's log. Big mistake. He scares me. Need to stay away from this family. I think they are still mob connected. Dangerous!'*"

"Notice the difference in her writing?" I asked.

"Yes. Instead of just notes, this is written almost as a diary entry. She knew her life was in danger. She wrote this to either the police or someone else—like us—who might take over the hunt. The question is, do we give this information to the police?"

Ahh, back to the question of how much to withhold from the police. I had changed from only a few days ago. There is no way I would give them my mother's secret carrot cake recipe now.

"Good question," I said. "There is no direct evidence that he did anything to her, but getting the police to investigate might slow him down some."

"If he's mob connected though, I question how much—if any—evidence they might find."

"I agree. It also means the police are going to want everything we have."

Sabrina sighed. "Normally, I'd be the first one to go to the police. I'm just not sure it's the right thing to do at this moment."

"Then let's sit on it. There's no reason we can't give it to them in a few days if we feel it necessary."

A decision made.

"So where do we go from here?" she asked. "We don't want to interview Mario Guidry, and I don't think we will get anything else from Mikey's grandson—Izzy did a good job with them. Fairfield?"

"I think so. Tracking down that painting seems to be the next step."

"I feel sorry for Izzy," said Sabrina. "She definitely inherited Ray's genes. She was just too greedy. If she had just gone about it a different way, she might be alive today."

"Would you have helped her with this if she had come to you?"

"I don't know. That's a good question. On one hand, she was family. On the other hand, she was a spiteful bitch who tormented me my whole childhood. It's hard to dismiss that. I just wish she had been a different person. She robbed us both of something that could have been special."

We still had to go down to Izzy's room and pack everything up, so we put away the papers and log book and got our bags ready to go. I went with Sabrina to her sister's room. She didn't need the help, but I think she appreciated the support. We threw all of her toiletries in the trash and her clothes in the suitcase. Sabrina put the $200 from the safe in her purse.

"If we go by a Goodwill store, I'll just donate the whole thing; money, suitcase and all," she said.

"We need to decide what to do with her room at the Residence Inn," I said. "She had almost nothing there, but if we don't go back, will they keep charging you? I'm just worried that the place might be under surveillance."

"I think we should chance it," she replied. "I'd feel better cleaning up after her."

We checked out, and they brought the car around. We got to the Residence Inn around 10:30. We were in and out in record time, and on the road to Fairfield, Iowa.

*****

It was a better part of a five-hour trip from Chicago to Fairfield. We spent a little while rehashing what we had read in the log and the notes, but eventually we realized that most of it was going to hinge on what we found in Fairfield. After that, I had Sabrina tell me what it was like to be famous.

"You have to understand," she said. "All this fame stuff is new to me. It's all been within the last year. Before that, I was a complete unknown. If Ellen—she's my editor—hadn't liked one of my first two books, I'd still be toiling away in obscurity. Besides, it's not like I'm a movie star or anything. I'm a writer. People know my books, not me. The fact that a few people have recognized me over the past couple of days is pretty rare."

"Or a sign of things to come," I argued. "Look at Stephen King. I bet he can't go anywhere without being recognized."

"In all honesty, I don't want that. Despite what you might think, I'm really a very private person."

"But as your books become more popular, so will you. Your face will start appearing on the cover of writing magazines, then more mainstream magazines like *People*. Like it or not, you will start to be recognized. Maybe not Stephen King recognizable, but you will have to start wearing sunglasses and big floppy hats."

She laughed at that, but I also knew she was thinking about what I had said.

"I'm sorry," I added. "I hope that didn't depress you."

"No, not really. My agent was warning me about that a few

weeks ago, but I guess I wasn't listening, because it really hadn't happened yet."

"On the other hand," I offered, "I'm sure I could pass most of my favorite authors in the street and not recognize them. Most likely, you will interact with people who will walk away thinking, 'Boy, she looks familiar. I wonder where I've seen her.'"

I didn't know if I was right or not, but she seemed to perk up a bit, so it did the job.

Once we shook loose of the city and suburbia, we entered flat farmland.

"There's something nice about this," said Sabrina, about two hours into the drive. "I don't think I could live here, but it's very peaceful to drive through."

I was getting a different feeling. It had just dawned on me that the same car had been about a half mile in back of us for the longest time. It was gray or silver, but it was too distant to see a make. We were on a major highway, Interstate 88, so it's not like it was just them and us on the road, but something was odd about it. Other cars either passed us or dropped further behind. Not this one. It always seemed to be right in that same spot. I broke the news to Sabrina.

"I think we're being followed."

I'll give her credit. She was cool about it. "Should I not look?" she asked.

"No, it's okay. They are quite a ways back there." I explained what I was feeling.

She watched for a few minutes, then said, "You might be right. What do you want to do?"

"Did you get the same feeling that I did from Izzy's

research that she hadn't told Mario about Fairfield?"

"Pretty much."

"Then I suggest we get off somewhere, try to switch cars, then find another way to Fairfield."

"Sounds like a plan."

It turned out to be one of those easier-said-than-done plans. We were passing Sterling, Illinois, a small town that actually had a Hertz office. However, the road was so flat, they would see us pull off. So we made the decision to keep going to Davenport and try to lose them there.

"What if Izzy did let it slip about Fairfield?" asked Sabrina. "What if these people are just keeping tabs on us but there is someone already in Fairfield?"

"Then they will be looking for a red Camry. The car switch might buy us some time."

By the time we reached Davenport, we were prepared to lose them. Sabrina had pinpointed the Hertz office on her phone's GPS app and had called ahead to have a car waiting for us. As for an excuse as to why we were exchanging cars, she explained that the Camry was too small and that we now wanted an SUV. They accepted that without question and said they would have a Toyota Rav-4 all set to go.

Meanwhile, the silver car was still the same distance behind us. By this time, there was no doubt in our minds that it was tailing us. We also knew that switching cars would work for a while, but eventually they would pick up the trail again. If Sabrina's fear that Izzy let more slip than she indicated was true, they'd be waiting for us in Fairfield anyway.

Traffic had become heavy the closer to Davenport we got, so by the time we were ready to make our exit off the highway, there were quite a few cars between us and our silver pursuer. When I could see them I noticed that they had closed the gap—probably in an effort not to lose us—but there was still a chance they wouldn't see us take the exit.

I didn't use my turn signal, giving them as little advance warning as possible, and shot down the exit ramp. Sabrina kept an eye out for them. I was turning at the bottom of the ramp when I heard honking.

"They saw us too late and missed the exit," she said in an excited voice "They tried to slow down, but that didn't go over well with the other drivers, as I'm sure you could hear. By the time they get off the next exit, we'll be at the Hertz office. We shook them!"

I wished that I could share Sabrina's enthusiasm, but it was beginning to hit me just how dogged these people were in their quest for the treasure. Did they know something about it that we didn't—like, what it was? Had Mario's great-grandfather passed down some information as to the nature of the treasure, and all they needed were the clues in Izzy's possession?

I was beginning to think that we were in way over our heads.

# Chapter 12

I said as much to Sabrina once we were outfitted in our new vehicle and again on our way.

"You think they know more than we do?" she asked.

"No, I think they know different information than we do. It's like having a puzzle in two pieces. Each piece is worthless without the other. But put them together and you have the solution. I think we have the means to find the treasure, and I think they know what the treasure is."

"And your reasoning?"

"We're looking for it mostly out of curiosity. We want to know why it got Izzy killed. We want to know how our families are connected. We're just looking for answers. If things get too hot, we can turn it over to the police and walk away. No harm, no foul. Izzy is the reason I think they know what it is."

"Izzy?"

"You don't kill someone because you are trying to satisfy your curiosity. You kill someone because they have information you need and either won't give to you or you extracted it from them and don't need them anymore. Mario—assuming it's Mario—knows what the treasure is, but until Izzy came along, it was just the stuff of legend. All traces of the map—or painting—had disappeared. Now he's presented with a way to get it. You think he's not going to take advantage of that?"

"But obviously she didn't give him the information he was looking for, so wouldn't he be better off keeping her alive?"

"He probably got everything he could from her—including my name. Remember, he had already met with her in Chicago. At this point she became an adversary. She had to go. So now he's still looking for the missing piece."

Sabrina was quiet for a minute. "If that's so," she finally said, "we're all in the same boat. In fact, we're actually in a bigger boat. In better shape than them. Wouldn't you rather know how to get the treasure and then find out what it is, than to know what the treasure is, but have no way of finding it?"

"Only two things wrong with that," I said. "First, we don't yet have the means to find it, which reduces the size of said boat, and second, they are willing to kill for it. That puts us in the middle of the ocean with floaties on."

Sabrina chuckled. "I'm sorry I ever brought up the analogy." Then she turned serious, but with a wild look in her eyes. "But Del, doesn't all this spark a sense of excitement in you? Doesn't the danger kind of drive you?"

There was definitely something to what she was saying. Besides, I didn't want to appear the wimp.

"It does." But hey, if I'm a wimp, I'm a wimp. Call it as you see it. "The curiosity factor is what gives me the adrenalin rush. I'm hoping that the danger factor will keep me thinking clearly."

While there was no direct road to Fairfield, there were three logical choices from Davenport. We took the fourth. The first three all had us entering Fairfield from the East. The route I decided on took us West on Interstate 80, way past Fairfield, then coming down through Oskaloosa and Ottumwa, entering Fairfield from the West. It wouldn't make any sense for us to do that, so if they were watching for us, the odds were that they would be waiting near the East entrance of town. All part of my caution campaign. Sabrina didn't sound an objection.

The long way got us into Fairfield mid-evening. We stopped at a nondescript chain hotel and parked around back. They had a sign out front: Riblets $8.95. Toast Buffet, 6am-10am. What the heck was a riblet? A little rib? A toast buffet? You had to be kidding me. We decided we'd be better off having a pizza delivered. We asked the front desk clerk who had the best pizza. When the answer came back Pizza Hut, I found myself seriously missing Boston. What would Seymour say about our predicament? Yeah, sometimes he ate crappy pizza, but at least he knew the difference.

Riblets and Pizza Hut. Was this Iowa cuisine? We ordered Chinese instead, knowing full well that whatever we ended up with would be a disappointment. It was.

We were both exhausted, so we laid in bed—our separate beds, of course—talking baseball. That's right, baseball. Over the years and all the dates I went on, I didn't once find a woman who liked baseball. That's actually odd for Boston. Everyone likes sports in Boston. Everyone, that is, except the women I dated. How exciting it was for me to find someone to intelligently talk baseball with. There were only two problems: 1) She was a Yankees fan, and 2) We weren't dating. The first I could live with, I suppose. She had probably been brainwashed at an early age to support the Evil Empire. So sad. The second … well, the second was beginning to have possibilities. The sexual tension we felt in Chicago was still there, and had even increased a notch. Was baseball an aphrodisiac? Or maybe it was the unspoken danger that we might be heading into. Whatever, I felt like saying, "Oh, let's just get it over with," but that seemed a bit crass. Then again, maybe she was just waiting for me to make the first move. God, I felt like a teenager.

In case she was, I thought I'd lead into it gently. When the baseball talk had wound down, I said, "Sabrina, I really like you. You are a breath of fresh air in my life."

And that was all it took. A minute later she was in my bed and we were naked. Go figure.

*****

We woke up the next morning wrapped in each other's arms. Despite the fact that she was the one who entered my bed, she was oddly hesitant about sex, as if she hadn't had a lot of experience. I found that strange. At thirty-four, and as gorgeous as she was, I would have expected her to be an expert. She certainly had the desire though; she latched onto me and wouldn't let go, as if the mere touch was all she needed. There was a story here. Hopefully I'd hear it someday.

The nice thing was, there was no morning-after awkwardness. After we woke up, we held each other for close to a half an hour, made love—still with some of the strangeness I felt earlier—then showered together. Not a lot was said, but it all felt good.

When we were back among the living, we talked about our plans for the day. But there was a different feel as we talked, the silent acknowledgement that we were now a couple. Our night together wasn't a one-night stand, and it wasn't simply two people thrown together using each other for support. It was deeper, and we both knew it.

As tempting as it was, we decided to pass up the toast

buffet and eat something later. Sadly, they had never heard of Dunkin Donuts in Fairfield, Iowa.

Our one and only goal was to find out what happened to the art gallery, and more importantly, the paintings. If we were able to figure out why Bruce had come to Fairfield to deposit the painting, that would be a bonus.

There was a light rain falling. We'd have to get rain gear. That was good. A hood would cover Sabrina's hair, her most noticeable feature. I'm not sure it mattered that much for me, I had a pretty forgettable face. But I decided the hood wouldn't hurt. Between the new car and the raincoats, if there was anyone in town looking for us, we were pretty invisible.

Before venturing out, we boned up on the history of Fairfield, or rather, Sabrina did. I decided it was time to find out a little about my ancestors. While Sabrina was gathering information on the town, I joined Ancestry.com and looked at my family history. I found what I was searching for almost immediately.

I put my name in and my birth information popped up. It showed my birthdate 38 years earlier, and my birthplace as Northampton, Mass. Then it listed my parents. I had no interest in my mother's side of the family, so I confined my clicks to my father's side. My father was Robert Bruce. His father was Robert Bruce. His father's father's name was a little more daring—Bruce Robert. You've gotta be kidding me. And I end up with Delmore?

My father's birthplace was listed as New York, NY. His death hadn't yet been entered. Whose responsibility was that anyway? His father's birthplace was also New York, with a death date of 1944. The death location was left blank. Yeah, that would be a hard one. And here was the kicker. Great-grandfather Bruce was born in Fairfield, Iowa!

It listed his death as 1935, in New York, so that was consistent with everything I had read. I also found the answer to one of those silly questions: Why was he Bruce Robert and not Robert Bruce? Turns out he had an older brother named Robert Bruce who died when he was a teenager. God, could my family get any more boring with the names? Delmore must have come from my mother's side, and knowing her, I bet she insisted that I not be another Robert Bruce.

An interesting little tidbit was that my great-grandfather's father—yes, yet another Robert Bruce—was born in Paisley, Scotland, in 1860. It would make sense for him to end up in New York and stay there with all the other immigrants. But he didn't. So how did he get to Fairfield in order for Bruce to be born here? Something for another day, I suppose.

I told Sabrina about the Fairfield link.

"He must have known the gallery owner," she replied. "And if so, how much did he tell him … or her? For all we know, the gallery owner found the treasure years ago and this is all just a wasted effort."

"Not completely wasted," I said.

She gave me a broad smile and leaned over and kissed me. "No, not completely. Besides," she added, "We have to assume Bruce had some brains. He wouldn't have given anyone the means to beat him to the treasure."

"Let's remember," I said, "He was still a Honeycutt. Stranger things have happened."

"Anyway, I found out some things about Fairfield. Did you know it is the home of Maharishi University? The TM people?

A lot of the culture of the town revolves around it. It used to be a college called Parsons. Started in the late 1800s. Evidently kind of a hotshot college back in the sixties. In the mid-sixties, it had the third highest paid faculty in the country."

"What happened to it?"

"Went bankrupt and closed."

"So much for their salary plan."

"The town has a couple dozen art galleries. I suppose we could go into some of them and ask if they've ever heard of the Simpson Gallery. Fairfield had the first public library in Iowa—one place I read said it was the first public library west of the Mississippi."

She continued, "Sounds like a cute downtown. There is an actual village square, surrounded on every side with stores, restaurants, and art galleries. It sounds like for most of its history, it was just a farm community"

"Did you get a job with the visitor's bureau?"

"I always do this when I travel. Just like to know where I am."

"And where are you?"

"In the middle of pig country, having the best time of my life."

The gorgeous world-famous author was serious.

"Hard to believe," I said. "I would've guessed that you've had more than your share of good times."

She looked at me. Her eyes had misted over.

"Then you'd be wrong."

# Chapter 13

I wasn't sure what to do with that comment, and she didn't seem to want to fill it in any, so I left it and moved on. We had reserved the room for three nights, just to be safe, so we left our luggage, locked up the log and the papers, and headed out to find a store to buy raincoats.

An hour later, we were walking around the town square. There was a chilly drizzle coming down, but we welcomed it for its potential to keep us hidden from view. Of course, I thought, whoever was after us might not have the slightest clue that we were here and might be three states away. But somehow I didn't think so.

After my "good times" comment, Sabrina had been pretty quiet. I asked her if I had said anything wrong and she said no. She took my hand as she said it, so I was pretty sure it wasn't me. I did know, however, that whatever nerve the comment struck was a pretty deep one. By the time we went into our first art gallery, however, she was back to normal.

It was kind of a hole-in-the-wall gallery, and looked as if it had been there a long time. I liked the looks of it specifically for that reason. My guess was that the Simpson Gallery probably hadn't been much bigger.

A middle-aged woman sat behind a crowded counter.

"May I help you?" she asked pleasantly.

"Are you the owner?" I asked.

Her eyes narrowed. "I am, but I should warn you right now that I'm not looking to buy anything and I'm not looking to be saved."

Our raincoats matched. Did that make us look like missionaries or salesmen?

Sabrina took over. Laughing, she said, "No, nothing like that. We have a historical question that we're hoping you can help us with."

The woman softened. "Sorry. You wouldn't believe how often I have to deal with that. What can I help you with?"

"Back in the 30s…" I started.

"Wow, you are talking historical. Okay, go on."

"There was an art gallery in town called the Simpson Gallery. We were wondering if you had ever heard of it."

"Can't say I have. Do you know when it closed?"

"Not really." I decided to give her a part of the picture. "My great-grandfather had loaned the gallery a painting. He died, and when my grandfather went by to claim it, it wasn't there. Now, I don't know if he meant that the painting was no longer there or the gallery, so I couldn't tell you exactly when it closed."

"Was your great-grandfather the artist?"

"No, it was somebody by the name of Lando Ford."

"Hmm, never heard of him."

"You're not the only one. I don't know anything about the artist, or about the painting, for that matter. It's become more of a quest—an ancestral quest, I guess."

"Obviously you don't have an address."

"No. I have the receipt, but oddly enough it only lists the name of the gallery and the town name, which, of course, is Fairfield."

"Probably didn't need the street back then. Fairfield isn't

very big now, but it was tiny then. It had to have been somewhere in the downtown section. I can't imagine any business surviving that wasn't downtown."

"Would you have any suggestions for us?" asked Sabrina. "Any gallery owners who might know?"

"I would doubt it. My gallery is one of the oldest. Most are owned by younger people and the vast majority by recent transplants. Even I'm not a Fairfield native. I think going the gallery route will leave you frustrated. You could try the library or the newspaper office. They might have something on it." She could see the disappointment on our faces. "The only other thing I could suggest would be to try all the Simpsons in the phone book. Maybe one of them is a relative of whoever owned the gallery."

We thanked her for the information, feeling a little guilty that we didn't buy anything, and went back to the car. We decided to look in the order she suggested, first trying the library. Between the library and the newspaper, we spent most of the day, and accomplished nothing. We went online, looked on microfiche at newspapers that hadn't yet been digitally transferred, paged through old picture books of Fairfield. Nothing. Finally, we got a clue, as meager as it was.

Someone at the newspaper office suggested we take a ride over to one of the nursing homes in town and talk to some of the most ancient of the residents. Maybe one of them would remember something.

We walked into one of the nicer facilities and explained our mission to the person in charge. She thought it might be a good brain exercise for the residents.

"A lot of them are in the activity room right now," she said.

"Maybe asking them all together would be a better plan. Someone might say something that will spark a memory in another."

We went into the room, occupied by about forty residents, and the woman—whose name I forgot the minute after she said it—got their attention. Thus began a comedy of errors.

I stood in front of the group. "We are trying to find out some information about an art gallery that was in Fairfield back in the 1930s. It was called the Simpson Gallery. Has anyone heard of it? We'd appreciate your help."

"I can't hear you."

"Speak up."

"Stop mumbling."

So I repeated it in a much louder and clearer voice.

"You don't have to yell. We're not deaf!"

Finally, I got my message across, ending with, "Has anyone ever heard of it?"

A woman who had to be about 800 years old raised her hand and answered simply, "Yes." That was all we got out of her.

"It was owned by a guy named Simpson," said an elderly man in the front. "Never knew his first name."

Well, that was a big help.

We checked out two more nursing homes and came away with just enough information to know that it actually existed—but nothing more than that.

"I was starting to wonder if this place was real," Sabrina said finally, as we were again walking through town, this time in search of a decent cup of coffee. "Can you imagine it as some sort of great prank by Bruce. Think about it," she was having fun with this, "you come up with a joke to play on your family. It could affect the lives of your ancestors all the way down the line. The ultimate practical joke."

I didn't get the chance to respond. We were passing an alleyway, when hands reached out and roughly pulled us in. I was thrown to the ground, landing on my left shoulder. I cried out in pain. I heard an exclamation from Sabrina, as well.

I looked up at a big guy holding a gun on me. I glanced over at Sabrina. She was sitting up, rubbing her elbow. An even bigger guy stood over her. I couldn't see a gun.

"What do you want?" I asked, knowing full well he wanted the painting.

"The painting."

I must be psychic.

"What painting?" I asked innocently. But I wasn't fooling anyone.

He kicked me in the side. It was meant to hurt, not to disable, and it did its job. As bad as East Boston was, I had never been mugged before. It was scary. I was wishing Mo and her martial arts skills were with us just then. But I needn't have worried. Turns out, I had Sabrina.

"You must be two of the stupidest crooks I've ever seen," she said. "And I've seen a lot of stupid ones. Do you think if we had the fucking painting," I had never heard her swear, "that we'd be strolling around the town? Don't you think it would have been a little more intelligent to just follow us until you saw the painting? God, you guys are an embarrassment to the crook business."

She had them off guard. And then she kicked her leg up from the sitting position and got the bigger guy right in the balls. It was vicious. He didn't utter a sound more than "umph," and dropped like a sack of manure. Then she swept her leg around and caught my guy in the back of the knee. He went down backwards and landed with a thud. She was up in a second and gave him a kick in the family jewels just as hard as the other guy. He dropped his gun and reached for his groin. Little good that was going to do. I took a shot there once. There is nothing you can do to stop the pain.

I quickly got up and grabbed his gun and held it on the two men. It was a pretty needless exercise. Both men were throwing up and had no interest in me. Meanwhile, Sabrina looked down at her guy and asked, "Who are you working for?"

"Fuck you," he answered between gasps.

She kicked him in the kidney and he screamed out. I was pretty sure she had done some damage. She moved over to my guy.

"You want a shot to the kidney too?"

The guy tried to roll over on his back to protect himself from her kick, but another rumble of vomit came up and he had to go back on his side.

"You've got two seconds," she said quietly, but with the kind of tone you don't ignore.

"Mario," he gasped. "Mario Guidry. He hired us to get a painting from you, that's all."

Sabrina nodded to me. I dialed 911 on my cell phone. I told the dispatcher that two men had attempted to mug us. She asked where we were, and of course, I had no idea. I walked out to the end of the alley and gave her a landmark. She assured me a car would be right there. I laid the gun on the ground out of reach of the two thugs. The last thing I wanted was to be mistaken for one of the attackers.

"You were fast," I said to Sabrina. "Where did you learn that?"

"Self-defense classes," she said off-handedly. I didn't believe her. However, I dropped it. But there was definitely more to this girl than met the eye.

The police arrived a few minutes later and we rode with them to the station. Before they got there, we decided we would tell them a piece of the story—just enough to implicate Mario.

When we were in the police station, I explained to the detective in charge that my great-grandfather had lent a Fairfield gallery a painting that I was trying to recover. Somehow, a guy named Mario Guidry got wind of it and tried to steal it. Supposedly his great-grandfather had tried to take it from my great-grandfather back in the 30s. I told them I had no idea why someone would want the painting. We embellished it a bit, but stayed pretty much to the truth.

It took them about five minutes to break one of the crooks, who confirmed that they were sent to steal the painting. While we were there, we asked if anyone if they had heard of the Simpson Gallery, just in case they could provide us with more information than our elderly friends, but again we struck out.

We were out of there in less than two hours. We told them we wanted to press charges, but they'd have to let us know if they wanted us to come back. They doubted it, seeing as how the muggers were admitting to everything.

As we were walking back to the car, I asked, "What did you mean back there when you said you had seen a lot of crooks? Are you some kind of cop and you're just not telling me?"

She laughed. "No. I'm just an author. In my research I've met with a number of crooks."

"Oh."

Did I believe it? I didn't have much choice, so I decided to go with it—for now, anyway.

"You think they will pick up Mario?" Sabrina asked, maybe to change the subject?

"No. He'll be long gone. If nothing else, his name is now on record related to this stuff."

"Back to the hotel?"

"Yeah, we can figure out what we're going to eat, and find out how many Simpsons live in Fairfield, Iowa. Tomorrow we talk to them. Hopefully we won't hit a brick wall."

"Even if we do, I'm determined to continue this"

"Me too. Otherwise it means I'll have to start job hunting. Oh, please let there be a Simpson who knows something about that gallery or the painting."

# Chapter 14

We made love again that night, and again Sabrina clung to me like I was the last man on earth. Could this possibly be the same person who didn't think twice about crushing a man's kidney? It was dawning on me how little I knew about her.

After breakfast the next morning we looked up Simpson in the phone book and found six of them. We decided it would be better to go see them in person, rather than calling, and we wrote down the six addresses. It was a beautiful morning, warm and sunny, so our raincoat disguises weren't necessary. We weren't worried, seeing as how Mario's men had been arrested. There was no way he would have anyone else watching us, so we felt pretty safe.

The first two visits were washouts—in both cases people who had recently moved to Fairfield—and the next two weren't home. The fifth turned out to be the one. An old guy answered the door. He was limping badly, most likely a bad case of arthritis, and seemed to be in a fair amount of pain. Despite the obvious discomfort, he was pleasant as he greeted us.

"Mr. Simpson?" I asked.

"That would be me. I'm Harry Simpson. If you're selling me religion though, I already have one, thanks."

Sabrina and I looked at each other. Sheesh! Did we really look the part? Even without the raincoats? I was seriously starting to wonder.

I gave him the friendliest, non-religious smile I had and said, "No. My name is Del Honeycutt, and this is Sabrina

Spencer..."

"Like the mystery writer," he said, interrupting me.

"Actually, one and the same, Mr. Simpson," said Sabrina. "Nice to meet you. We are tracking down an old mystery and were hoping you could help us."

"Seriously? You're the mystery writer?"

"I am."

I may as well have disappeared.

"Yeah, you look like your book cover." He turned toward the inner part of the house. "Edna. Get out here. There's someone you have to meet."

A large woman of about the same age waddled in from the kitchen.

"Edna, This here is Sabrina Spencer, the mystery writer."

"Oh my word!" exclaimed Edna. She touched her hair, as if it would magically fix anything that was out of place. "You look like your picture."

Duh...

"Come in, come in," she said. "Harry, get out of the way. Let them in."

Harry was moving as fast as he could, which wasn't very fast at all. I felt for him. At this point, even if they knew nothing about the gallery, we had to visit. The delight in their faces upon meeting a real live mystery author was priceless.

They were rattling on to Sabrina about what great fans they were and that they had all of her books. They did, too. They brought them out for Sabrina to see, and she offered to sign them. You'd think they'd just won the lottery.

"My new one is coming out around Christmas," said Sabrina. "I'll get some copies earlier than that. If you give me your address, I will send you a signed one."

Edna screamed with joy, then got up and went into the bathroom. Could she have peed her pants in excitement?

Things eventually calmed down and Edna returned from the bathroom.

"How can we help you?" Harry finally said.

Sabrina turned it over to me. I had reappeared.

"We were wondering if you knew anything about an old gallery in town called the Simpson Gallery."

"That was my grandfather's place," said Harry.

We had found it!

"We're trying to locate a painting," I began, then told them the abbreviated version of my great-grandfather's story. "Do you know when the gallery closed?"

"Yeah, sometime right before the war. When he went to jail."

"What did he do?" I asked.

"What didn't he do? He was a real crook. You name it, he was involved in it. You say your great-grandfather was a friend of his? Was your great-grandfather a crook too?"

"Everything is pointing that way," I said. "Do you have any idea what might have happened to the paintings in the gallery?"

"Most of them went back to their owners. But there were about twenty or so that my daddy inherited. I guess they couldn't find who they belonged to."

The million-dollar question. "Do you know what happened to the twenty?"

"I most certainly do. They are somewhere in my basement."

Sabrina and I looked at each other with raised eyebrows.

Could it be this easy?

"Well some of them anyway. I gave some away."

Of course it couldn't.

"I could go down and look, if you like."

"I know you're having trouble getting around," I said, "and I'm sure going down to your basement must be hard. We wouldn't ask it of you if it wasn't important."

"No, I'd be happy to," said Harry. "It'll probably take me a couple of days to get to it though."

My heart sank and I groaned inwardly—at least I hoped it was inwardly, because Sabrina shot me a glance. But Sabrina saved the day.

"Unfortunately, we have to leave town soon," she said, "but I have an idea, if you and Edna would agree to it. Would you be okay if Del and I went down and searched for it? You could tell us where to look."

Edna, who probably would have agreed to anything to make sure she got that free signed book, said quickly, "We'd be happy to let you, wouldn't we, Harry?"

"I guess so. It's kind of messy down there, though."

"Not a problem at all," I said, anxious to get the go-ahead.

An hour later we were sifting through the most crowded basement I had ever seen. Edna said she and Harry had been married over fifty years, and had lived in the same house the entire time. I could believe it. There was about fifty years' worth of garbage piled around us. Harry had given us a general idea where to look, but I was honestly having questions about how long it had been since Harry had last been down there.

Finally, we found the boxes we were looking for. There

was a small corner devoted to junk from the gallery. There were about a half a dozen boxes in all. Two were labeled *Sculptures,* one labeled *Records,* one labeled *Christmas Decorations,* and two labeled *Paintings*. Each had about an inch of dust built up on it. I wiped off the boxes and said, "Here goes."

It wasn't there.

There were ten paintings in all, ranging in size from about three feet by three feet, to one that was only six inches in diameter. But the Lando Ford painting wasn't one of them.

"Shit," I exclaimed. I felt like crying. "So what now?"

"I guess we find out who he gave them to. If he knows, we continue on. If he gave them to Goodwill or someplace like that, then we go home."

Disappointed, we wiped ourselves off, both looking forward to getting back to the hotel and showering, then went upstairs.

"Any luck?" asked Harry.

"I'm afraid not," I answered. "We found the paintings, but there were only ten there, and it wasn't one of the ten. Do you happen to remember who you gave the others to?"

"My brother. We split them up when our father died." He held up his hand as I was about to say something. "And before you ask, my brother died about five years ago. I assume his son—his only kid—has them. What he did with them, I can't tell you. The fact is, I'm not in touch with my nephew. He's—excuse the language—an asshole."

"Harry!" scolded Edna. "Don't use that language in this house."

"Well he is."

She turned to Sabrina and said in a conspiratorial voice, "He is, you know."

"Last I knew," said Harry, "He lived in Wahoo, Nebraska. A few hours from here. We lost contact a long time ago when he cheated us out of some money my brother left us. He pulled a fast one, and we never saw a dime of it."

"That's horrible," said Sabrina with a look of disgust. She struck me as someone who would always root for the underdog.

"Wahoo?" I asked.

"I assume he still lives there. This is the Midwest. People stay where they are. His name is Russell. Russ Simpson."

"I probably have an address for him," said Edna. "I'll get it for you."

She found the address and we slowly extracted ourselves from the house, and a few minutes later we were back in the hotel room. Sabrina was already in the shower and I was looking at a map online.

This was going to be our last chance. Sabrina was right. If Russ didn't have it, we were going home. And I didn't want to go home.

# Chapter 15

We spent a quiet evening in our room, after dining at one of Fairfield's finer establishments. We were both subdued after the high and then quick low at the Simpsons' house. We certainly didn't want to have to go home. It wasn't so much about the supposed treasure as it was the curiosity of why people died for it. Plus, I think we were both wondering what would become of our relationship if we had to return to our normal lives.

It occurred to me over dinner that we had, in fact, solved one mystery. The Brooklyn Museum heist had been unsolved all these years. We thought we should inform them of the news. Then we figured that they had waited this long, they could wait a few more days or weeks.

We made love again that evening, and again it was strange. Not bad strange, just unusual. If she had been a virgin, I could maybe understand it, but she had been married. Then it hit me. It was like making love to a puppy dog. She was crying out for affection and couldn't get close enough to me. And yet, to protect me—protect us—she laid into those attackers like nothing I'd ever seen before.

"You're a very complex individual," I said just before we drifted off.

"Mmm," she replied, half asleep.

We slept in the next morning, then I went out for bagels and coffee. When I got back, she was on the phone to her editor talking book business.

While she was involved with that, I went back onto Ancestry.com to see if anything else popped out at me regarding my family. But no. My family—for better or worse—was as clear as it was ever going to be.

Sabrina was still deep in her conversation, so just for fun, I typed in Sabrina Spencer, with the parameters that would narrow it down. Nothing. That was strange. I thought for a minute and typed Isobel Worth, along with the same parameters. I found her almost immediately. Like my father, her death hadn't yet been added, but it was the right person, showing that she was forty-one.

I clicked onto her parents. It displayed their birth and death dates and locations, and also showed their children, Isobel and Patricia. Patricia? Patricia was adopted, and would now be thirty-four. Sabrina was Patricia? Why wouldn't she have told me that? Hadn't we reached a point of trust in our relationship?

She was off the phone and had opened her laptop to check her emails. Casually, I asked her, "So is Sabrina Spencer a pen name?"

Without looking up from her computer, she answered. "No. My real name. Why?"

Her response may have sounded relaxed, but it wasn't. Her radar had gone on alert, I could feel it.

"No reason. Just curious." I counted to ten silently. "So do you go by Patricia or Patty?"

I looked over at her. She was unmoving, still staring down at her computer, but now seeing nothing in front of her. And then slowly, tears began to form and she started to shake.

"How did you find out?" It came as a whisper. "Were you

checking up on me? Didn't you trust me?"

She attempted for it to come out as an accusation, but it failed miserably, and she knew it.

"I was on Ancestry.com and I just did it for fun. But to answer your question, yes, I trusted you implicitly. Now I don't know what to believe."

"I was going to tell you, I promise I was." The tears were flowing freely now. She wasn't faking it. These tears were real.

"Why didn't you?"

"Because I didn't want you to question my character. If you found out about me and my history, you would lump me in with Izzy, and I'm nothing like Izzy."

And then she broke down—a break-down like I had never seen before. Starting as almost hiccups, they quickly turned into sobs, sobs that seemed to emanate from the deepest part of her soul. At one point she couldn't catch her breath and began to hyperventilate. She was beginning to scare me. I went over and put my arms around her and helped her to the floor. She latched onto me the way she did in bed, as if I was all she had in the world. Suddenly, I could see that she was going to throw up. The waste basket was within reach, so I grabbed it and put it in front of her. Just in time. She threw up, while at the same time choking on her lack of breath. I tried to pull her hair back, but wasn't in time. The ends were caked in vomit. I had never seen an emotional reaction like this. Whatever was in there was ever so dark. I wasn't so sure I wanted to hear what was behind it. What could scar somebody so horribly as to leave them in this state?

We just sat there for what seemed like an hour—and maybe it was. When she was able to sit on her own, I extracted myself from her arms and went into the bathroom for a couple of wet face cloths. One, I gave her for her face. The other I used to gently wipe the vomit from her hair. Finally, she spoke. Her voice was soft, almost a whisper, and had a distinct quaver. It dawned on me: it was fear—an all-consuming fear, like I had unearthed something that was better buried.

"I didn't divorce my husband. I killed him."

What could I say to that? So I said nothing.

"Most of the story I told you was true. We were married for five years. At first it was blissful, like I said, and the whole part about me not being able to have children was true. What I didn't tell you was how abusive my husband became—emotionally and physically. He would hit me sometimes, but even worse was that he would always play with my mind. The emotional abuse was horrible. And then he would force himself on me, as if that would somehow fix me and I would get pregnant. He would fly into a rage when I got my period. When it was confirmed that I was sterile, he almost killed me. He had beaten all the confidence out of me—everything I had once been. Somehow though, I was able to plan my escape—I don't know how my mind was even working at that point. It took weeks from the moment I decided to do it until the time I killed him—weeks of more abuse and weeks of fighting with my desire to just lie down and die. He came home one night from work, and I was waiting for him with a shovel. I meant to just hit him over the head with it—even with all the planning, I'm not sure I really had it in me to kill him—but the shovel turned as I swung, and I hit him with the edge of the blade, splitting his head wide open. He was dead immediately."

She talked in a monotone, the quaver gone. It was as if she

had long ago lost any feeling for her actions of that night.

She continued. "The police arrested me and I stood trial for murder."

"Did they know you had been abused?"

"I told them, and they could see the old bruises, but I had never called the police and he had never hurt me badly enough to go to the hospital, so there was nothing to back up my statements. You have to understand, I was young and I was scared. My parents were dead and my sister was not in my life. This was his hometown. I had no close friends. It was my word against his family's word. I had no hope of winning that battle. The only thing that saved me from life in prison was the fact that the judge believed me. Maybe he had dealt with that family before. I don't know. But when it came time for sentencing, he took pity on me: Eight to fifteen years, with the chance of parole after six. I served the six and was released from prison four years ago.

No way! She didn't have the prison mentality, the crudeness, or the hard looks of someone who had done six years in prison—other than the way she had dispatched Mario's guy. Now Izzy I could believe, but not Sabrina. Not at all. I told her as much.

"I was lucky ... if you could call it that. Not my first year. My first year was the most absolute hell you could ever imagine. I was beaten by the other inmates and raped repeatedly by the guards. If I had been resourceful enough to find a way to kill myself, I would have."

She was quiet for a moment, revisiting a memory probably best left alone. "Then my life turned around. The beginning of the second year things changed suddenly. I heard the head honcho inmate, a very large and intimidating woman in her thirties named Terri, say to someone that she was trying to write a letter to a guy on the outside she liked, but didn't know what to say. I told her I had experience writing and would help her with it. I needed some way to get on the good side of people. Of course, I was lying through my teeth. I had no experience writing. What I did have, that most of these women lacked, was an education. Some of them couldn't put two words together. Anyway, Terri took me up on the offer. The day a letter came back from the guy showing interest was the day hell ended for me. Terri wanted me to write all of her letters and she put out the word that I was not to be touched—even by the guards.

Over the next five years, I wrote letters for everybody—including the guards. I was writing letters to lovers, family members, lawyers, the media—I even had an article published, not under my name, of course, but under the name of the inmate I was writing it for. Things got a lot better for me, and for the first time since early in my marriage, I was gaining confidence. I would trade writing for facials, haircuts, manicures, pedicures, you name it. It's why I don't have the hard looks associated with prison. Some of the girls taught me how to defend myself—real self-defense—effective stuff that causes the most pain to your attacker. These girls were tough, but they also had needs and my writing fulfilled so many of those needs. One of the guards who had raped me early on even apologized for his actions after I wrote a loving letter to his mother for him. Prison is where I wrote my first two books, although I didn't try to get them published until I got out."

She went on. "Once I was released, I legally changed my

name and found a job. I did live in an apartment with other women—none of whom knew my story, by the way—but I never worked as an editorial assistant."

She caught a breath. I was mesmerized by her story and still couldn't say anything.

"That part of my life is something I will never be able to forget, obviously, but I'm doing everything possible to move on and create this new life as Sabrina Spencer, author. Someday the story will come out, but by then, hopefully I will be strong enough to lay it out without shame. I'm so sorry I didn't tell you the truth, but you have to understand, I didn't know you well enough at first. I've thought a few times about when I would tell you, but I kept chickening out. Only three people in my new life know this story—my agent, my editor, and my therapist." She smiled for the first time. "My therapist, by the way, will be thrilled that I had this breakdown. She has been trying for four years to get me to let it out like that, but I've been unable to. Maybe it took finding someone I really cared about for it to happen."

"I think that answers a question I had as to why you seemed so tentative in bed, and also why you clung on so hard," I said.

"Del, I haven't had sex for nine years, and before that, I hadn't had willing sex for another three or four. I held onto you—and will continue to hold onto you, if you still want me—because you are the first person in my life I feel totally safe with. I've never known that feeling. I'm so sorry I didn't tell you."

I reached over and pulled her to me. "Sabrina, I understand. I wouldn't have told anyone either. Of course I still want you—but only if you take a shower. Your hair smells like puke."

She laughed, but her laugh quickly turned into tears. They were different this time, though. They were happy tears. They were tears of sheer relief.

"But I go back to my original question," I said after she had come out of the shower, now with the strawberry scent that I liked so much. "You spent six years in prison, and yet, one would never know. How can that be?"

"Believe it or not, I owe a tremendous amount to my fellow inmates. Yes, most of them terrorized me in the beginning, but I came to realize that that was their own form of self-preservation. Deep down they were still people with the same hopes and fears as anyone else. It was just that their hopes had to be customized to their life behind bars. Once we established my worth to the group, they became fiercely loyal to me—as I was to them. My fifth year there, a new guard tried to rape me. Because of the skills these girls taught me, I almost killed him. I thought my hope of a parole was dead, but my friends—and even the other guards—came to my defense. The guard was charged with attempted rape and is now in prison himself. By the time I walked out those gates I was nothing like the person who had gone in. Other than the fact that I didn't trust anyone on the outside, I was confident, I was attractive, and I could take care of myself. It wouldn't have happened without them. I still write to them all the time, and send them copies of my books."

"So they know who you are now. Are you surprised no one has leaked your story to the media?"

"Not at all. As I said, they are fiercely loyal. It will

eventually come out somewhere, and until now I wasn't sure I was ready for it. But these last couple of hours have cleansed me. If my story comes out, it comes out, and for the first time, I'm totally prepared."

*****

We took the rest of the day off and explored the town of Fairfield. There were actually some pretty spots. We drove a ways out of town and stopped next to a field full of cows. As we approached the fence, some of them came over to check us out. We spent well over an hour talking to them and petting them. It was just what we both needed, but especially, it was what Sabrina needed.

She was even different in bed that night. A calm had pervaded her whole being. There was none of the desperation I felt before. I woke up before her the next morning, and I could have sworn she actually had a smile on her face while she slept.

# Chapter 16

We were in the car on the way to Wahoo, Nebraska, each of us deep in our own thoughts. Somewhat appropriately, John Cale was on the radio singing *Hallelujah.*

The song ended. Finally, I spoke. "I'm going to ask you a weird question."

"Oh?"

"Not so much weird, as embarrassing—embarrassing for me, not for you." She looked at me expectantly. "It kind of takes a whack at my manhood. Hell, you're supposed to be coming to me with this question." I hesitated. This really was embarrassing.

She gave me a smile to let me know it was alright, then said, "So out with it."

"I'll start with a preamble. My life for the last ten years has been my job. It gave me little time for anything else. Before that, I took care of my mother while she was sick. There are a lot of things I've thought about doing, or wished I had done, and one of them was self-defense classes. A couple of years ago I asked Mo, my martial artist neighbor, to teach me some moves, but they all seemed so complicated—grab here, push there, turn this—and there was no way I would remember it all. You took care of those two guys in the alley like you were taking a stroll in the park. How did you make it look so easy?"

"Because it was. I think what you are trying to ask me, but it's doing quite a number on your male ego—which I think is cute, by the way—is, will I teach you some of those moves?"

"Yeah, that's what's trying to come out, but it's fighting me all the way. I feel like such a wimp. I assume it's all stuff you learned in pr ... your former life."

"Del, it's okay to say prison. It's where I was. In my mind, I didn't deserve to be there, but when all is said and done, it was an experience that has made me who I am now, so I have no regrets. Yes, I learned it there. I can definitely show you moves, and that's valuable. But the most important part of it is something I can try to teach you while we drive. It will cost you, though."

I looked at her, thinking she was joking. I could tell by her face that she wasn't.

"I'll teach you how to fight, but only if you teach me how to trust."

"Trust?"

"When we were on the plane and that autograph seeker approached me, I was fine with that. I could tell she was sincere. But I didn't trust any of the others and I was very uncomfortable. The flight attendant saw that, which is why she put a stop to it. When I do book signings, I'm always on edge—on guard. I'm always wondering what the person's motive is. What's their hidden agenda?"

"People don't always have a hidden agenda," I said.

"Exactly. And that's why you have to teach me to trust. I spent six years in an environment where everyone had an agenda—even I had one. Nothing was done for the sake of doing it. There had to be a reason. Trying to figure out someone's motivation was all part of the game. An agenda was part of life there. At first for me it was all about trying to survive—and when you come right down to it, that was the underlying motivation for us all. But once you figured out the basics, it got more involved. You needed something, you found a way to get it. Sometimes you had to take advantage of someone, but usually it was a simple trading process. I have what you need and you have—or can get by trading with someone else—what I need."

She took a breath.

"I distrust everyone, Del. Everyone but you. You are the only person since I was a young girl that I trust implicitly. And I've only known you for a few days."

"Your editor and agent?"

"I like them, and obviously I had to open up to them about my past. But I can't honestly say that I trust them."

"Your therapist?"

"Oh God, no. I mean, she's a sincere person and I like her, but I'm always on guard with her. She can get me to talk about almost anything, and yet, I can't allow myself to trust her because I don't like the control she has over me when I'm there."

"Why me?" I asked. "I mean, why is it me that you trust? Here I am, ashamed of the fact that I don't have the street smarts or skills that you have. I'm a middle-management drone. I'm boring. I'm still trying to figure out why you like me at all."

"Because you're honest and you're caring. You sacrificed your life for three years to take care of your mother. Do you have any idea how rare that is? You had the humility to allow yourself to ask me for fighting tips. You've got more street-smart skills than you think. You just need to find your passion. I found mine with my writing. You'll discover yours."

I had to think about that for a minute.

"Okay. I will do my best to teach you how to trust, but I don't think there are any tricks to it. Eventually it all comes down to what's inside you. That will be the defining test."

"Funny," Sabrina said. "That's exactly what fighting is all about. Maybe we will be treading on similar ground in our teaching."

"You said the gist of self-defense could be taught in the car. How?"

"By changing your attitude. The reason Mo can't teach you is because to her, it's meant to be complex. I don't know her, but I can guess that she strips every move down to its basic form, and then builds on it from there, adding complexity as she goes. I bet she thrives on that."

"Knowing Mo, I'd say you are probably right."

"You can take self-defense courses and martial arts classes, and you will learn some cool stuff. But in the vast majority of those classes, you will probably miss—unless you have an extraordinary teacher—the one thing that will determine your success in the real world: the inner ability to kill someone. If you don't have that, all the training in the world won't help you."

"How can you teach that? After all, I'm a pretty civilized guy. Killing someone doesn't exactly come naturally."

"Right, and that's where most self-defense courses go wrong. When I first got married, Kevin insisted I take a self-defense class. His heart was in the right place—at least, at that point in our marriage. He wanted me to be able to protect myself. So I took the class and I learned all the moves. They were all simple and effective ways to repel an attacker, and we practiced on our classmates. But in the end, I didn't feel any safer. Even though they were simple moves, I was afraid of ever having to actually use them. Why?"

"Bad teacher?"

"No. He was actually a good teacher for technique. But he forgot an important part of it—or maybe he just didn't know it himself—the part of it having to do with the fact that we were all civilized. Civilized people don't do that sort of thing. In prison, on the other hand, there is nothing civilized. Everything you do is for survival. If you are in a fight, you don't have time for fancy moves. If you are attacked by a man, you go for the groin with the intent of making sure your attacker will never have children. You go for the eyes, not with the intent to hurt, but with the intent to blind—to push your thumbs right through the eye sockets. In classes you are taught about the vulnerability of the pinky finger and how you can subdue someone by bending it back. If I'm going to grab the pinky, it will be with the intent to rip it off their hand. You have to bring yourself down to the level of your attacker. Even if their purpose isn't to kill you, the minute they seriously threaten you, it's all fair game."

I just looked at her and shook my head in wonder. She was a strange combination of vulnerability and strength. The image she put out to the world was the person she would like to be, but was still light years away from actually becoming. In bed, she was like a child who was craving love and acceptance. But her strength was an animal strength, a survival instinct that had been honed sharp as a knife. She was someone you didn't want to mess with.

"You can't go into a fight hoping to overpower your

opponent," she continued. "You have to go into it *wanting* to break your opponent into little pieces. There is nothing subtle about it. I can tell you all this, but in the end it comes down to your ability to find that part of yourself, because I think we all have it in us. It just depends on how deeply buried it is."

"You gained all this in prison," I began. "Do you think there was any part of yourself that you lost while there?" I asked.

"There was nothing to lose, because I hadn't yet found myself. I was a young bride dominated by a very powerful man. I had already lost my innocence because of him and I didn't yet have an identity. No, what I lost was time, the time to find myself like a normal person would. I ended up finding the dark side of myself, something I'm not especially proud of. But I really didn't have any choice."

And now I knew. She was simply a lost soul trying hard to find her way.

I had to learn to kill. She had to learn to trust. I think I had the easier part of the deal.

# Chapter 17

We were quiet for a while, both of us reflecting on our life experiences—the heartaches, the missed opportunities, and the strange path that led us to each other.

"This is exciting, don't you think?" Sabrina said, breaking the silence.

Okay, so it was only me.

"Yeah, I guess," I answered. "A question. Assuming we find the painting, will there be enough clues to lead us to the treasure?"

"I guess we take it one step at a time. We find Russ Simpson and hope he has it."

"And hope he gives it to us. Sounds like he's kind of an asshole."

"You've got the original slip. He has to give it to you. If I have to, I'll call my agent. He's also a lawyer."

"The slick big-city lawyer calls the bumpkin from Wahoo?" I asked. "That should be fun."

Not even close.

*****

Russ Simpson was a weasel. A smart weasel. The kind of weasel lawyers hate. Needless to say, things didn't go well.

Wahoo, stuck in the middle of nowhere, wasn't exactly a metropolis, but it seemed to be thriving nonetheless. My travel agent passenger, reading from Wikipedia, informed me that

Wahoo, once a small farming town, had become a bedroom community of Omaha. It was clean and well-cared for, with a strange combination of the old and the new. The town even once had a college. Thankfully, that was about all she could tell me about it.

Russ Simpson lived in one of the newer neighborhoods. It was a rather plain house, but there was something about it that hinted at money. Maybe it was the Jaguar parked in the driveway.

We pulled up to the curb and sat for a minute, re-evaluating our tactics. The original plan called for politeness followed by intimidation, if he wasn't accommodating. Now we didn't exactly know where we would go with it.

"I guess all we can do is ask," said Sabrina.

"Based on the description we heard, I can't picture that going well," I said, "but we can try."

We got out of the car and walked up the path, the grass on each side meticulously landscaped. We rang the bell. From inside the house we heard the chimes of Big Ben informing the Lord of the manor that he had visitors. We had looked him up online and it didn't seem that he was married.

Russ Simpson opened the door.

He might have been a weasel, personality-wise, but appearance-wise he was a bull. Well over six feet, he had a massive upper body and a thin waist. A large ring in his nose would have completed the bull image. But no ring. He was dressed casually—not jeans and a ratty t-shirt, like I would wear, but country club casual. The type of casual that looks good but couldn't possibly be comfortable.

"Amway? Jehovah's Witnesses? Either way, don't want

any." His condescension was almost withering. If I had been selling something, I would have felt like slinking away. He started to close the door in our faces. I noticed though that gave Sabrina more than a cursory look.

"Mr. Simpson," Sabrina quickly said. "We're not selling anything. We were given your name by your aunt and uncle in Fairfield."

That stopped the door from closing, but not for long. We were going to have to get it out quickly. If he felt any of the same feelings for them that they felt for him, it was going to be a short conversation.

I knew what he was thinking. Could there possibly be anything in it for him?

"One of them dying?"

"Not that we're aware of," I answered.

Okay, so he wasn't inheriting anything.

"Then I can't imagine what we'd have to talk about." The door was inching closed again.

"It has to do with a painting from your great-grandfather's gallery."

The door not only stopped closing, but actually reversed direction slightly. His radar was up.

"What about it?"

"Can we come in?" asked Sabrina.

He hadn't taken his eyes off her, the lust apparent. It wasn't enough though.

"We can talk out here."

We had no choice but to lay it out for him. We kept it simple though—old family quest, emotional value, and all that. He didn't buy it, and I can't say I blamed him. I wouldn't have believed me either.

"So who are you?"

I gave him my name and was about to introduce Sabrina, when she said, "Patty Worth. I'm Del's girlfriend. Nice to meet you."

Of course. If he knew he was dealing with someone famous, it would just kick up the ante.

"My family has been looking for this painting for decades," I explained. "The artist saved my great-grandfather's life, and has had almost folk-hero status in our family. It would be so important for us to get it back. Patty's been helping me track it down. I can't believe we might have finally found it." I tried to say it with an innocent wide-eyed enthusiasm. I doubt that it worked.

Didn't even come close.

"I've never heard such bullshit in all my life. That's the best you could do?"

"It's the truth," I said weakly. God, I was terrible at this.

"Uh huh. So assuming I even have this painting, what's in it for me?"

I looked at Sabrina for help. I really had no idea what to do at this point.

"You'd be helping a family answer some questions about its past," said Sabrina truthfully.

"Couldn't care less." He started to close the door.

"Legally it's mine," I said quickly. "I can get a lawyer and force you to give it up."

"You could," he said, momentarily stopping the door from closing. "But you won't. First, you don't even know if I have it. Hell, I don't even know. Second, it would take months—maybe years—for this thing to work its way through the courts, and I don't think you want to wait that long. You need this painting now, I can tell."

He was good. I had to give him that. I guess when you're a life-long asshole, you assume everyone else is too. He knew we had an agenda.

He closed the door, leaving us standing there.

"Wow," said Sabrina.

"He can afford to close the door," I said. "He knows he's got us. Now he'll expect us to knock on his door and bargain with him."

"Then let's not," Sabrina replied, turning back toward the car. I followed along.

"And your thinking?" I asked.

"He'll pull out the painting and do some research on it. He'll discover that it's not valuable, and then he'll be as stuck as we are."

"Of course, we don't know that it doesn't tell exactly where the treasure is."

"It doesn't. I can't believe they'd go to the trouble of painting a picture as the clue and then put explicit instructions on it."

"But it has to have enough of a clue to set us in the right direction, I would think."

"But we might already have enough to set us in that direction," she answered. "We have notes and family history to go on. Russ has nothing. No, I say we go to a hotel and wait for him to find us. We have each other over a barrel. We need him for the painting and he needs us because he has no idea what this is all about. We should talk about what we can offer him when he shows up."

We found a better than average steak house and took some time to decompress. Sabrina had me describe my now former job. She seemed genuinely interested in my story. She must have liked me. No one else would have willingly suffered through that.

After dinner we found a decent hotel. After our experience in Fairfield, things were definitely looking up. When we arrived in our room and had closed and double-locked the door, Sabrina grabbed me and kissed me. It wasn't just any kiss. It lasted almost five minutes. She was probing and exploring, and I was willing to let her explore. And of course, it didn't end there.

An hour later, with the bed covers in a heap in the floor, we lay in each other's arms, completely naked, just savoring the moment.

"It was different," I said finally.

"Different?"

"You were different. Less tentative. More forceful. You seemed more at ease."

"I was. I am."

"Are you trusting more?"

"I trust you." The implication was clear. Trust of others was going to be a long road.

"Well, it was nice," I said.

"Given a little more time, who knows what will emerge." She snuggled in closer.

"Even better than this? I can't wait."

A knock came at the door.

"Shit," I said. "Just a minute," I called out.

We quickly threw on our clothes and picked up the sheets from the floor and laid them hurriedly across the bed.

I went to the door, expecting Russ.

He didn't disappoint. Even better, he was holding the painting.

# Chapter 18

He may have had the painting, but he wasn't ready to give it up. As expected, he had conditions.

Russ Simpson was surly, even more surly than he was that afternoon. The reason was clear. He had to come to us, and that bugged him to no end. He looked like the kind who was used to people coming to him. He was in some sort of commercial lending business—we determined that when we looked him up. He was successful, so he was probably a big man in town—possibly just in his own mind—and this wasn't supposed to happen. But it was obvious that he was also greedy, and his greed-o-meter was clanging away loudly. The problem for him, of course, was that the message of the painting meant nothing to him—he didn't even know it held a message. Finding nothing of interest in the painting, he probably did his research online and came up empty. He knew we were lying, and it was frustrating him that he didn't know the story.

Sabrina had called it. Now we just needed to convince him to hand the picture over.

He walked into the room without saying a word. I saw his eyes go from me to Sabrina to the bed. The scene and the sweaty smell of sex told him all he needed to know. It probably just intensified his lust for Sabrina. I looked at her. She was blushing—embarrassed that we'd been caught so soon after the act.

"You ready to tell me why you want the painting?" he finally asked.

"I guess we could be a bit more forthcoming," I answered.

"I guess you could. And if I don't like the explanation, I walk and you'll never see the painting."

"And what'll you get out of it, Russ?" asked Sabrina.

"Mr. Simpson."

"I'll stick with Russ." She wanted him to know exactly where he stood with her. "You brought the painting here, so you're obviously ready to deal. If you leave, all you'll have is a totally worthless piece of art. You can either hang it over your fireplace or throw it in your basement."

"The thing's ugly. Not worth the canvas it was painted on," he replied. "Which means it must be fucking valuable. Let me guess. It contains some sort of message or clue?"

Wow, a shot in the dark and he hit a bulls-eye. Impressive.

"So what do you want for it?" I asked, ignoring his comment.

"I want in."

"In what?"

"In whatever you've got going here. I don't know if it's a scam, a treasure hunt, or something else. Whatever it is, I want in. And I want the whole story."

"And?" I asked, waiting for the other shoe to drop.

"Fifty percent."

"Thank you very much, Russ," said Sabrina, going over and opening the door. "But we don't need it that much."

Silence. He looked at me, at her, at the door, then down at the painting. He knew when he said it that he'd never get fifty percent. Now the negotiating would begin.

"Thirty."

"Door's still open," said Sabrina.

"Twenty, but that's the lowest I'll go."

"Ten, and that's the highest we'll go," I countered.

His eyes narrowed. "What are we talking here?"

"A million," answered Sabrina. "Maybe more.

Prison certainly taught her how to lie with a straight face.

"We don't know for sure ourselves," she continued. "But the fact is, we've put in all the work. You just happen to be lucky enough to have a small clue. It'll speed up the process, but that's all. That doesn't warrant twenty percent."

Dollar signs hovered over Russ's head. "Okay, let's split the difference," he said. "Fifteen."

I looked at Sabrina, who gave an imperceptible nod. We had already decided we'd go as high as twenty, so we were making out on the deal.

"Okay."

"With the agreement," added Sabrina, "that your contribution ends here. Don't get it in your head that you're coming with us. The fact is, I don't like you, and I don't want you anywhere near us." Thoughts of how he cheated the sweet couple in Fairfield were obviously at the forefront of her thoughts.

He was staring at her—more specifically to one area of her anatomy.

"And if I catch you staring at my boobs one more time, I'm going to shove that painting down your throat."

That was the thing I was learning about Sabrina. She was all sweet and kind—even shy—most of the time, but if you got in her space ... look out. I was beginning to learn what space must mean to a prisoner.

Russ quickly looked away. Somehow he could sense she meant business. I wasn't sure if he had planned to ask to come along for the ride—wherever that was—or if he was only out for the money. Sabrina settled that quickly with her comment.

"And one more condition," he said. "I keep the painting."

"No way!" I exclaimed.

"You can take all the pictures of it you want, but it stays in my possession. Just a little proof if down the line you try to screw me out of my share."

"Forget it," I said. "What's to stop you from going after it yourself?"

"You think I haven't already taken pictures?" he asked, as if I was really stupid. "If I wanted to go after it, I certainly wouldn't have brought it to you." He thought for a minute. "If we all determine that you need the physical painting, then take it, but I've looked it over. You're not going to want it."

Sabrina looked at me. "If the photo will suffice, I don't see any problem with it."

"Okay," I said, turning toward Russ. "You've got a deal."

He reached into his pocket and pulled out two copies of a contract. Figures he'd have that already.

We read it over—it was simple and straightforward. We changed the "fifty" to "fifteen" and all initialed it. Then we all signed both copies and gave him back one of them.

"So let's see the painting," I said.

"Not until I get the story."

"Let me at least see the signature, so I know you're not trying to con us. You seem to have a reputation for doing that."

The comment just rolled right off him. He must have cheated so many people, it was just a way of life for him. He pulled away a piece of the paper on the bottom right of the painting. There it was: *Lando Ford*.

So we gave him the story. Obviously not all of it. He didn't rate that. We told him enough so he'd know why we were looking for the painting, but nothing that could give him any ammunition to go out on his own—not that we had a whole lot of ammunition ourselves. We told him about the museum robbery and how it was all because of this painting. We told him about the Guidrys, without revealing their name, and about Izzy and how the search began.

He seemed satisfied.

He ripped off the rest of the paper wrapping, wrapping that he had so carefully re-taped after looking at it earlier, then held it up for us to see.

I couldn't fault his taste. He was right, it was ugly. The funny thing was, it wasn't just hurriedly dashed off, it really looked as if it was painted by someone who was trying. Mr. Lando Ford just wasn't very good.

We already knew that the painting wasn't going to reveal anything obvious, or Russ would have run with it. We just hoped it would tell us something ... something at all. But it didn't look as if that was going to happen.

It was a simple scene: A white, one-story wooden house set on a newly cut lawn, a bright sun hovering overhead, and a single tree in the yard. The tree had a white rounded gash about a foot long down its trunk. About ten feet from the tree—assuming the perspective was correct—was a single headstone. On it was RIP. No name. No date. Just RIP.

The house resembled an old Cape Cod vacation cottage—but there was something that told me it wasn't in the states. Or maybe a southern state. Maybe it was the apparent lack of insulation on the house, but I couldn't tell for sure. But really, the picture reminded me vaguely of the tropics. Anyway, at first glance, that was it. That was the whole painting. Disappointment hung in the air. I looked at Sabrina. I could see it in her eyes. We came all this way for this?

"Well?" asked Russ.

"Well, nothing," I answered. "I don't have a clue. It means nothing to me."

"Don't fuck with me."

"He's not," said Sabrina, coming to my aid. "It tells us nothing. There isn't anything in the picture to indicate where this house could be. No signs, no people ... nothing." She was avoiding mentioning the tree. Would he catch it?

He caught it.

"That slash in the tree," he said. "Could be a clue. The headstone. Or maybe the type of tree itself. Do you know what it is?"

"I don't," I replied, "and we will research it. There might be a clue there, but at best it might lead us to a general area of the world. What then? We Google Earth it and hope we hit on this scene? And remember, this was painted in the '30s—what are the chances of that house still being there? Or even the tree? The painting might be of some use further down the line if we can find some other clues, but for now, it's pretty worthless."

While I was talking, Sabrina was taking pictures of the painting with her cell phone—all different angles. Then she picked it up and scoured every inch—front, back, and the edge of the canvas—for any writing that may have faded over time. Then she gave it to me and I did the same thing. I didn't bother handing it to Russ when I was finished. I was sure he had already inspected it from top to bottom.

Russ stayed another few minutes, getting our cell phone numbers—and trying them in case we were giving him fake numbers. A trusting soul. We took his information, and he left, painting in hand, with a simple statement. "Keep me informed."

*****

There was nothing more we could do about it that night, so Sabrina took some time to answer emails from her publisher and agent. Then we took a long shower together and headed for bed.

We had just closed our eyes when our door burst open and two men rushed in.

So much for security locks.

Both carried guns, and both guns were pointed at us.

# Chapter 19

I didn't see where Sabrina's magic could get us out of this one. We were under the covers. They had us just where they wanted us. But they also knew that the noise of breaking through a hotel door at two in the morning left them precious little time to do what they came for.

They were pretty nondescript—average height, average weight, late-twenties to early thirties, and dark hair. It's not like they were twins or anything; they just had the same general look. The only distinguishing feature was a full arm tattoo of a dragon on one of them. The artwork wasn't very good.

"Where's the painting?" demanded tattoo-guy.

"What painting?" I asked with a dumb expression. My strong point.

"Don't fuck with me. A man was seen coming in the hotel with a painting. Where is it?"

"Why don't you ask the man?" said Sabrina.

Tattoo-guy hesitated, and I knew immediately what had happened. They had one person covering us at a time. He had seen Russ come in, but couldn't do anything about it until his friend arrived, and he didn't arrive in time. He either didn't see Russ leave, or chose to stay on us rather than to follow him. He should have followed Russ.

"I'm asking you."

"Someone came with a painting and wanted to sell it to us, but we refused."

"What was his name?" Tattoo-guy kept glancing at the

hallway. I could hear some activity. They didn't have much time.

"He didn't give us his name," I said. "He was trying to be mysterious. We told him to get lost."

The other guy quickly searched the room and announced, "No painting here."

"Shit," said tattoo-guy. Then he spied our cell phones on the table. He broke into a smile. "But I bet you took pictures. He snatched the phones from the table. He pointed his gun again. "Get out of bed and come with us."

"Yeah, right," I answered. I could hear a walkie-talkie in the hallway. Obviously an employee. And then I heard a siren. "I think you've got about three seconds to get out of here before the police come. No way we're going with you. Besides, I'm naked. No one wants to see that."

"I do," said Sabrina.

We were playing with them now. We knew we weren't in danger. They weren't masked, and there were too many potential witnesses. Besides, they didn't strike me as killers. Killing was above their pay grade. The guns were simply for intimidation.

They ran. As they reached the hallway, they tried to cover their faces with their arms, without much success. By this time, most of the guests on our floor were standing out there.

Sabrina reached for her pajamas next to the bed and put them on under the covers. Mine were across the room.

"Um," I said.

"I'll get them for you," she said, getting out of bed. A minute later we were standing in the middle of the room. Sabrina had added a robe to her outfit, and I had gone into the bathroom to put on my jeans. The hotel employee was in with us, asking if we were okay. Everyone else was crowded around the door. A dozen heads peeked around the door frame. Thank God there weren't any Sabrina Spencer fans out there.

When the police arrived and everyone else had been chased away, we recounted the incident and suggested they call the Fairfield police for more information about Mario Guidry. We were pretty certain he was behind this event too.

"Do you know Russ Simpson?" asked Sabrina.

A cop rolled his eyes. "We do." Ah, he was just as popular with them as he was with us.

"You might want to warn him," she said, letting them know that he had the painting the men were after.

Finally the police left, and the hotel staff moved us into a room that had a working door.

"Your photos are gone," I said. "We can take more photos, but now Guidry's men have them. That might give him the clue he needs."

"They don't have them," she said. "My phone is locked. There is no way they can access anything. And we don't have to see Russ again. All my pictures were uploaded to the cloud. As soon as I buy a new phone, I'll download them. This didn't set us back at all. The only thing it told us is that Guidry is still on our trail."

We were wide awake now, so I went online to see if I could find the tree in the picture. After two hours of searching with no success, weariness once again set in. Sabrina had collapsed an hour earlier. It was no good. We were going to have to find an expert. Then the thought popped in: what if the tree was just a figment of the artist's imagination? If so, we were definitely screwed.

*****

We were eating a late breakfast the next morning at The Cracker Barrel. Sabrina had been strangely silent.

I was trying to give her some space, but finally blurted out, "You okay?"

She focused in and smiled. "I am. I was just thinking that you're ahead of me in school."

"Huh?"

"You're learning how to fight faster than I'm learning how to trust. All those people in our room—all the hotel guests, the hotel staff, and the police—gave me the creeps. I wanted to go hide in the bathroom. I was actually more comfortable with the crooks. I guess I can relate to them better."

I gave her a look.

"No, seriously. They were crooks, but they were at least clear about their intentions. All the others ... yeah, a few might have been genuinely concerned, but most were there for the thrill of it, or out of nosiness, or if there was anything worth putting on YouTube. In that case, who do you believe? Which one of them is being honest? And I'm supposed to trust people?"

She had a point.

"Sometimes you just have to assume they have the best intentions."

"Why? If I assume that and they don't? I just put myself in a bad situation."

"But most people do have good intentions."

"Do you really believe that?"

"I do."

"Then I have a long way to go with this trust thing."

I couldn't disagree with her.

"But what did you mean about me learning to fight. I didn't fight anyone."

"Sure you did. You were staring down the barrel of a gun—two guns—and you cracked a joke."

"It was either that or pee my pants."

"You weren't wearing pants."

"Pee the bed, then."

"But that's my point. That's the first rule of fighting, remaining calm."

"But I didn't feel calm."

"But you acted calm. A big part of the battle. You think I wasn't scared? I was naked under the covers with two men with guns standing over me. I had other fears besides getting killed. Who cares that you didn't actually fight them. They had guns. You would've lost. This way, you won the battle without having to physically fight them. Most battles are won without ever having to throw a punch. No, trust me, that was a major leap in your training."

It was my turn to be silent. I thought about all that had happened in the past week and suddenly felt ashamed that I had wasted ten years stuck in that meaningless job and doing nothing with my life.

"What next?" I asked, changing the subject.

"I think we've kind of reached the end out here," she replied. "What do you say we head back to Boston? You can pursue the tree angle, and we'll see if that leads anywhere.

Meanwhile, I need a day or so to catch up with the publisher. That annoying publicist has left about a million messages for me. First though, we get new phones and I download the app that will let me erase my other phone."

By dinnertime, we were on a plane back to Boston.

# Chapter 20

I was sitting with Mo in my living room the next afternoon, bringing her up to date on our trip to the Midwest. I told her everything, except Sabrina's secret past. Even though I knew I could trust Mo to keep it to herself, it would have been an invasion of Sabrina's privacy to tell anyone. I did tell her of our adventure in the alley with Guidry's men and how easily Sabrina had dispatched them. I think I sensed a little envy on Mo's part. There was probably nothing more she'd like to do than to take apart two low-life men piece by piece. Oddly, Mo didn't ask where Sabrina picked up the skills. A secret code amongst bad-ass women? Or maybe she sensed there was more to Sabrina than I was telling and knew it would do no good to ask.

When I finished my story, she said, "Well, it's about fucking time."

"For what?"

"To do something with your life. Look what happened the minute you quit that shit-show you called a job. Your life completely turned around. You found a woman—an incredibly hot woman, by the way—have embarked on a treasure hunt, fought off attackers, and got to spend time in Wahoo, Nebraska. Who else can claim that?"

I had no answer.

"So what's next?" she asked.

"I find a plant or tree expert who can tell me if the tree in the picture really exists, and if so, where?"

"I know someone."

"Of course you do. What's her name?"

"Believe it or not, it's a guy. The husband of a co-worker. Met him at a staff Christmas party. He teaches botany at Boston College. I'll call up Marci and see if I can get you an appointment with him."

"Thanks, Mo."

"Just do me a favor and don't get yourself killed over this. It would be sad if you died just as you finally started living."

After Mo left, I called my mother and gave her a sanitized version of the story. She knew I was holding back some information, but knew better than to ask. She invited me over for dinner and asked if I wanted to bring Sabrina, but I took a rain check. I'd end up spilling the whole story, and I wasn't ready for that.

I didn't bother seeking out Seymour to bring him up to date. I wasn't in the mood for his grouchiness. Besides, I knew Mo would fill him in.

I met Sabrina for dinner and we spent the night together at her hotel. I think we were both feeling that this relationship was real, and not just a by-product of the adventure. In fact, other than a few moments of catch-up about the events and where we were going from there, our conversation was spent on the normal things that two new lovers talked about.

*****

The next day I found myself in the office of Richard Santos, in the botany department of Boston College. He was a throwback to the '60s and '70s, when college professors all tried to look like their students. The students he was trying to look like, though, were still from that era. He was in his mid-sixties, tall and lanky, with a gray ponytail halfway down his back. He was dressed in jeans, a t-shirt advertising some botanical conference, and Tevas. I had a feeling he desperately missed the hippie days.

He was looking at the picture of the painting Sabrina had emailed to me. He tried to increase the size on my phone, and finally had me email it to him so he could look at it on a normal-sized computer screen.

"The artwork sucks," he said.

"Yes, that's been established."

"I mean, really sucks."

"Got it. So can you tell me what the tree is?"

"It would help if I knew where the painting is set."

"That's the whole reason I'm here. We're hoping that by you telling us what the tree is, we'll be able to figure out where it is."

"Why's that important?"

I'm sure he was just making conversation and didn't mean anything by it, so I tried to be diplomatic.

"Kind of a long story." I left it hanging, and he picked up on it, quickly turning to the task at hand.

He peered closer, then shook his head. "Looks familiar. Painting sucks though," he repeated. He glanced at his watch. "Go get a coffee or something. Give me an hour. That's about as much time as I have. I can concentrate better without an audience, so get lost."

Subtle.

I got lost. I found a Dunkin Donuts a few blocks away and

ordered an iced coffee and a bagel. Ten minutes later the bagel was gone and I was bored. I walked back to the campus and sat under a tree. It was sunny, but there was a nip in the air. A few minutes later I was cold. I looked at my watch. Forty-five minutes had elapsed. Close enough. I made my way back to his office.

He looked up from his desk when I walked in the door.

"That was a fast hour."

"Sorry. I'll stay out of your way and not say a word."

"No need. I know what it is. If it wasn't such a sucky painting, or if you could've given me a general location, I could have told you an hour ago. It's a Hevea brasiliensis."

Was there going to be more? He caught me staring uncomprehendingly at him.

"A rubber tree. More specifically, a Pará rubber tree. Found in the Amazon. Most likely in the Pará state of Brazil."

Brazil? The Amazon jungle? Well that certainly narrowed it down to a few million square miles.

"You were kind of lucky. The tree in the painting resembles a rubber tree, but as I said..."

"Yeah, I know. The painting sucks."

He ignored me. "What finally tipped me off was the white slash in the trunk. It hit me that someone had cut into the bark. The white is latex oozing out. That's what they make the rubber from. How important is the tree to the picture?"

I wasn't sure how far to go with an explanation. Luckily, he saved me the trouble.

"I'm not asking to pry. I just have a theory."

"It might be very important. I'm hoping it's a clue to a bigger mystery. I don't know yet."

"Well, if it is, I think the artist put the white slash there on purpose."

I gave him a questioning look.

"There is no real reason the tree should be sliced like that. There's no tap in it, or bucket at the end of the slice to collect the latex. If you've got latex flowing out, you're going to want to collect it. I think the artist knew he sucked and drew the latex into the picture to help identify the tree." He threw up his hands. "Just a thought."

Not a bad one.

"Your idea is something to keep in mind. So can you pinpoint it any closer than that?"

"The Amazon jungle in Brazil doesn't do it for you? You want latitude and longitude? Directions?"

He was starting to sound like Seymour. It was time to leave.

"No, the Amazon narrows it down nicely. I appreciate your help."

"Yeah," he said, looking at the clock. He gathered up his class notes and beat me out the door.

I called Sabrina as I walked to my car and gave her the news.

"Wow, the Amazon," she said. "So where does that leave us?"

"Not quite sure."

"No colorful relatives who lived there?"

"Not that I kn..." I stopped because Sabrina was interrupting me.

"Didn't you tell me you had a relative who got thrown out of South America?"

"Oh my God, yeah. And it was the same great-grandfather who started this whole thing. But it was never specified where."

"What do you want to bet?"

"I don't. I'm sure you're right, but it still doesn't get us any closer."

"Nowhere you can find out more information on his early life?"

"His early life? Look how long it has taken us to find what we have so far."

"Well, there's got to be something."

"Let me work on it." Well, it sounded good anyway.

"Okay, keep me apprised. I love you."

"I love you, too." How many years had I waited to be able to say that to someone?

Think. There had to be something. Was it Brazil he was thrown out of? If so, where? And was it related to the picture? It had to be. It was too coincidental otherwise.

I arrived at my apartment just as my cell phone went off. I looked at the caller's info before answering it. "Private number." Of course it was. Caller ID seemed to mean very little these days. I answered with a fake exasperated tone, figuring it was a telemarketer. It wasn't.

"Mr. Honeycutt, this is detective Sorenson of the Nebraska State Police."

I had a bad feeling.

"Uh, hi. How can I help you?"

"I was given your name by the Wahoo police. Can I ask where you were last night around eleven?"

A really bad feeling.

"I was with my girlfriend all night at her hotel in Boston.

Why?"

"Can anyone else confirm this?

Why couldn't they ever come right out and say why they were calling?

"Probably a lot of people. She had calls from her agent and publicist while I was there, and I think she mentioned me to them. My downstairs neighbor saw me go out around seven. Need more?"

"No, that's fine." His voice took on a friendlier tone. "You are not a suspect. I just like to cover all of my bases. Do you know a Russ Simpson?"

"He tried to sell me an old painting that used to belong to my great-grandfather. So I only met him two days ago. Did something happen?"

"Yes, he's dead."

All the air was sucked out of my body.

"Dead?"

"Quite brutally. Simply stated, he was tortured."

I had a feeling he said it for effect, to make it easier to extract information from me. It worked.

"Can you tell me about the painting?"

"Are you sure it had something to do with the painting?" I had no doubt it did, but I had to ask it anyway.

"He was still alive when we found him. He actually lasted six hours before dying. There was very little the doctors could do, and in fact, they were surprised he lasted that long. At one point he woke up and seemed almost lucid for about fifteen seconds. During that time he said 'Damned painting' twice before lapsing back into unconsciousness. The Wahoo police said you asked them to warn him about some men. Can you give me the story?"

I told him. The whole story this time, not the condensed version. This violence had reached a gruesome level, and Sabrina and I were right in the thick of it. So I told him everything I knew. Sadly, other than Mario Guidry, who was probably long gone, it didn't give him anything to go on. I told him I would email him the picture, but warned him that it wouldn't help any.

I think he sensed my sincerity (read: fear), and thanked me for the information, but not before warning me to be careful.

The morons who accosted us in the hotel didn't do that to Russ. No way. The big guns had been called in.

This was serious. I had given Sorenson everything I knew, but it wouldn't do any good. This wasn't a problem the police could solve. It all lacked context for them. Guidry now had the painting, but I knew he wouldn't stop there. He still needed more pieces to the puzzle, and that was us. No, the best we could do would be to stay one step ahead of him.

What had I gotten us into?

# Chapter 21

I called Sabrina and told her we needed to meet. She could hear the fear in my voice and wisely didn't ask me to explain it over the phone. On my way out, I stopped at Seymour's apartment. He answered the door—without a scowl for a change. Maybe I hadn't woken him up this time? Or maybe Mo told him the story of my adventures and he had developed a new respect for me? Somehow I doubted that. In fact, though, he knew everything that had gone on. When did Mo ever find the time to tell him these things? It was a mystery, for sure.

I only had a moment to talk, which was just fine with Seymour.

"Don't open the front door unless you know exactly who's out there," I said, anxious to get to Sabrina.

"Never do."

"Yeah, well, it's especially important now." I updated him on Russ's death. "Can you get a message to Mo?"

"I don't need to, but I will. She can take care of herself."

"I'm well aware of that," I said, "but these people mean business, and they have guns."

"I remember. The house still has bullet holes from your last encounter. Do they know where your mother lives?"

Shit! My mother. Of course they did. They followed me there that first night.

"I'll call her on my way to the hotel," I said. "Thanks, Seymour."

"You carrying?"

"Carrying what?"

"Carrying. You know. Your gun? You do have a license to carry, remember?"

"Right." Not counting my initial meeting with Sabrina and my trip to my father's house, I had never actually carried a concealed weapon. Even going to the range, I transported it in in a case. "I feel kind of awkward doing it. You know, like I'm doing something wrong."

"Sometimes you're a real idiot," he said. "You got the license to be able to carry it for protection. You don't think this qualifies?"

"I guess it does. I'll go get it."

"Smart boy. Don't forget to load it."

I went back up to my apartment and retrieved my gun. I was kind of wishing I had bought something smaller for concealment purposes. I spent ten minutes trying to find the best spot to put it so that it wasn't digging into me, or if it accidently went off, it wouldn't blow off some vital part of my anatomy. I finally decided it was the least uncomfortable in my pants in the small of my back—the same place I put it when I first met Sabrina. Luckily, the chilly weather required a jacket, so the spot would be covered. How did they make it look so easy in the movies?

Then I called my mother. I had no idea what I was going to say. Thankfully, she made it easy. I told her a shortened version of events, this time without sanitizing it. Of course she was worried for me, but oddly, not as worried as I thought she'd be. I questioned her about that.

"Del, I've been worried about you for the last ten or fifteen years. You've had nothing in your life. *That* worried me.

Obviously I'm concerned, but I hear a confidence in your voice I've never heard before."

"Really? And I thought it was fear."

She chuckled. "Maybe I should be more worried than I am," she continued, "but I have faith in you. What you're involved in is dangerous, for sure, but you're finally living. You have excitement in your life. You've never had that. Anyway, don't worry about me. I was going to visit a friend in England next week. I'll re-book it for tomorrow."

"Thanks. That'll make me feel better."

"And Del, remember, you are traveling with a famous author. She's going to bring her publisher a lot of money over the next few years, so they will do anything to keep her safe. One phone call from her and they'll send in the Marines. Use that lifeline if you need to. Stay safe and keep in touch by email. I love you." She hung up.

Okay, so that was weird. That was nowhere near the reaction I expected. Was my life really so empty before this? Yeah, it was.

I finally made it to the Weston an hour later. Sabrina greeted me with a hug. Her eyes widened when I took out the gun and laid it on the coffee table.

"That's ominous," she said.

"'Ominous' doesn't begin to cover it." We sat on the couch and I related the call from Sorenson. She began to cry. I wasn't sure what reaction I would get from her, but the tears surprised me. I thought they were tears of fear, but once again, I was mistaken. They were for Russ.

"I couldn't stand the man," she said, wiping her eyes, "but nobody deserves that. We got him into it, and now he's dead.

He didn't do anything wrong."

There was nothing I could say.

"So what now?" she asked.

"We're kind of stuck," I said. "We can't move forward until we can narrow down the clue in the picture. At the same time, we can't abandon it, because Guidry is going to keep coming at us. He might need something else from us or he might just want us dead. Either way, he's dangerous."

"And we can't hand it all over to the police," added Sabrina. "There's nothing they can do with it."

She looked me in the eyes. "We really have no choice but to take this as far as we can."

I started to shake my head. I must have had a mournful look on my face.

"And Del, before you say it, you didn't get me into this. Remember, I came to you."

Wow, she could read minds, too.

"Let's switch gears," she said. "Supposedly there is a treasure. What could it be? Gold, silver, jewels?"

"I don't know what they produce in Brazil," I said. "We can look it up. He referred to it as a fortune, so it has to be something tangible that they could determine was valuable."

"So gold, silver or jewels certainly fit the bill."

"Maybe."

"What about an icon of some kind?"

"What do you mean?"

"You know, like some ancient religious artifact. Isn't South America famous for them?"

Something clicked in my head. The words 'South America' set it off. Sabrina sensed it and went silent, giving me the time to process it. And then it hit me. I might have been looking at one of the clues that very first day, the day I went to my father's house.

I shook my head in wonder. Could my family get any more confusing? "All this time," I said, "I've been under the illusion that my father knew very little about this. And yet, he was the one who hid the book and the bag in the boxes in his attic. Why would he hide them so carefully if he didn't know? So it's obvious that he had to know at least a part of the story. He realized that there was danger associated with it."

"And?" Sabrina was waiting for the other shoe to drop.

"He was working on a book for about ten years—at least, that's what I thought. I saw all the notes on his laptop. I just assumed inertia kept him from making much progress. But maybe it wasn't a book at all. Maybe he was looking into the same thing we are, just from a different angle. I think he knew—to some degree, anyway—what the treasure was. I think he also knew it was somewhere in South America."

She was still waiting.

"He was doing research on South America."

"On what aspect? Brazil? Treasure? Religious artifacts?"

"Um, I have no idea. I just know it was on South America."

"It's a big place."

"I get that. You have to understand my relationship with my father. We never talked about anything of substance. He would ask the safe questions like 'How's work' or 'How's school' or 'Do you have a girlfriend'. And he shared nothing about his life at all. Once, about five years ago I asked him—more just for something to say—if he was getting anything published. I was remembering how he published articles when

I was young. At that time he said he was working on a book about South America. That's it. He never elaborated."

When I went through his stuff, I found the notes on his laptop—just a single file labeled 'Book Notes." I opened it and saw South America mentioned a few times, so I closed it and went on to other things."

"It's certainly worth checking out," said Sabrina. "Who knows? All these years your father may have been researching the treasure right under your nose."

# Chapter 22

We had to solve the mystery. This one act of ... of what? Stupidity? Greed? One act, committed so many years ago, was now in its fourth generation. That was three generations too many. It had to stop, and it was up to me to end it. My great-grandfather died because of it; my grandfather died because of it; my father died ... well, my father died because he couldn't keep it in his pants, but he was responsible for keeping the whole thing going. He could have destroyed all the material and it would be over now. But no, he couldn't do that. And now, two more people were dead, and my life and Sabrina's life were in jeopardy.

It was too late in the day to go across the state to my father's house, so we stayed in and ordered room service. The good thing, at least as far as we knew, was that Guidry's people didn't know Sabrina's name, so we felt pretty anonymous in the hotel.

We tried to have a nice romantic night, but finally gave up. Sabrina's publicist called four times, and she couldn't ignore him this time. He was putting the finishing touches on her book tour, and there were too many time-critical issues to be taken care of. So I played with my new phone until boredom set in. I finally fell asleep fully clothed, on top of the bed. I had a vague memory of Sabrina taking my pants off at some point and pulling the covers over me. I think she even whispered "sorry," but I guess our adventures out west wore me out more than I knew.

I woke up refreshed, but disturbed. In those early morning minutes, when dead sleep had ended, but I wasn't quite awake, my interaction with Seymour the day before took over my brain. What was it that disturbed me? It was related to his comment about the bullet holes in the side of the house, that much I knew, but it wasn't connecting. It was what finally woke me up—that and the fact that I had to pee.

When I got back from the bathroom, Sabrina was awake.

"Sorry again about last night. I ... what's wrong? Are you mad at me?"

I looked at her in surprise, then realized I must've had a scowl on my face. I got rid of the scowl and sat next to her on the bed. "God, no," I said, and kissed her lightly on the lips. "How could I be mad at you for anything?"

She relaxed. "You had such a strange face when you came out of the bathroom. Everything go okay in there?"

"Just dandy. No, the face was me pondering a dilemma. It was something Seymour said to me yesterday when he was telling me why I was an idiot for not carrying my gun. He referred to the people who tried to kill me outside my house."

"And?"

"And why? When the thugs burst into our room in Wahoo, they weren't there to kill us. They wanted the painting. When the morons in the alley in Fairfield jumped us, they were looking for information. So why did they suddenly go from trying to kill us, to trying to pump us for information?"

"Not the same people?" She said it almost without thinking, as if it was the logical response. And then she realized what she had said and stared at me. "If we follow that a step further," the wheels were turning now, "who actually killed Izzy? We've assumed Guidry killed her after getting the information he needed, but maybe it wasn't Guidry at all."

"So there could be a third party involved?"

"It's not even worth asking who," said Sabrina. "But I guess it means we have to be even more vigilant than we already are."

"Is that even possible?" I asked.

A text came in from my mother telling me that her flight was boarding and warning me to be careful.

I wished her well and assured her we would be. Like I would say to my mother, "No, I won't be careful, but thank you."

We had breakfast in our room and got ready to leave.

"When you travel, do you usually eat in your room?" I asked.

"Always, unless I'm meeting someone. Is that a window into my life?"

"A picture window. Am I helping any with the trust thing?"

"Well, like I said before, I trust you."

"That's a good start. Only seven billion more people to go."

"Piece of cake."

*****

We arrived at my father's house around noon.

"Nice," said Sabrina. "It feels like an academic neighborhood."

"A lot of faculty and staff from the various colleges in the area live here. It's quiet."

"Could you live here?"

"No. Too many memories of a broken childhood. I'll sell it when the time is right."

"You're happier living in a third floor apartment in East Boston than here?" she asked incredulously.

"Says something about the memories, doesn't it?"

"What if you weren't living in it alone?" she asked.

I looked at her. Was it an invitation? She had turned bright red. It was a feeler.

"I suppose that could change things."

I left it at that. Sabrina had just taken a giant leap forward. If I put too much attention on it, she might retreat. By positively acknowledging her veiled suggestion, but not taking it any further, it would give her the comfort of having taken a step without an actual commitment.

Everything was as I left it from my last visit, my father's laptop still sitting on his desk. We took off our jackets and Sabrina threw them on the couch in his office. How often had that couch been used for grade-raising purposes? I picked up the jackets and put them on a chair in the corner. Sabrina gave me a questioning look.

"Trust me. And I don't suggest sitting on it, either." She nodded in understanding. I pulled a comfortable chair over to the desk, next to the office chair. We both sat and I opened the laptop.

I found the folder marked "Book Notes" and opened it. As I knew from my previous foray into his computer, the folder only contained one file. I guess he never felt the need to divide his research into topics.

It was a hodgepodge of his own notes interspersed with

pasted articles. It was one of the reasons I hadn't spent too much time looking through it. Frankly, it was boring. My initial impressions from when I first looked at it were definitely wrong though. This was not research for a book. Sabrina saw that immediately.

"A book has a certain feel to it," she said. "Even in the research stage, you have a sense of where the book is going. I don't mean you have the story figured out. Heck, I never know where my books are going. I just let the characters take the story. What I mean is, if you were to look at my early notes, you might not know exactly what the story is about, but you know that it's a story. You might mention a character's name or a piece of dialogue that you want to stick in it. If it was meant to be nonfiction, you'd sense a theme. This has none of that. It's just a hodgepodge of downloaded articles—or parts of articles. Also, if it was a book, there would be more than one file. You'd have separate files for dialogue, research, characters, etc. Not one big file."

His early notes seemed be generally about South America, but there didn't seem to be much rhyme or reason. We read on … and on. His notes seemed endless, but they led nowhere. He jumped from topic to topic: idols, religious artifacts, jewels. Although he never used the term *treasure*, his notes intimated that it was where he was going. And then there was an abrupt switch. He stopped his research on South America and changed to Russia, pre-revolution.

"I don't get it," I finally said. "What just happened?"

"He's stuck."

"In what way?"

"He's brainstorming with himself," she said. "It's like when

I get writer's block. Sometimes I will just jot things down, hoping it will get me going again. Your father was in the same spot we are. Well, not as far along as we are, but just as stuck. He suspected that the answer was in South America, but he hadn't pinpointed where. I'm not quite sure why he jumped over to Russia."

"How did he even know that South America played a part in this?" I asked.

"Deduction, I guess. He knew your great-grandfather was thrown out of South America and was trying to find a connection."

"Doesn't look like he found it."

"We're not done with it yet."

Truer words were never spoken. The breakthrough came twenty minutes later. I was in the bathroom when Sabrina yelled out, "Found something!"

I zipped up and quickly washed my hands.

"What did you find?" I asked as I took my seat next to her.

"It's not what I found, but what your father found. Look." She pointed to a line on the page.

*"Did Mikey die? His body was never found."*

"Where did that come from?" I asked.

"He must have found something. There's more." She was almost jumping in her seat with excitement. "But not much. It's interesting though."

*"Why didn't Mikey go back for it?"*

*"In Fordlandia?"*

It ended there.

"What the heck is Fordlandia?" I asked. "What?"

Sabrina was laughing.

"Do you know something I don't?"

"No," she answered, wiping her eyes. "It's just funny. We've been sitting here for almost three hours, and the answer comes on the last page. If your father figured it out, wouldn't it have been nice of him to delete the rest of the notes? No, instead, he makes us slog through pages and pages of nonsense. Two keystrokes would have saved us three hours of agony.

"Well, he *was* a Honeycutt," I offered.

"Obviously." She was looking at me with a funny expression.

"What?"

"You don't see it?"

"See what?"

"I can wait." Oh, she was having fun with this. I was missing something obvious and she was going to torture me until I found it. I looked back at the computer screen.

It *was* obvious. So obvious.

"Fordlandia," I finally said. "Lando Ford."

"The picture was only part of the clue," she said. "The artist's name was the other."

"But what does Fordlandia mean?"

She was way ahead of me. She was Googling it.

When the result came on the screen, the answer became clear.

"We're going to Brazil," Sabrina said.

# Chapter 23

Fordlandia. A fascinating story that somehow they neglected to mention in history class. It was too bad, really, because a story like that was so much more interesting than most of the snooze material I was taught.

We spent the next couple of hours immersing ourselves in the history of Fordlandia through the many articles that had been written on the subject.

It was the brainchild of Henry Ford. Built in 1928 on the banks of the Rio Tapajós river, Ford bought up 3900 square miles of remote Amazon rainforest with the idea that he would produce his own rubber for his car tires. Whether the idea was a good one or not was questionable, but it really didn't matter, because the execution made it all moot. It was a poorly thought out and mismanaged plan from the very beginning.

Besides being clueless about growing and caring for rubber trees, whoever was in charge of the project knew nothing about culture and the cultural differences between Americans and the native rainforest Brazilians. In an attempt to make the American workers' home so far away from home seem more familiar, they modeled the town after a contemporary U.S. town, completely mimicking U.S. life. They paved the streets and constructed houses that you would see in the heart of middle America—with running water, sewage lines, and street lights. Lawns were mowed and flowers planted. They provided the workers with the food—hamburgers, hot dogs, and such—that they were used to. They held dances and barbeques, church services, and ice cream socials. The familiar life, if you were an American, that is. Many of the workers, however, were locals, not used to eating such rich fare or having to conform to American life. But it was a requirement. Ford also banned alcohol, loose women, gambling, and other vices from the town—even in the privacy of their own homes. The natural result was the establishment of a community—nicknamed the Island of Innocence—eight miles upriver that promoted all of the missing vices. Needless to say, Fordlandia was a complete failure in every respect. In addition to the collapsing business, crime ran rampant throughout the town, and the local workers revolted in 1930. Although the revolt was quashed, the conflicts continued to the very end.

Despite his statue greeting people as they got off the boat—the only mode of transportation to the town—Henry Ford never actually visited the town himself. Fordlandia was a massive failure, and in 1945, his grandson sold the land back to the Brazilian government for a loss of twenty million dollars. No rubber was ever produced from the venture. A few people still lived in the dilapidated town, some of them descendants of the Brazilian workers.

"Wow," I said when we finished. "I had no idea about any of that."

"Me neither," said Sabrina, "but it looks like dozens of articles and even a book have been written about it. I guess we lead a sheltered life."

"So do you think Bruce was a worker there?" I asked. We had stopped calling him my great-grandfather and just referred to him as Bruce.

"He was involved in running illegal booze," replied

Sabrina. "What if they were making shipments to the 'Island of Innocence'?"

"From the states? Would it be worth it?" I asked. "Couldn't they get it cheaper from Mexico, or pretty much anywhere down there?"

"Yeah, but as you reminded me, this was *your* relative."

She wasn't wrong. "But he worked for others," I said. "They would have sent him down. Wouldn't they have had enough brains to see the stupidity of that?"

"You're kidding, right?"

I shrugged. "Maybe they only made the one attempt before figuring out it wasn't going to be lucrative."

"So I think we now know *where* we need to go. Now the question is *why*?"

"And going back to my father's notes, what did he mean with all that about Mikey? And why did he stop there? It seemed he was on to something. I think we can assume he read the material in his attic. Maybe the fact that Mikey's body was never found bothered him."

I was getting no response from Sabrina. She was back at the computer.

Finally she said, "I was thinking the same thing, so I wanted to check something. You ready for this?"

"Probably not."

"As you said, your father had been dabbling with this for a long time. Up until the Mikey stuff, your father hadn't made any notes for over three years. Those last entries, however, were added only a week before he was shot. It seems the minute he got onto this new topic, he was killed."

I didn't know what to say. Even as I learned that the deaths of my grandfather and great-grandfather were in fact murder, I still assumed that my father's death was totally unrelated to all of this. Hell, it had to be. They had the woman's husband in jail. He admitted to it. So was it just coincidence? The trouble was, I no longer believed in coincidence. But this would be hard to explain any other way.

I sat staring at Sabrina. She let me stare. That was good, because I had nothing to say. What could I say?

"Fuck it," I finally said, throwing my hands in the air.

"I expected something a bit deeper, but we can go with that," she answered.

"It doesn't make sense," I said, "and I don't think I can deal with that right now, so let's concentrate on something different. Izzy wrote that the Flynns seemed nervous. What if they knew that Mikey wasn't really killed and they were afraid to let out the big family secret?"

"I'm sure he died long ago, but I suppose some families are very protective about their ancestors. It's possible."

"I'd give my ancestors up in a heartbeat," I said.

"I don't blame you."

"So, another road trip?" I asked.

"Did Izzy say where they live? I seem to remember seeing Vermont, but I'm not sure where in Vermont."

"She had it listed as Brattleboro. That's only an hour or so north of here."

"Her itinerary is becoming clearer," said Sabrina. "She must have gone from New York to Vermont to see the Flynns, then on to Chicago to see Mario."

"And then her unfortunate trip to see me."

It was getting late and didn't make sense to head back to

Boston if we were going to Vermont the next day, so we found a hotel nearby. I couldn't sleep in that house yet, and I didn't want to use my mother's house while she was away.

*****

In the morning we were on our way to Brattleboro. Having grown up an hour south, I was actually pretty familiar with the area. An old mill town, Brattleboro came to life in the sixties and seventies as a refuge for hippies and ex-hippies. It developed quite the counter-culture reputation. I was too young to experience it, but I was told that whether or not you agreed with what Brattleboro had become in those couple of decades, it certainly had personality. Before they split up, my parents spent a lot of time there and later filled me full of stories of that era.

But as always happens, the hippies grew older and started donning suits and ties (or the ex-hippie equivalent) and became bankers, store owners, and insurance or real estate agents. Many ran for public office, and although they wanted to stay true to their counter-culture ideals, the reality of compromise set in. Many even found themselves starting to believe in the very things that they had fought so hard against in their protest days.

These days the town was sorely in need of a personality. It was now a strange mixture of art galleries and dollar stores. I had only been through there a couple of times in the last ten years, but both times felt that the town had gotten dirtier. Maybe it was reverting back to its mill town roots.

I explained all this to Sabrina as we drove up Interstate 91.

"Now who's the travel agent?" she asked.

We found Bill and Amanda Flynn's address in Izzy's notes. Being a Saturday, we were hoping to find them in. We did, but not until late that afternoon. We spent the day exploring Brattleboro, coming back every hour or so to check to see if they had returned home. Finally, at about four o'clock, we saw a car sitting in the driveway.

They lived in an old three-story Vermont house, kept up as well as you could keep up a 150-year-old house. To me it looked like a spider breeding ground.

A rather nondescript man about my age answered the door—was that how people referred to me? He was shorter than me by a couple of inches and had wispy red hair, the edges trying to turn gray. He didn't look particularly friendly or unfriendly, just not interested why two people were at his door. He was holding a beer can.

"Yeah?"

"Mr. Flynn, my name is Delmore Honeycutt." The reaction was almost imperceptible—almost. He knew the last name. "And this is Sabrina Spencer." We had decided to go back to Sabrina's pen name—partly because he knew the name Worth from Izzy, and partly to see if her fame would get us further. So much for that. It didn't generate any response at all.

"Our great-grandfathers knew each other."

"How nice for them." He was trying to be uncaring, but when he licked his lips I knew that he was, in fact, nervous. He didn't say anything more.

A normal conversation would follow some form of politeness—"What can I do for you," or some such thing. The fact that none of that was forthcoming obviously meant that he knew—or suspected—why we were there.

Sabrina got it going. "You recently talked to my sister, Isobel Worth."

"Can't say that I did."

"Well, yeah, you did," I said. "We have her notes."

He went quiet again.

"Can we come in, Mr. Flynn?" asked Sabrina. "This is important."

With an audible sigh, he moved aside and let us pass.

Despite its ancient exterior, the inside was pretty modern and comfortable. No spiders that I could see. He motioned us to a couch. His wife came into the room from the kitchen. She was a female version of Bill—around the same height, with the same color hair. She even had the same lack of personality.

"Amanda, this is Delmore Honeycutt and ... I don't remember your name ... the sister of that woman who came by with all the questions."

"Oh, not again. Why can't you people just leave us alone?"

"We would ... I'm Sabrina, by the way ... but we are involved in something that we have to find the answer to."

"Your problem, not ours," she said.

"Not really," I said. "Like it or not, we are all involved. And it's become dangerous. If you can tell us what we need to know, we can be out of your hair for good."

"We saw on the Boston news that your sister was killed. Sorry." Was Bill opening up? "But she was killed by a mugger, right?"

"No. She was killed in connection to this," answered Sabrina. They looked at each other. "Look," Sabrina continued, "we didn't ask to get involved in this any more than you did.

We were happy in our ignorance. But the fact is, we're stuck in the middle of it now, and unless we can solve it, all of our lives are in danger."

"What did you say your name is?" asked Amanda.

"Sabrina. Sabrina Spencer."

"Like the mystery writer."

"That's me."

"Huh. Heard of you but haven't read any of your books. So let me guess. You're writing about it?"

"I'm not going to be in any book," said Bill.

"No." Sabrina replied. "It's all a little convoluted. Your great-grandfather and Del's great-grandfather were friends. They also committed a crime together. My grandfather killed Del's grandfather over that same crime. Now my sister is dead and a man in Nebraska is dead because of it. We're trying to stop anyone else from dying. If you can just answer a few questions, we'll be on our way and, hopefully, you won't have to deal with any of this ever again."

She had them. I think the pressure of family secrets, and now dead people, finally got to them. Bill looked at Amanda. She gave a nod.

"What do you need to know?" he asked.

"What do you know about everything that went on with Mikey?"

They looked at each other again, this time with a puzzled look.

"Who's Mikey?"

It was our turn to look at each other. Did we have the right person?

"Your great-grandfather."

"His name was Preston. Preston Flynn."

I must have looked confused, so Bill cleared it up.

"I suppose it's possible that he went by a different name when he was young. He robbed a museum in New York and skipped town."

"Same person. He was known as Mikey back then."

"And you're looking for the paintings he stole."

"Uh, no. Why, do you have them?"

I could tell by his face that he did.

"You've got to understand," explained Bill. "These fucking paintings have been the bane of our existence. Did you know that this was his house? I'm like the fourth generation to live here. He put those paintings in the basement and told my grandfather not to breathe a word about them. He, in turn, told my father, who told me. I'm sick of it."

"Why didn't you just turn them in?" asked Sabrina.

"Because we were told that there was a lot of danger associated with them and that we'd be better off keeping our mouths shut. And now you show up looking for them."

"We're not," I repeated. "There were eleven paintings stolen, but only ten reported missing. We were looking for the eleventh, which we've already found."

"Frankly," added Sabrina, "if you turned those over to the authorities—and you could make up some story about finding them in your basement—you'd be heroes. Those paintings aren't dangerous at this point. The one we have is."

"Then what are you here for?"

"We need information about Mikey. He was involved—in some way, anyway—in a crime before that one. The eleventh painting that I mentioned was the one they were robbing the museum to get. That painting holds a clue to the earlier crime. But we're missing something and we're hoping that any information you can give us about Mikey will give us the missing clue."

"I don't think we can help you. I don't really know that much about him. He died around 1960, I think. Other than this painting shit hanging over our heads, it's ancient history."

"So that's it?" I asked. "You know nothing more about him?"

"Nothing."

"Except," said Amanda, "that he wrote a book."

# Chapter 24

"A book?" Sabrina and I blurted out almost simultaneously.

"Oh yeah," said Bill. "Forgot about that."

"That was a pretty big 'forgot'," I said.

"Hey," he said, showing a bit of anger. "Unlike you, we've tried our best to forget about him and anything associated with him. Up until your sister," looking at Sabrina, "and that other guy long before her came by, I had forgotten all about him ... except for the paintings."

"Someone else came by?" I asked.

"Yeah, some Italian guy. Nice enough. When he found out I didn't know anything, he left."

"When was this?"

Bill looked to Amanda for help. "I don't know. Couple of years ago maybe."

"More than that," said Amanda. "Closer to four years."

"Did you tell him about the paintings or the book?"

"I've never told anyone about the paintings—sort of the family curse..."

"I know all about that," I mumbled.

"As for the book, I forgot we had it."

"You have a copy?" asked Sabrina.

"I just said that, right?"

The longer I knew Sabrina, the more I realized that there were things you just didn't say to her. Anything that violated her personal space in some way—such as when Russ was staring at her boobs. Bill had just committed a verbal violation—a snide comeback. She probably had to deal with those on a constant basis in prison when she first got there, but probably not so much toward the end. I could see why. Her face turned to stone and she just stared at Bill. And this was no ordinary stare; there was venom behind it.

Bill caught it. He had to. He would have had to have been dumb as a stump not to. The room went deadly silent. I didn't say anything. This was Sabrina's battle to win—and winning was the only option.

"Uh, sorry. Didn't mean it that way," Bill finally said, looking down. We had a winner, and the pecking order was now firmly established.

Amanda got up, coming to Bill's rescue, and went over to the built-in bookcase on the wall. It only took her a minute to find what she was looking for. She came back with a fairly new looking hardcover, minus a dust-jacket, and handed it to me.

Etched on the front cover and spine were *My Criminal Life: A Novel*, by Preston Flynn. I quickly looked through it, then handed it to the book expert. Sabrina opened the cover and looked at the first few pages.

"It was self-published in 1958," she said.

"Self-published?" I said. "They had that back then?"

"Yes, but back then you had to pay a publisher to publish it for you. They were known as vanity presses. You still hear the term, but not as much, as self-publishing becomes easier and more accessible for people to do it themselves. Back then it was assumed that you were some kind of hack and could only get published if you paid someone to do it for you. The publisher he used was probably one of the smaller ones. I've never heard of it ... which means nothing."

"It looks so new," I said.

"I can answer that," said Bill, his manhood slowly returning. "I doubt if anybody in my family ever read it. We certainly didn't. I have a vague memory of my grandfather—Preston's son—calling it a piece of crap." He hesitated. "I think he was also ashamed of his father. You know, having a criminal in the family.

"May we borrow it?" asked Sabrina, all memory of the previous incident already vanished.

"You can have it, for all I care. If it will help end all of this, then you're welcome to it."

"If you turn in the paintings," I reassured him, "I think you will finally be free of it all. They were stolen from the Brooklyn Museum. I'm sure they'd be mighty happy to get them back."

We left them with smiles of relief on their faces.

As we were walking out to my car Sabrina said, "So Mario—at least we have to assume it was him—has known about this for a long time."

"Well, unlike the Flynns, the Guidrys probably kept the story alive. My guess is that each generation of that family has been as greedy as the one before it."

"No doubt. And four years ago he probably came across some information on Mikey he didn't have before, looked up the Flynns, and then went away disappointed. Then when Izzy showed up, the door was once again opened."

We started on our way. Dusk had fallen and a light rain was falling. The highway was shiny in the headlights. I said, "You read, I'll drive."

Sabrina spent a few minutes flipping through it, getting a feeling for the book.

"Well, I can tell you right away that the book isn't any better than the painting in terms of quality. Simply stated ..."

"... It sucks, right?"

"Right. He wasn't a very educated man, but he had a story to tell. And he's telling it in the form of a novel."

"Let's just hope it's the story we're look..."

We were hit from behind ... hard. The car swerved across the lanes as I frantically tried to regain control. I avoided going off the highway and finally pulled over to the side. The car stalled. Because of the rain and the darkness, the road was fairly empty of traffic. I wasn't sure anyone else had even seen the accident.

"You okay?"

"I think so." She rolled her neck. "Yes, it just caught me by surprise. You?"

I didn't answer. I was looking at the side mirror, then the rear-view mirror.

"What's wrong?"

"Can you get my gun out of the glove compartment?" Before we left, I had looked up the gun laws in Vermont—basically there were none—and found that I'd be perfectly legal bringing my gun into the state from Massachusetts.

This was real, and in response, my hands were shaking. I think Sabrina saw that. She retrieved the gun, but didn't hand it to me. Instead, she hid it under the jacket on her lap. "They'll never expect me to have it," she said by way of explanation.

There were two of them and they split up, each taking a different side of the car. If I had any doubts about their intentions, that certainly erased them. Sabrina put the book under the seat. I could have tried to start the car and pull away before they reached us, but was it worth it? That would be assuming the car would start, and then what? It would result in a high-speed chase down the highway. What would it accomplish? So we waited.

My guy was right outside my door. He rapped on the window with the butt of a gun. Not a good sign. I rolled down the window, the light rain quickly coating the inside of my door.

"Can I help you?"

Without warning, he smacked me on the side of the head with the butt of his pistol. I fell into Sabrina's lap. In my dizzy state, I saw him raise his pistol. He was going to shoot us! Then I heard a gun go off. *Heard* was putting it mildly. The explosion was right in my ear. I looked up, afraid that Sabrina was the victim. Needless worry. She was holding the gun. A split second after shooting, she whipped open the passenger door, and I heard—with my one good ear—an *umph* on the other side of the door. She jumped out and I heard her kick the other assailant. As I was finally starting to move, she handed me the second man's gun.

"Check the other guy." I was oddly pleased to hear—again, with my one good ear—a tremor of fear in her voice. Or maybe it was just adrenaline. I opened my door and looked down at Sabrina's victim. He wasn't going anywhere—ever again. He caught one in the throat.

I was regaining my senses. I pulled out my phone and dialed 9-1-1.

"We've just been attacked on Interstate 91, just south of Brattleboro," I reported to the dispatcher. I was still shaking, and it was reflected in my voice. "We've killed one of our attackers and have the other one subdued. I will lay their two weapons and my own—which I have a license for—on the hood of the car."

"Officers are on their way. Is anyone hurt?"

"Well, other than the dead guy, I don't think so." I was calming down. "I can't hear out of one ear from the blast of the gun in the car, and my girlfriend kicked the other guy, but I don't know his condition."

"Do you know why you were attacked?"

"I have no idea. A carjacking, maybe?" I was learning to lie with the best of them. "I have to check on my girlfriend. I hear the sirens now." I hung up, retrieved the dead guy's pistol, and went around to the other side of the car. The live guy was sprawled on the ground in that ever familiar position, holding his crotch. Sabrina was good at that.

She handed me the two pistols and I put the three of them on the smashed-in trunk of my car. Then we waited. A Vermont Highway Patrol car pulled up, and the officer got out, pointed his gun at us and told us to lie on the ground, with our arms spread. Easy for us, not so easy for the other guy. A minute later another patrol car pulled up, and then a couple of Brattleboro cop cars. Once they assessed the situation, they cleared us and we were able to get up. A few minutes after that an ambulance arrived. They put a bandage on a cut on the side of my head and determined that my eardrum probably wasn't ruptured. The other guy's balls definitely were.

It took a while, and we had to accompany them to the local State Police barracks to give our statements. We never mentioned the book, which Sabrina had retrieved and put in her pocketbook, but we did talk about the mystery to some degree and referred them to Sabrina's detective in Boston. Our attacker wasn't talking. In fact, he didn't say a word. When they found out who Sabrina was, they were fawning all over her. I was invisible, once again. By the time we got out of there, several Boston news stations had their trucks parked outside the police barracks. After all, a murder in Vermont was big news. A murder in Vermont by a famous mystery author was even bigger news. Sabrina talked to the press for a few moments, and even though she did well, considering the situation, and charmed them to no end, I could see that she was uncomfortable almost to the point of shutting down. After a few minutes, I hustled her away.

We decided to head back to Boston and the privacy of her hotel room. Sabrina hadn't said a word since getting in the car, and once I was away from the circus we had just left, I pulled over in the first rest area we came to.

We hugged, and that's when she let it out. The tears came and she shook in my arms. Oddly enough, I had already done my shaking and was able to be a support to her without breaking down myself. I just let her cry. I didn't know if it was memories of killing her husband coming through, or memories of prison. It was probably a combination of both of them—and maybe other things as well. After all, she had just killed someone, and her name was going to be plastered all over the news. I wisely refrained from telling her that it would help her book sales.

Things were better after the cry and we talked a bit while I drove. Then Sabrina fell asleep. I let her sleep and drove in silence, thinking about all that had happened. We arrived at the hotel around daybreak. A few minutes later, we were both sound asleep in the safety of her room.

# Chapter 25

We only slept a few hours. Between the leftover adrenaline and cell phones vibrating all over the table—shutting them off would have been the smart thing to do, but we were zombies when we got to the hotel and clear thinking eluded us—we were up by eleven.

I called my mother in England. She heard the news and had left six messages. I also called Mo, who had left three, and Seymour, who had been asleep and hadn't heard the news yet. I wasn't sure if he would have called me even if he had heard.

Sabrina had concerned calls from her editor and agent, and another from her publicist. Thirty seconds into the third call she slammed down the phone.

I raised an eyebrow.

"They can find me a new publicist. I'm done with him."

I waited while she fumed.

"Do you know what he said?"

"I can guess."

She didn't hear me. "He didn't even ask if I was okay. He said that this is the best thing that could've happened. My new book will soar to the top of the lists and my author signings will be even more packed." She was shaking with anger. Or was it anger? "Do you know what I'm going to do?"

"I do."

She didn't hear me again. "I'm going to cancel all my signings. It'll be a circus now. People won't come to hear about my book. I bet most of the people couldn't care less about my book. They'll just want to gawk at the famous woman who killed a guy. And do you know what else?"

"Yeah, I do." Why did I even bother? She was in a different zone. The fact was, I knew precisely what was coming into her life.

"They're going to learn about my past. It might not be tomorrow, but it'll be soon. They'll be looking at my life with a microscope." She looked at me with tears in her eyes. "I don't mind them finding out about all that. I was prepared for it. I knew the coverage would be pretty intense, but with you in my life, I knew I could handle it. But not this. Not now. I've killed a second man. They'll all be vultures. People will come out of the woodwork. 'Entertainment reporters'"—she made quotation marks in the air while making a face—"will be hounding me, not for my books, but for the 'story behind the story'."

She sat next to me, her body language saying she needed a massive hug. I obliged. All the trust issues she had been so valiantly working on had just gone out the window.

"What can I do?" Her voice had taken on a pleading tone. I had to answer, and I had to say what she needed to hear.

"Cancel your signings for this book. All of them. Hey, you have a perfect excuse. You've just been through a traumatic experience. Then you announce your past."

She looked at me in alarm.

"The suspense of it all is killing you. You know they are eventually going to find out—you knew it before all this—so meet it head-on. Tell your story. You don't have to do it yourself. Let your publisher do it. Give them as many facts as you think pertinent. And then have your publisher also announce that you will not be available for interviews about it.

Put it to bed. Let them also announce that you won't be doing any book signings for the foreseeable future. It'll never go away, but over time it will dissipate. Maybe to the point of someday resuming your signings."

She was silent. I let her think. After a couple of minutes, she gave a little smile.

"I like it."

"One more thing," I said. "You don't stop writing. You might gain a whole new audience from this—and I don't mean it the way your ex-publicist meant it. People might discover you through this, but if you keep writing, they will appreciate you for the stories you tell. The rest of this nonsense will eventually fade into the background. Your writing won't. Someday you might be ready to do signings again. But if not? Hey, there have been plenty of reclusive authors. You'll be the J.D. Salinger of the mystery world."

She was smiling broadly now. I think she approved. Much like the pressure that was relieved when she opened up to me about her past, I could feel her relief in her body language as she melted in my arms.

*****

The rest of the day was spent ignoring phone calls and knocks on her door, as she crafted her life story as succinctly as possible. She would tell of the abusive marriage and of finally reaching her breaking point; of the judge who was lenient with her sentence; and the first year of hell in prison followed by the five years of rediscovering herself.

"I'm not going to name any of the other inmates, but it's

important—no, more than that. It's essential—that people understand how these women changed my life. As much as they almost killed me in the beginning, these women saved me in the end. I never want to compromise the relationship that we had ... and still have."

"And then," I said, "you disappear for a while."

"Which will give us the time and freedom to see this through to the end." Then she added, "Under the cloak of secrecy."

"Well, not total secrecy. They are all camped out in this hotel waiting for you to show your face. And although I'm not the focus, my name is now out there. I'd say we could stay at my place, but they might be watching that too."

"Your dad's house?"

"That might be the safest option. Of course, depending what Mikey says in his book, who knows where we might be headed. Brazil, probably."

"At least they won't know me down there."

"Speaking of that, be prepared to be recognized from time to time. Your picture is going to be plastered everywhere, so it won't be like before, when you'd get noticed by a few fans here and there."

"I know. But I have to tell you what a relief it is that I'll be cancelling my signings."

"Don't get too used to it. As your teacher, I'm not letting you off that easily. You're not going to learn to trust by sneaking around in the middle of the night. I'm just giving you a free pass for a while. Class starts again when we solve this."

"You're not giving me a lot of incentive to solve it any time soon," she said with a smirk.

"If this leads us to Brazil," I said, "I'm going to have to brush up on my Spanish. Haven't had to use it since high school."

"Well, you could do that," Sabrina answered, "but considering they speak Portuguese down there, I'm not sure it's going to help you much."

"Oh."

That evening she had a three-way call with her agent and her editor, and explained her plans. There was no objection. Sabrina had suddenly become a cash cow for both the agent and the publisher, and would only become more of one after the announcement.

It was decided that the story would be presented by her agent. He would also ask the reporters to give her the space she needed, but we all knew that wasn't going to happen. He would break the story the next day, giving them no time to dig it up on their own.

When the call was finally done and all the details had been hammered out, it was close to midnight. And by the time we finished making love, it was almost two. Another late night. Before we fell asleep this time, however, we remembered to turn off our phones.

*****

We broke out of our hotel prison the next day at noon. It was decided that Sabrina's agent would make the announcement about her past from a conference room at the Westin, and he flew up from New York early that morning. Her editor and a lawyer from the publisher would also be attending. Although nothing specific was said, it was assumed that Sabrina would be present at the news conference. As a result, the reporters camped outside our room stampeded to the conference room to get good seats, leaving the hallway empty. Well, almost empty. There were two tabloid photographers who weren't fooled and hung out waiting for a glimpse of the gun-toting mystery author.

But I anticipated that. Mo had called during a break at school asking if there was anything she could do. I explained about the news conference and Sabrina's past—with Sabrina's permission—and mentioned my fear that the news conference wouldn't draw them all away from the door. She arranged for another teacher to watch her students for a while and took a ride down to the Westin. So when Sabrina and I left the room, there she was, entertaining the two wayward photographers with her charm and beauty.

When they saw us and started to follow, she said she had something else to tell them and gently laid her hands on their shoulders. They sat on the floor with a thud and didn't try to move. Mo turned her head toward me and winked. Her day was complete.

We arrived at my father's house two hours later, free and clear of the hordes of reporters. We didn't know when our fortress of solitude would be discovered, but for now the peace was the most glorious thing we had experienced in days.

But even more than the peace, we were looking forward to cracking open Mikey's book and seeing if it held the clue that would finally explain all the lies my family had covered up for decades.

We got comfortable on the couch—the living room couch,

not his questionable office couch—and we took turns reading aloud. The writing was pedestrian, but not annoying. As a novel, it was terrible. He basically laid out the facts of his life in first-person novel form, but with little artistic flair. Every character seemed to be a character from his real life. The names weren't even changed. If he had any illusions of becoming a bestselling novelist, it wouldn't have been with this book. Besides the poor grammar, the book was laced throughout with profanity, more than any conventional publisher of the time would tolerate. We were just hoping it would give us something we could use.

It started out slowly ... oh so slowly ... describing his—or his fictional character's—childhood in New York and his slow integration into a life of crime. It was the "good boy caught up in events he couldn't control" type of story. He didn't like the life of crime, but was in too deep to escape it. None of it was of any interest to us, but we continued to read every word for fear of missing an important clue. None came for most of the book.

Finally, at around the three-quarter mark, he began the story we had so patiently been waiting for. It was the story that would answer so many questions. And in the process, would raise so many more.

# Chapter 26

*It started with the Russian. The damn Russian. He wasn't even one of us. Tony met him down there and he convinced Tony to help him look for the treasure. Now Tony is dead, Bruce is dead, John is probably dead, and they think I'm dead. All because Tony got greedy. Vlad (we never did know his real name, but he was Russian, so that's what we called him) thought he was so smart, but in the end he wasn't.*

*It was supposed to be an easy job. Flanagan had a friend who told him he'd get rich delivering booze to this place in the middle of nowhere down in South America. I didn't see it the same way, but I was low man on the totem pole, so what I thought didn't count. Well, you didn't have to say the word rich to Flanagan twice. He put the four of us on a boat with the biggest shipment of booze we'd ever delivered. We were going to a town in Brazil owned by Henry Ford. Imagine, the guy was rich enough to own a whole town in another country. I guess he didn't allow booze in the town, but there was a place upriver that did. That's where we were going.*

*I could have told him he wouldn't make any money, but as I said, nobody cared what I thought. I looked the place up on a map. It was going to take us three weeks in the ship just getting to Brazil, then another week to get where we needed to go. And what if they didn't need our hooch? Or what if they paid us in Pesos, or whatever worthless shit money they used down there? It was a big risk, but when Flanagan saw dollar signs, you didn't argue.*

*By the time we reached Belém, the port city in Brazil, we all knew it was going to be a bust. Even Tony, who was almost as greedy as Flanagan. But we had no choice at that point, we had to go through with it.*

*We hired a river boat to take us to this place called "The Island of Innocence." We knew from the name that it was going to be a wild place. The boat cost us a fortune. It didn't matter which one we used, as soon as they saw what we were transporting, they tripled their price. Flanagan was going to lose his shirt on this one. It took days to get there.*

"No description," said Sabrina.

"Huh?"

"He just took a ship to Brazil, then a multiple-day trip down river. Where's the description? Did he not notice his surroundings? He could have added so much to the book with a little description."

There was no doubt in my mind that the quality of writing in the book was annoying Sabrina.

*The trouble started when we met Vlad. He was a little older than us—probably around thirty—and caught a ride with us down river. Thinking back, he planned it. He was waiting for the right group of lunks to come along to help him pull a job. When he saw us, he knew he'd found them. We were a little desperate. We knew we were going to go back to Flanagan empty-handed, and none of us wanted that. So on the second day on the river when he brought up the job, our ears perked up. Especially Tony, but I can't blame him alone. Vlad told a good story. His English was good, but his Russian accent was a little hard to understand at times. Even so, he had us, and he knew he did.*

*So the story was this (at least, this is what he told us. I came to find out that there was more to it than what he let on): It was all about eggs. That's right, eggs. He wouldn't go into any more detail than that, except to say that they were valuable. Someone in Fordlandia (yeah, can you imagine naming a town that?) had some valuable eggs, and Vlad needed help stealing them. Eggs! Were they from a golden chicken or something? To this day I've never seen them, so I have no idea what made them so valuable. Bruce thought they were maybe dinosaur eggs, but Bruce was a little soft in the head. I liked him. He was a good guy. Just a little soft. Like me, I don't think he was cut out for a life of crime.*

"Sounds like a Honeycutt," I said.

*Anyway, so this guy we were supposed to steal them from was also a Russian. He was some bigwig there, so he lived in one of the big houses. Vlad said he couldn't do it alone. He needed help. He said the guy who hired him would pay us a fortune for them. At first we thought it would be a way for Flanagan to make money on this deal, but then we all thought, "Fuck Flanagan. He doesn't have to know."*

*So we land at the Island of Innocence and deliver the hooch. The one thing Flanagan never thought about was that they had us over a barrel. That wasn't meant to be funny, but I guess it is. They knew we were stuck. We had to sell it to them because we couldn't very well turn around and take the whole shipment home. So they gave a us a fraction of what it was worth, and we had to take it. Flanagan lost thousands on that deal.*

*We took the money and put it aside for Flanagan. One thing we all knew: he wasn't going to pay us a dime. He'd accuse us of taking a bad deal, losing the money, or even worse, stealing it from him. However you looked at it, he was losing big and he'd have to pass the loss onto someone. We were the someone.*

*When the deal—such as it was—was done, we went to*

*Fordlandia and rented a house for a week. They let us do that in the hopes that we'd want to stay and work there. Seems they were always hiring. They especially liked Americans. As it turns out, John did stay. He said he liked it down there, but I'm not so sure that he wasn't just afraid of going back and facing Flanagan. Truth be told, he was like Bruce and me; he was too nice a guy. He was a struggling artist—back then everyone was a struggling something—who just needed a steady job. We all liked John and didn't mind him deserting us. When I think back, the only real criminal in our group was Tony. He was bad. We were all a little afraid of him, I think.*

*So Vlad gave us the lowdown on the job. He made it sound easy. At least I think he did. I still had trouble understanding him. But Tony seemed to understand him okay, so I went with that. I still didn't know exactly what we were stealing. The rumors were that a lot of the bigwigs there were smuggling gold out of the country, so naturally I assumed that was the treasure. Turns out I was right … and wrong. They were smuggling gold, the whole lot of them, all those guys who lived in the nice houses on the hill. And we got some of the gold, but we got something else too, something that Vlad said was worth ten times what the gold was worth. I assume it was the eggs.*

*I never saw them myself, so this is all second-hand. You see, we split up to do the jobs. Bruce and I had one house and Tony and Vlad had another. Tony said we should concentrate on the two houses that they had scoped out as having the most gold. To try to break into all of them—there were about six—would be too risky. What Bruce and I didn't know was that the house Tony and Vlad were going in was the one the Russian was living in. And they weren't going after any gold.*

*Tony spent a few days scoping things out. He talked to people and he watched the men who lived in the big houses. He even broke into a couple on his scouting mission. He said as tempting as it was to steal some of the gold, it was important to wait until the time was right. Finally, two days before we were going to leave, he set the plan into motion. He told us which house had the most gold and where to find it. I have to say, Tony was good. His directions led us right to the horde. And let me tell you, there was a lot of it!*

*It was the easiest job I'd ever pulled. We did it during the day when everyone was at work. We found the stash in the wall of the bedroom—right where Tony said it would be—and spent an hour getting it out. There were a few bags of gold ore and dust, but mostly it was gold that had been melted into bars. I didn't know how much it was all worth, but I knew it was a fortune.*

*Bruce and I took it out the back door into the jungle. It took about five trips each—the stuff was damn heavy. We put the boards back exactly the way we found them. If we were lucky, the guy who lived there wouldn't check on his gold until after we were long gone. Once we were in the jungle, we found a small gully just the right size. We piled in the gold and covered it with dirt, leaves, and rocks. No one would find it there. The day we were leaving we would pack it into some of the empty liquor crates and put it on the boat.*

*We were in heaven. We were rich! All five of us would have enough to last a lifetime. We included John even though he didn't do the actual stealing. We figured we might need him later. As it turns out, we did.*

*So when Tony and Vlad met with us later and told us that they didn't get any gold, it was a surprise. But then they said that what they got was even better than gold. We were a little dubious, to say the least. Tony said they hid it and would show us the next day. The made a reference again to the eggs and said it was the find of the century. It didn't make any sense to me.*

*Sadly, it never made any sense, because I never got to see the eggs. To this day I have no idea what they were talking about. The next day all hell broke loose. First, Tony and Vlad got into a big fight. It seems that Vlad needed to bring those eggs to a contact in the states. He was working for someone. Never found out who, because Tony killed Vlad. Just like that. They had an argument about something and Tony stabbed him right through the heart. Tony says he was defending himself, but we all knew better. He didn't want to share the eggs with Vlad. Since he didn't want to tell us anything about them, he obviously didn't want to share them with the rest of us either.*

*After Tony killed Vlad, all hell broke loose and we knew it was time to go. Three of the Fordlandia guys had Tony cornered, and Bruce—who didn't even like Tony—shot one of them. I don't think he meant to, but Bruce wasn't so great with guns and I think it went off accidently. I figured that because Bruce dropped the gun and ran into the woods. He spent half the trip home crying like a baby about how he had killed a guy.*

"Definitely a Honeycutt," I said.

*Well, we hightailed it to the boat—the same boat we had hired to get there. They hung around because Tony had promised them a big payoff if they'd wait. In the end, he stiffed them, but that was Tony.*

*We made it back to New York a few weeks later, broke and tired. I thought Flanagan was going to kill us all, and he almost did, but somehow Tony talked him out of it. But we were done with Flanagan and he was done with us. We all got legit jobs, but with the knowledge that as soon as we got the word from Tony, we'd be involved in the biggest score anyone had ever seen.*

*Which brings me back to John. Tony put John in charge of hiding the treasure. We had to get out of there so fast, Tony didn't have time to do it. The plan was, when things quieted down, John was going to send Tony word of where it was hidden. And that's just what he did. A few months later Tony called us together with a plan. We had to rob a piece of art from the Brooklyn Museum. Tony and I did the heist, while Bruce acted as lookout. We were supposed to get one specific painting, but I said, "What the hell?" and took a whole pile of them.*

*John sent us instructions to where the treasure was hidden. Did he send us a letter with clear directions? No. Instead, he sent us a clue. A painting. The painting we were after in the museum. It was a clue, but really it was a "fuck you" message to Tony. Turns out John hated Tony (big surprise, everyone hated him). I saw the painting. There was nothing in it Tony didn't already know. Fordlandia, a rubber tree, a house that looked like all the others, and a headstone.*

*Anyway, things were hot for a while after the heist, so Tony gave the painting to Bruce and told him to hide it. Right after that, Bruce left town for a while; I think he found a good hiding place. As for me, I skipped town. I heard later that everyone assumed I was dead.*

*As for the others, Tony was killed a short time later. Bruce lasted a little while longer, but was killed in an accident. Last I heard about John, he left Fordlandia when Ford abandoned it. He developed some sort of fever and died before he could even leave Brazil.*

*Me? I took the name Preston and settled in the sticks, doing odd jobs. I never made it back down to Fordlandia.*

# Chapter 27

That was it, at least for us. The rest of the book went into his life in Vermont, his failed attempts at writing, and his regret that he never got to bring home the gold. Other than that, no further mention was made of Fordlandia, the heist, or the eggs.

"What do you think?" I asked. We had somehow ended up curled in each other's arms ... and legs. Kind of like a giant pretzel. Extracting ourselves from that position was going to be interesting.

"Terrible novel. He had no imagination. He was only able to write about what he had experienced. He could have made up a story of going down to find the treasure. Gun battles. Intrigue. Anything. There was none of that."

"Other than that," she continued, "I think the location of the treasure died with John. Unless someone discovered it by accident, I think it is still there."

"Are you suggesting that it's time to go to Brazil?"

"I do."

"So what about the eggs?" I asked. "Any thoughts?"

"No, but I can try to find out. I need to go online."

I looked at her, then down at our entangled limbs.

"Really?"

"Uh, I'll look it up on my phone."

She ended up at the computer. We were both beginning to cramp up. Untangling ourselves seemed prudent.

Sabrina typed in "Russians" and "Eggs" and almost immediately we knew what we were looking for.

"Oh my God, of course. Faberge Eggs." She said it in a quiet voice, almost one of reverence. "It has to be. I can't believe I didn't make that connection before."

I didn't say anything. For a different reason than Sabrina's awe, though. It didn't really mean anything to me. I mean, sure, I had heard of Faberge Eggs. Just some ornate eggs, right? Yawn. Well, I guess it was a little more than that. As she read about them out loud to me and showed me the pictures, I gained a little more respect for them. Actually, I gained a lot of respect for them. This Faberge guy was a master craftsman. They weren't just ornate, they were truly treasures. Most of them were now in museums or private collections.

It was when Sabrina came across a reference to some "lost" eggs, that we perked up. It seems that Faberge had created a collection of fifty or so "Imperial Eggs" for the Russian Royal Family. When the Romanovs fell in 1918, the House of Faberge was ransacked and the fifty Imperial eggs were taken by the Bolsheviks. But of the fifty, eight mysteriously disappeared and were never found.

"Want to bet some of those eight found their way to Fordlandia?" Sabrina asked.

"I can see why Tony was so excited," I answered. "Even back then they were pretty valuable. Eighty-five years later, they are priceless." Then I added, "Yeah, I think it's time to go to Brazil.

*****

Traveling to Brazil wasn't like traveling to Iowa. It took us a couple of days to plan, pack, and let the important people in our lives know where we were going. For me that meant my mother, Mo, and Seymour. It was a bit more complicated for Sabrina, who had to deal with her agent and publisher. Now that she had cancelled all of her signings, at least she didn't have to deal with the publicity troll.

But it still wasn't easy. Sabrina was one of the hottest commodities in the country at that moment. There were Sabrina sightings all over the place—including one by an elderly couple named Simpson in Fairfield, Iowa. Her greatest fear had been realized. She was on the cover of magazines; she was in the news; she was exactly where she never wanted to be.

"So much for the J.D. Salinger life," she said during a quiet moment on the couch after turning off the news.

I felt guilty ... massively guilty. After all, I was the one who suggested she go public. I said as much to her.

She turned toward me, cupped her hands around my ears and pulled me to her with a sudden strength. Good thing she liked me. Looking me in the eyes she said, "Del, you have no idea how much you've saved me. This was all going to come out eventually. I knew it, my editor knew it, and my agent knew it. Heck, even my therapist mentioned it. You know my ... um ... eccentricities, my distrust of people. No, more like my fear of people. Imagine me trying to deal with all this on my own. And that's exactly what would have happened. All of those people—my supposed support—would have been no help at all. I would have retreated. I probably would have quit writing. There is only one person in the world who truly understands me—with all my baggage—and only one person I can truly lean on for support.

"Me?" I asked innocently with a slight smile. Actually, it

wasn't a smile. She was holding my head so firmly my lips were being pushed together. I imagined it looked like a smile, but it probably just gave me fish lips. She was latched onto my head the way she had latched onto my body when we first made love—like she didn't want to let go.

"Yes, you idiot. You." And then she jumped me. Oh my God. It was like nothing I'd ever experienced. The complete opposite of our earlier sexual forays, she was totally in charge. I let her. Hell, if I hadn't let her, she might have hurt me. It wasn't rough, just forceful. More inner demons—or inner somethings—were being released. I certainly didn't mind being the recipient. As we lay there afterward and I caught my breath, I kind of expected her to talk about it. But she didn't. Not a word. Another mysterious side to her. Well, she certainly wasn't boring anyway.

*****

We were about to leave for Boston the next morning so I could say my official goodbyes to Mo and Seymour, when Sabrina's cell phone rang. Not an uncommon occurrence, but in this case, it was Detective Marsh from Boston. Sabrina put it on speaker and let him know that I was listening too.

He got right to it. "Do you know two thugs named Freccetti and Danza?"

What, were we suddenly the expert on thugs?

"Should we?" asked Sabrina.

"Considering you almost put both of them in the hospital, I thought you might."

We looked at each other. "Fairfield?" she asked.

"Your attackers." He said it with an edge. Was he trying to scare us? Probably. Cops seemed to live for that.

"You are bringing this up for a reason?" Sabrina's demeanor had changed. Someone was stepping into her space. Whoa. Big mistake. If he thought he was going to intimidate her, he was sadly mistaken.

"I'm bringing it up because they are dead."

"They were in a dangerous business," she responded with a marked coolness. She was going to give back exactly what she was getting. I just stayed silent. I figured I'd know when—or if—I was needed.

"Where were you yesterday?"

The second time we were asked that question by a cop.

"You seriously think we had something to do with it?"

"Not you, Ms. Spencer. Mr. Honeycutt."

Moi?

"A witness described someone who looked suspiciously like you, Mr. Honeycutt."

My turn. "Well, I have a dozen witnesses putting me at the Westin yesterday."

"What time?"

"C'mon Marsh, you know better than that. To get from here to Iowa, kill two people, and back in the same day? It's a little ludicrous."

"Who said anything about Iowa? They were killed here in Boston."

That shut me up.

Sabrina took over ... thank God. "You're pissing me off. What reason in the world would Del have to kill those guys? That incident began and ended for us in Iowa. We had no reason to pursue it further. Why don't you talk to Mario Guidry? He was their employer."

He hesitated just slightly, but I caught it. "He's disappeared. His known associates haven't seen or heard from him in days. The word on the street in Chicago is that people are worried about his disappearance."

"And you believe them?

"We do."

"So because you people can't do your job, you are picking on Del. He was with me all day yesterday. Are you going to suggest now that I had something to do with their deaths?"

I loved it when she got into this mode.

Marsh hesitated again, this time a little longer. "I don't like your tone," he said finally. "Remember who you're talking to."

"Are we done?" she asked.

"For now. Honeycutt, don't leave town."

"We are leaving town," said Sabrina. She was all business now. Maybe because she knew exactly who she was dealing with. This was her territory and there was no fear. She lived in an environment for six years that saw no gray areas. Everything was black or white. Her conversation with Marsh was just as clear. "We are leaving the country tomorrow on business. If you try to stop us, I will have so many lawyers on your ass, you won't be able to sit down."

Silence. He could sense the change in her. He'd have to be a moron not to. He also knew I had nothing to do with their deaths. He knew that even before he called. He was probably trying to see if we knew anything that we were withholding from him. His tone suddenly changed.

"Sorry, this has been a stressful time. A double homicide is a big deal. And when we factor in your sister's death and the Chicago connection, it becomes complicated. I apologize if I went about it the wrong way."

I'll say this for Sabrina, she didn't hold a grudge. Probably another thing she learned in prison—take care of business and move on.

"How did they die?" she asked.

"They were tortured. It was pretty gruesome. I talked to the Fairfield police, who put me in touch with the Nebraska State Police about a similar incident in Wahoo, Nebraska. I was told that you were involved in that one too."

"Involved?" I asked.

"You knew the victim."

"Barely," I said.

"The Nebraska State Police said you thought Guidry might be responsible for the incident in Wahoo."

"Can I call you back in a few minutes?" Sabrina suddenly asked. "This opens up a possibility that we haven't thought of. Del and I need to talk it out first, then I'll call you back."

"Make it fast." Uh oh. "Please." A last second save.

Sabrina hung up and stared into space. The wheels were turning. I was pretty sure they were turning in the same direction as mine.

"Guidry is not our enemy," she said. "Or at least he's not the one we should really be afraid of." I was right. The same direction.

"And I'm thinking that maybe Guidry might even be afraid of this third party. I'm thinking he went underground," I added.

"So who is it?" she asked.

"If we trace all this back to Vlad and his scheme to steal the eggs, and add to the mix the magnitude of the original heist from the Romanovs and the sheer value of the eggs, there can only be one answer. Who would still be in search of the eggs?"

"Russians."

# Chapter 28

"So what do we tell Marsh?" I asked.

"The truth ... or at least enough to get him looking in the right direction. He has a job to do and I wouldn't feel right withholding a vital piece of information. I don't know if he can do anything with it, but at least he'll have it."

"I don't think we have to tell him about Fordlandia."

"I agree. But we can tell him about the eggs. Honestly, I don't think it will help him much, but if he knows he might be looking for some Russians, it might put him in the right direction."

"Think it's the Russian mob?"

"Who knows? Maybe, or it could be like us and the Guidrys—a story passed down through the ages from family member to family member."

"And in the long run it really doesn't matter," I said.

"Exactly."

She called Marsh back. "You might be looking for some Russians," she said as he picked up. She kept the phone on speaker.

"Withholding information from me?"

"No. It's an angle we just figured out when you called. We had to discuss it to decide if it was a viable direction. We think it might be. I think early on Del gave you some of the story, but there wasn't much to give you—a missing painting that supposedly held a clue to some treasure that had our two families connected. It seems that Mario Guidry's family was connected too, and it all leads to Brazil, which is where we're going. Up until now, that's really all we knew. We did finally find the painting..." He tried to interrupt, but she talked over him. "...which has since been stolen again. It was with the man in Nebraska who was killed. The painting was of almost no help anyway. However, something that kept popping up, but that we kind of ignored, was something about eggs."

"Eggs," he stated flatly.

"Our thought exactly, which is why we put it on the back burner. However, it came up again just in the last day or so..."

"How?" he interrupted.

"Hard to explain."

"Try."

"No, I won't. Look, we are trying to be as honest with you as we can. There are aspects to this that would make no sense to you that might or might not be related to the case."

"Why don't you let me be the judge of that. I'm good at what I do."

"I have no doubt about that. We are not trying to keep you out of the loop. These are personal things that take on a whole new dimension. But they might only be family issues."

She was good. She was managing to skirt the issue by being just vague enough to give him no ammunition to come back with.

He sighed. It must have been frustrating for him, but dealing with a hot celebrity was always tricky and he knew he had to tread lightly.

"So, tell me about the Russians."

"Back in 1918, a collection of Faberge eggs was stolen from the Russian Royal Family. Some were never recovered. We think some of the treasure that has been referred to revolves around those eggs."

"Why?"

She was silent.

"Yeah, I know. It's part of what you can't tell me."

"What I can tell you is what we just found out. There seems to have been a Russian involved with our families. In fact, he may have been the one who got them into this whole mess. We think he was searching for them and got Del's great-grandfather and Mario's great-grandfather involved. Anyway, we don't know his name or anything about him beyond that, but we are deducing from all of this that there is a third party involved in this treasure hunt and we think it might be a Russian ... or Russians. We are now thinking that it wasn't Guidry who killed my sister or tried to kill Del in front of his house. We also don't think he was responsible for Russ Simpson's death in Nebraska. We think it was people connected to that original Russian."

"So I'm looking for Russians. There might be one or two of them in Boston."

"Sorry. If we had a name, we'd give it to you."

"I'm not so sure about that."

"We would," I interjected. "Look, both of us have respect for what you do. Both of us have been threatened and almost killed. Trust me when I say that I'm scared shitless. If there was anything else we could give you, we would, but most of what we have relates to our families. For every ten pounds of crap we shovel through, we find one nugget, and then maybe we find another. But the problem is, they don't seem to be related. We've given you all the nuggets we can. Our families are interconnected in so many ways, and yet, things still don't make sense. And believe me, if they don't make sense to us, they certainly won't to you. If we find a pattern, we'll let you know immediately."

Marsh was silent. He finally said, "What about Guidry?"

"He's caught up in it too," said Sabrina. "He's a crook. No doubt about that. But we think he bit off more than he could chew and has run into someone even more crooked. We think he's on the run."

More silence, then, "So what's in Brazil?"

"We don't know."

"That's no answer."

"It's the best we can give you," I said. "Honestly, we don't know."

"Why do I get the feeling you people are fucking me over?" He sighed, started to say something, then abruptly hung up.

"That went well," I said.

"I feel bad for him," said Sabrina. "He's got so little to work with. He's treading water. He knows that we are holding back, but he thinks we are holding back a lot more than we are. Maybe after this trip we'll have something substantial for him."

*****

Two hours later we were back in East Boston. We both thought it prudent to avoid the Westin for now, at least until we could figure out how to gather her belongings without attracting a horde. As we entered the outer front door, Mo opened her door and greeted us. Sabrina introduced herself and thanked Mo for running interference for us in the hotel.

"Hey, that was my fun for the day. Took those guys ten minutes before they could move again."

She invited us in. Her apartment amazed me every time I saw it. It was always a mess. It wasn't dirty, by any means, but it was messy. There were piles of clean laundry that hadn't been put away, books and magazines piled high on bookshelves, and stacks of artwork given to her by her students. Knowing how precise Mo was in her martial arts and how perfectly groomed she always was, it just didn't seem to fit. She once caught me looking around and stated simply, "Priorities." I guess clutter was very low on her priority list.

We brought her up to date on our adventures. Impressed at first, her mood changed when we told her of our plans to travel to Brazil.

"You're going into the jungles of friggin Brazil? Do you have even the slightest clue about what you're getting into?"

Friggin? She must have been impressed by Sabrina to clean up her language like that. So what did that say about her respect for me?

"Absolutely no clue," answered Sabrina. "That makes it more exciting!"

Mo looked at me. I shrugged.

"This is how she is. She lives for adventure."

"It's not Sabrina I'm worried about."

"Oh."

"Del, I'm not saying that you are helpless, but you've been stuck in an office for ten years. Are you ready for this?"

"Aren't you the one who told me I have to start doing something with my life?"

"I thought you might do it in increments, not jump off the

cliff the first chance you got."

"Don't have a lot of choice now."

"We always have a choice."

"Del's right," said Sabrina, coming to my aid. "We've kind of put ourselves in a situation where we have to see it through. We have the Russians on our tail now..."

"Russians?"

"Long story. We'll tell you about it in a minute," I said.

Mo rolled her eyes.

"I think," continued Sabrina, "the only way to get them off our trail is to solve the mystery. Then they have no reason to go after us."

We told her about our speculation about the Russians. When we were done, she just shook her head. "I don't know whether to be scared for you both, or ..."

It suddenly dawned on me. "You're jealous!"

"Hell, yeah, I'm jealous. I'd give anything to go with you." She turned to Sabrina. "Take care of him. Don't let anything happen to him. If you don't hold onto him, he'll get lost."

"Actually, he's the one who's kept me from getting lost."

I got the feeling that sometime down the line Sabrina and Mo were going to become good friends. Sabrina wouldn't have even hinted at her issues with anyone else. That showed an amazing amount of instant trust. Maybe there was some progress after all.

# Chapter 29

The flight to Belém was long. We could have traveled across the U.S. three times in the time it took to get to there. If we were going to Australia or China, I could understand it, but wasn't Brazil just somewhere south of us? Of course, the seven-hour layover in Miami didn't help.

We had tried to time it so we'd arrive at Logan as close to boarding as possible to avoid excessive contact with people. Up to that point we had managed to avoid the press, but our luck didn't hold. When we arrived in Miami, two sleazy tabloid photographers were there to greet us. We managed to give them the slip thanks to some good planning on my part—yes, me for a change, not Sabrina—and some help from the very people Sabrina didn't trust—the public.

When we were buying our tickets, I suggested that since we had such a long layover in Miami, we should buy each leg of the trip separately. That way, someone smart enough to track us would see us going to Miami, with no connection to the flight to Brazil. A room at a local hotel would further shield us from the possibility of detection.

My second suggestion was that we each take only a carry-on bag. No checked bag meant we were going to have to rough it, but it also gave us more freedom of movement, particularly in the airports, where Sabrina would be more likely to be recognized.

The flight to Miami was uncomfortable enough for Sabrina. She was convinced that everyone on the plane recognized her, a paranoia that wasn't totally baseless. She had chosen not to radically change her appearance for the flight—her attempt at rebellion. She was regretting the decision by the time we arrived at the gate. I knew she was recognized by a half a dozen or so of the passengers—which meant, of course, that by the time we landed in Miami most of the plane knew. We had seats in the second row so we could be off the plane the moment the doors opened.

We were standing up waiting to exit the plane when we heard from somewhere in the middle of the plane, "We love you, Sabrina," whereupon the rest of the passengers broke out in a spontaneous applause. Sabrina turned bright red and looked at me, as if to say, "What should I do?" I gave her a nod to say it was okay. It seemed to reassure her. She gave the passengers a shy smile and wave, and said "thank you" in a small voice.

When we reached the end of the gateway, the two photographers were waiting for us. How did they get through security? It occurred to me later that they must have bought tickets to a flight just to allow them access to the gate. Diabolical. I had to give them credit though, they were determined.

We never heard the press conference by her agent, although we knew what he was going to say, but he must have been effective as he gave her history and emphasized her shyness and need for privacy. Sabrina was someone who was easy to root for, and let's face it, people were tired of abuse. Her story must have resonated with people all over the country. So when our fellow passengers exited the plane and saw the cameras in Sabrina's face, they took action. They could smell sleaze a mile away. As a single body they moved in and wedged themselves between Sabrina and the photographers. Nothing was said, but the message was clear: Leave her alone. That gave us a clear exit. As we scurried away, I turned and shouted out, "Thank you, guys!"

We were free. We jumped into the first taxi available and were delivered safely to our hotel. It was only going to be our sanctuary for a few hours, but it was enough to give us some space.

We didn't sleep, but it was a chance to shower and prepare for the second leg. I didn't bring up the incident in the airport. I didn't want to belabor the obvious: that not everyone is out for themselves. It was going to have to sink in on its own.

I found myself excited and scared at the same time. I hadn't traveled much in my life, and had only been out of the country a couple of times. But those were planned trips. This was altogether different. Not only was I going to a completely foreign place, I wasn't even totally sure why. Add to that Mario Guidry and the Russians, and I felt about as unprepared as one could be.

We returned to the airport two hours before our flight to Belém. When we were researching the trip we noticed that Santarém was closer to Fordlandia than Belém and had a busy airport. However, we decided against it for one main reason: Sabrina wanted to reenact the trip the four stooges took. Fordlandia was accessed only by river boat and a good portion of the river looked much the way it did eighty-five years ago. She wanted the full experience, not an abbreviated version.

"If we're going to do this, we need to do it right," she said by way of explanation. "We should get a feel for what they went through."

I had heard of mystery writers who never left the comfort of their homes. Sabrina was not one of them ... by a long shot. I was coming to realize that mystery writing was just an extension of who she was—or more accurately, who she wanted to be. She wanted to feel the excitement she wrote about in her novels. Maybe it was because she lost six years of her life and wanted to make up the time. Maybe she just came to understand that living life to the fullest was what it was all about. I was beginning to understand why her books were taking off. It wasn't just her writing ability, it was her passion. When I was researching her, I had run across numerous reviews of her books. The word *passion* came up a lot. Maybe I would be able to find some of that passion myself.

*****

We arrived in Belém without incident. To the best of our knowledge she wasn't recognized on the flight, maybe because there were few Americans on board. I heard a lot of what I assumed to be Portuguese being spoken.

Belém was a modern city. It was actually kind of a shock. We kind of expected it to look like it did in the early 1900s, but when we passed our first Starbucks we were pretty sure that wasn't the case. Would Fordlandia turn out to be a theme park? No, that much we knew. Fordlandia was a ghost town, inhabited mostly by squatters.

We hadn't had a lot of time to research the river travel before we left, but had done some on the plane. There were numerous tourist-oriented boat trips down the Amazon, which we wanted to steer clear of. We were searching for something small, partly for the "Mikey experience" and partly for the anonymity. How quickly would word get out the minute some American tourists recognized Sabrina? After making numerous inquiries of locals—luckily most people we encountered spoke English—we were directed to a small family-owned boat.

We knew we had found our ride the minute we met the family. The boat was only about thirty feet long and had seen better days, but it looked sturdy. The family was large—about eight, including grandparents and grandchildren—but it would only be the father and son taking us on the journey. The father, Luis, was about fifty, small and wiry, and with the leathery skin that came from a lifetime in the sun. He was shy with foreigners and spoke little English. He let his son do most of the talking. Paulo was close to thirty and was the exact opposite of his father in appearance. He was tall and stocky, with a gleaming bald head that we only saw the few times he removed his baseball cap—which also looked to be about thirty—and a perpetual smile. Unlike the father, Paulo spoke English. It wasn't great, but it would get the job done, communication-wise.

The price they quoted to take us to Fordlandia and back seemed low—especially considering the trip to Santarém was going to take almost four days, with another twelve hours after that to Fordlandia. It was going to be a bit slower than some of the tourist boats, but Paulo assured us that it would get us there and back with no problems. They were obviously desperate for the business, but in the process were probably only going to break even by the time the trip was over. We talked about it and offered them three times what they had quoted. It was nice to have money. They were thrilled. By way of explanation as to why we were paying so much, we were honest with Paulo and told him that there was some danger involved. Sabrina, whom he was immediately taken with (duh!), explained some of the story, which he then related to his father. If anything, it made them more excited for the trip. Treasure hunters must not have been their normal passengers. Paulo proudly showed us the two rifles they kept on board.

They needed to buy some supplies and told us that they would be ready to go the next morning. As a sign of goodwill—and because they needed it to buy the supplies—we gave them half the money up front. They directed us to a small hotel within walking distance of the waterfront.

Our night was relatively quiet. We were exhausted from the traveling and just wanted to get a good night's sleep. The hotel had a restaurant that served decent food. We took a guess since we couldn't read the menu, and ended up lucking out with tasty fish dishes.

Luis and Paulo were waiting for us at the dock bright and early. Paulo sported a wide smile and informed us that the boat was stocked up and ready to go. As we boarded, he looked around, then motioned for us to follow him into the cabin, where he produced two revolvers with holsters. He handed them to us.

"For protection," he said quietly. "Good, huh? Take with you to find treasure."

I was glad we had been honest with him. "Thank you very much."

Sabrina went a step further. She gave him a quick hug. "Thank you, Paulo."

Well that certainly cemented their relationship. I was going to have to pry him off her with a crowbar from that point on.

We stowed the guns in our bags and went back out on deck. Ten minutes later Paulo cast off as Luis put the boat in gear. As we motored into the river Sabrina said quietly, "Del, look back at the dock. Who do you see?"

It took me a minute, but then I saw them, the goons from the hotel in Wahoo.

"How the hell ...?"

"Do you think they followed us down here?" she asked.

"Or did they assume we were coming and came down before us?"

"Maybe they were watching the flights from the states. Could they have followed us from the airport?"

"I suppose they could have," I answered. "We weren't really looking for anyone."

"Do you think they know where we're going?"

"If they followed us from the states, then they might not know. But if they were waiting for us, then they have to. Either way, we have to assume that we won't be alone when we reach Fordlandia."

"I guess that's not a total surprise."

"If we were right and the guys in the hotel were Mario's men, I don't think they're the ones we should be most afraid of."

"So the question is," said Sabrina, "where are the Russians?"

# Chapter 30

We were pretty sure that for the trip anyway, we wouldn't have any trouble—an assumption we almost came to regret—so we tried to settle down and enjoy the scenery.

The head of the Amazon was busier than I expected, and many of the boats were tour boats. We passed several that had dozens of brightly-colored hammocks covering the deck. I had read that many of the tours gave the option of private cabins or hammocks. Each time we passed one of these boats was just a confirmation that we had made the right choice in hiring Luis and Paulo. We appreciated the privacy of a smaller boat, and somehow felt a little safer in their presence.

Luis, probably because of his lack of English, kept to himself piloting the boat. Yet despite that, we felt a closeness to him. Paulo, on the other hand, was gregarious and informative, spending much time narrating our trip in his broken English. Most of the tour boats kept to the center of the river. Luis, maybe at the suggestion of Paulo, brought us closer to shore to get a better feel of the jungle. The farther we went, the fewer boats we saw.

There were long stretches of unspoiled jungle, full of some of the most beautiful plants we had ever seen. But as gorgeous as it was, it was the animal life that blew us away. We had never seen such brightly-colored birds. And they were everywhere. It was like passing through the world's largest zoo. And it wasn't just the birds that filled the color spectrum. Millions of butterflies of all sizes and hues dotted the shoreline, often coming out to the boat and flying around our heads.

Sabrina had a constant smile. I didn't ask, but I wondered if she reflected back at all to her years in prison, and each day filled with drab gray surroundings. If it hadn't been for the lenient judge, she could still be there today.

We saw enormous river turtles, and on occasion Paulo would point out a caiman sunning itself on shore. A couple of times we looked down in the water to see bulbous eyes peering back at us.

"What are those?" I asked Paulo.

"Baby Caimans," he answered. "Eyes and snout maybe all you ever see."

Late in the second afternoon on the river, Paulo called to us from the other side of the boat and frantically motioned for us to join him. When we got there he pointed down at an enormous shape passing us in the water. It had to be fifteen or twenty feet long and five feet wide.

"Manatee," said Paulo. "Rare to see. People kill them for skin and oil. Once there were many in the river. No longer."

The wildlife we weren't happy to encounter were the mosquitos and black flies. They came out in force in the evening and we had to use bug spray and cover up. But somehow, it was all part of the experience—one I could have done without, I suppose.

Luis and Paulo took turns operating the boat and also took turns resting. At night, however, we stopped for a few hours so that they could both catch up on some sleep. It was the third night of our journey and Luis had just turned off the engines. Every time he did that at night, we almost collapsed in appreciation for the silence. We had gotten used to the constant throb of the engines, but the silence was heavenly. In reality, it wasn't silent. The jabbering of the birds and the monkeys never let us forget the paradise we had stepped into.

This particular night, though, there was a different sound—a cry. No, not even a cry, really. It was the most chilling sound I had ever heard in my life. It came from the jungle—not very deep in the jungle though. At the sound of it, it seemed like all the other jungle noises came to a sudden stop. Paulo got up from his hammock on deck and joined us at the rail.

"Jaguar," he whispered. "You are very lucky to hear that."

One more time the cry came, longer than the first time. And then it stopped. Eventually the other jungle noises resumed and all was back to normal. But it took many minutes for the goose bumps on my arms to disappear.

"I think that was the most amazing thing I've ever heard," Sabrina said quietly, almost reverently. "It was the epitome of nature at its most spectacular—of life like I've never heard it." There was nothing more to be said.

Meals aboard the boat were simple, but tasty. They usually consisted of some combination of rice, beans, chicken, and local vegetables. Dessert was fruit or sweet bread. Paulo was the official cook and took great delight in our reactions to his meals.

At Santarém we turned off the Amazon and onto the Rio Tapajós river. About twelve more hours until we reached Fordlandia. River traffic was heavy around Santarém, but most of the boats were continuing down the Amazon on their way to Manaus. A speedboat passed us going at a high rate of speed—the only other boat heading our way. We were always on alert for trouble, but only one person was visible and didn't seem to be paying any attention to us, so I didn't worry unduly.

If it weren't for the fact that we were on a mission—and a dangerous one at that—the river trip would have been a wonderful vacation. It was so different from anything either of us had ever experienced, every minute seemed to hold a new surprise.

An hour after making the turn onto the Rio Tapajós, Sabrina, who seemed to be staring into space, suddenly sat up straight and pointed.

"What's that?"

I stood and looked in the direction she indicated. At first I saw nothing, then something jumped high out of the water and gracefully sliced its way back under the waves.

"I'd swear that was a dolphin," I said.

As if they heard me, three more jumped in perfect synchronicity.

"They are," said Sabrina. "They're beautiful."

"River dolphins," said Paulo from behind us. "They often follow the boats. They like to play."

We watched their antics for another half hour, until they got bored and moved on. We sat back down and dozed. I guess the excitement was too much for us.

When the attack came, it was sudden and violent. Sabrina and I were sitting on deck next to the cabin holding hands. After an animated conversation as to whether we saw a log or a Caiman, we had lapsed into a comfortable silence. I don't know what Sabrina was thinking of, but for me, it was another time of reflection about how my life had changed in just a very short time. Sabrina, sitting to my right, put her head on my shoulder—a move that probably saved her life. A second later, a horrific clang sent us diving for cover.

Reflecting on it later, I think what happened was that the bullet hit the railing where Sabrina's head had been and ricocheted down through the sole of my boot. I can't say with any certainty that I heard the gunshot, but I didn't need to. The shot came from ahead of our boat. It was the same boat that had passed us at such a high rate of speed a few hours earlier. Sabrina came within inches of dying. That made me angry—beyond angry—but not until later. At that moment, we were scrambling for our lives as a hail of bullets tore up the boat.

Most of my reactions came after the fact. There just wasn't the time to think at that moment. However, I noticed how cool and calm Luis was during the whole attack. He reached for his rifle and—while also trying to steer the boat—calmly aimed and shot. One after another. Paulo was brave as well, and hid behind the cabin, letting shots fly at the other boat. But it was obvious that this was new territory for him and the nervousness showed.

Sabrina and I were near Paulo behind the cabin, and had pulled our pistols from their holsters when it dawned on me: Other than in the alley in Fairfield, which didn't count, I had never even pointed a gun at anyone before, much less shot at them. This wasn't the movies, where the hero just whips off a few shots. This was real life. I had seen Sabrina shoot someone right in front of me and she didn't seem altered in any way—thanks to her years in prison, most likely.

She must have sensed my hesitation, because she said in a very clear and forceful voice, "Someone is trying to kill you. Are you going to allow that to happen?" The underlying message of my self-defense training.

"Hell, no," I answered, and aimed my pistol and fired. There was something about it that felt good.

Luis yelled something back to us.

Paulo interpreted. "My father says to hold your fire. A pistol will not hit its mark so far away."

The boat was coming closer, so I knew it was only a matter of time before I could fire back with a reasonable chance of hitting something ... or someone.

Our boat was a mess, but it was mostly cosmetic. With a steel hull, it would take a lot to disable it. Meanwhile, the bullets continued to rain down on us. There were three of them. The other two must have been hiding when the boat passed us earlier. These guys were serious. They had chosen their attack location well; it was a fairly remote section of the river—no civilization on either side and no other boats in sight.

Luis did whatever he had to do to stabilize the boat—I had no idea what that was—and jumped to a more secure location to continue his firing. He was calm and methodical. He yelled something back to Paulo.

"You can fire now," said Paulo.

And so I did. I was actually trying to kill another human being. When, just a few minutes earlier, I was reflecting on how my life had changed, this possibility hadn't come up. But it was real now and I took Sabrina's words to heart: If I wanted to protect myself or someone I loved, I had to be willing to kill. I was willing now. In fact, with each shot I fired, I became more comfortable with the idea. They had no right to do what they were doing, and I was going to make them pay.

Their boat was getting dangerously close to ours, but so far no one had yet been hit on either side. The only casualty was a hole in my boot that I could now stick my toe through.

In the end, it was Luis—calm, cool, and collected Luis—who got us out of there. He began to change the direction of his shots away from the attackers themselves and more at something on the boat. Unlike our boat, theirs was a fiberglass hull. Luis, who had spent his life on the river in boats, knew exactly where to shoot once their boat swung around a little. Suddenly, I heard a "ka-chunk" come from their engine compartment, followed by silence. He had destroyed their engine.

Quickly, he put our boat in gear, somehow avoiding getting hit. I didn't know if these guys were just poor shots, or if the movies made it all look a lot easier than it was to shoot moving targets. Judging by the fact that some of my shots weren't even hitting their boat, I'd say it was the latter.

A minute later, we were out of range, leaving our attackers standing in their disabled boat and looking around at the desolation. No AAA out there.

It would take them a few hours at least to fix their boat or commandeer another, but I had no doubt about one thing: We were going to see them again, and it was going to be ugly.

# Chapter 31

The dock at Fordlandia was old, but still usable. It had never been updated. There was no reason to. After all, the town had been abandoned for over seventy years. But boats still came on occasion and I could see spots in the dock that had been haphazardly patched. Beyond the dock, a large statue of Henry Ford welcomed us. It was almost eerie. He must have had high hopes for the place. What did he feel when it failed? Was there a sense of loss ... of mourning? Or was it all business and he just moved onto the next scheme? After all, he never actually visited the place.

Many of the buildings still stood, but they were in a bad way, overgrown and sagging. From my reading I knew that some of the larger ones were the factory buildings and one or two were used as dining halls and for social gatherings.

It may have been a ghost town, but there were enough squatters to erase the "ghost" part from the equation. We didn't know what kind of reception we were going to get from the residents, so we were pleasantly surprised when we saw smiles on most of the faces of those who met us at the dock.

A man approached us even before we got off the boat and said something in Portuguese. Paulo answered him and then said, "He say welcome. Ask if you are tourists."

"Please tell him we are looking for something," said Sabrina. Of course, asking Paulo to interpret for us was just marginally above useless.

"Could you ask if anyone here speaks English?"

Paulo put out the request. Secretly I think he was relieved. He liked to think his English was better than it was, and to have to interpret would only show off his deficiencies.

"Come," motioned the man. Probably his one word of English. "Follow." Okay, two words.

He brought us up a road that was once paved in brick to a small cottage that wasn't showing the ravages of time. In fact, it had been recently painted and the yard was nicely kept. He knocked on the door, which was answered by a man about Sabrina's age—maybe even younger. He was a handsome man of indeterminate heritage. He definitely had some South American blood in him, but there was something else, too. Our guide said something to him—I was pretty sure I caught the word English—then turned around, gave us a wave, and walked away.

"You're looking for someone who speaks English, I'm told."

Except for a very slight accent, he could have almost passed for an American. He must have seen the surprise on my face.

"I went to college in New York. SUNY Albany. Majored in business." I looked around and he laughed. "So what am I doing in such an out-of-the-way place?"

"It crossed my mind," I said. "I'm Del and this is Sabrina."

He held out his hand. "Emil." I cocked my head. "My father was German," he said by way of explanation. "And to answer your question, I came here at the request of some friends who wanted to restore the town and turn it into a tourist destination. A few days here convinced me that their idea would never fly. So they abandoned it—much like Henry Ford did—and I stayed. Suddenly my business background seemed silly. I loved the peace here, so I moved into one of the abandoned houses. That was five years ago."

"How do you earn a living?" asked Sabrina.

"Don't really need to here, but I cheat. My family has money. I keep a boat on the river and any time I feel the need to remember why I'm living here, I'll take it and go to a city or town for a few days. I'm always ready to come back." He opened his door wide. "Come in. Have a beer with me and tell me why you're here. You don't look like tourists."

"We're not. It might take two beers. It's a long story."

So we told him. Sabrina and I were quickly on the same wave-length and knew that we didn't want to mention the eggs. We did use the word treasure, though. When we finished, he said, "so what is the treasure?"

We liked him. He was intelligent, friendly, and forthcoming. His eyes didn't light up when we said treasure. He seemed more interested in the story and in the hunt.

"Part of it is gold," I said. "There is supposedly something else, but we'd rather not say what it is until we can confirm it."

"Fair enough. If it is gold and you find it, what are you going to do with it?"

We looked at each other. We had never actually talked about it.

"I suppose," said Sabrina, "if we find gold here, it should go to the Brazilian government or the people of Fordlandia. Like you, we both have money, and to be honest, it's not the gold we're after. It's the other thing. And even that we wouldn't keep. We'd turn it over to a museum. Believe it or not, this is more about clearing up the past than it is about finding treasure."

"I could use something to do right now. It may be peaceful, but it does get a little boring around here sometimes. What can I do to help?"

"We have a photograph of a painting. It holds a clue, at least we hope it does," said Sabrina. She took out her phone and showed him the photo. I had to give him credit, he didn't critique the quality of the artwork.

He looked at it carefully, finally shaking his head. "We have a cemetery here, but this picture doesn't look like any part of it that I've seen. The house could be any one of a couple of dozen. The tree? Well, it's a rubber tree, so it could be anywhere around here. And then there's the gravestone. It doesn't have a name on it—which probably wouldn't have helped, by the way—just RIP. If I had seen that, I would have noticed it."

I suddenly had an idea. "Suppose the stone had fallen down? After all, I think we can assume that John erected it for the purposes of the painting. Maybe he didn't put it far enough into the ground. Maybe it just fell over."

"Then good luck with that," said Emil. "The yards around most of those houses are completely overgrown. If the tree is still there, it would be fully grown by now. But it might not even be there. A lot of the rubber trees died. Not to sound pessimistic, but if the tree died and the headstone fell over, you've got your work cut out for you."

"We saw some houses, like yours, that have been fixed up. Maybe it was one of those houses," said Sabrina.

"I can ask around, if you like," suggested Emil. "If so, someone would remember it. Where are you staying tonight?" he asked, completely changing gears.

"We had hoped we might be able to solve this in one day," answered Sabrina, "but I think that was a pipe dream. We can stay on the boat."

"Believe it or not, we have a Bed and Breakfast here."

"Here?" I asked.

"We do get tourists . Not a lot, but they usually need a place to stay. I've heard it's not too bad, considering the location, and the food is pretty good. I know three guys checked in yesterday, but they might still have a room available."

We both perked up. "Three guys?" I asked. "Did you see them?"

"No, just heard they were here." Then it dawned on him. "Oh shit. Are they looking for the same thing?"

"It's possible," I said. I turned to Sabrina. "Could be Guidry's men. But if they knew about Fordlandia, why didn't they come earlier?"

"It could also be the Russians. If that's the case, we could be in a lot of trouble. But they never passed us again after we disabled their boat, so it's probably not them." She added, "Whoever it is knows we're here. They probably even know that we're in this house." And like a bad movie, that's when the knock came at the door.

"What do you suggest?" I asked Sabrina. I was suddenly having trouble breathing.

"I guess we answer the door. It's time we confront whoever it is. Maybe we can take them by surprise." As she said it, she pulled out her revolver. "Maybe they won't be expecting this."

"Emil, we're sorry we brought this to your doorstep," I said. "You might want to stay hidden. As I said it, I heard a shotgun being snapped shut. I looked around and saw Emil crouched behind the kitchen counter, with a double-barreled shotgun aimed at the door.

"No need," he said. "We're pretty good at taking care of ourselves here. Let them in. I just hope it's not the woman down the road bringing me eggs. She'll never bring them again."

The knock came again.

"Ready?" I asked.

"Ready," answered Sabrina.

She yanked open the door and we stuck our guns in the faces of three very surprised men. The two bigger men we knew from the hotel room in Wahoo. The third was unfamiliar to us. He was short, maybe 5'8", and he couldn't have weighed more than 150. He was a few years older than me, with jet black hair cut conservatively. He wore an outfit that he must have picked up at the "pretend you're going on safari" store. He also wore glasses that made him look like a college professor.

After getting over his initial shock at having guns thrust in his face, he held out his hand.

"Nice to meet you, Mr. Honeycutt. I'm Mario Guidry."

# Chapter 32

"I hope we're not intruding. May we come in?"

I looked over at Sabrina, then back at Emil. Finally, I stepped back from the door indicating that he could enter, ignoring his outstretched hand.

I'm not sure what we were expecting, but it certainly wasn't the scene before us. Chicago mobsters didn't look like ... well ... him. They also didn't sound like refined, cultured gentlemen. Didn't they use words like *yous* and *joiks* all the time?

"We finally meet," he said, again holding out his hand. I just looked him and he dropped it.

"We've already met your friends," I said.

"Ah, yes," he answered. "I apologize for that. I will make sure you get reimbursed for the phones they took."

Emil came into the living room, relaxed, but still holding the shotgun.

"Have a seat," I said. Mario sat, but his bodyguards stayed standing.

"All of you," I added.

Mario made a motion with his head and the other two looked around, saw that there were no more chairs, once Sabrina and I sat, and hunkered down onto the floor. I could tell that it annoyed Mario to have his men in such a vulnerable position, but it said to me that he truly intended for this to be a peaceful call.

Dead silence. Mario came to us, so he was going to have to

speak first.

"I'm sorry about your sister," he finally said to Sabrina. "I liked her."

"Nobody liked her," Sabrina answered.

"I was trying to be nice. In all honesty, she was somewhat unpleasant. But I'm still sorry to hear about her death."

"So you had nothing to do with it?" I asked.

"Heavens, no. You don't know me, but I don't kill people. I have business interests that sometimes require a firm hand," he motioned toward his men, "but never to that extreme. No, I'm afraid that was someone else, most likely the same people who killed two of my men. I was going to ask if you had anything to do with their murders, but I can see that it's an unnecessary question."

"So why did you follow us down?"

"Actually, we didn't. I think we had the same idea at the same time. And I assume we are all after the same thing—the elusive treasure. So tell me, how did you find out about Fordlandia?"

"Why don't you answer it first," suggested Sabrina.

"Fair enough. Like you I'm sure, Mr. Honeycutt, I've known about Fordlandia my whole life." He obviously didn't know much about me or my family. "But I had tucked that piece of family history away. I never had any interest in it. I had also heard rumors my whole life about treasure, but I never made the connection to this place. Nothing was ever specified, so I just assumed it was hidden somewhere in New York. Frankly, I had come to believe that the whole thing was just a tale, that is, until Ms. Worth approached me. She made it sound as if you had more of the story, so I put some men on you. I apologize, by the way, for stealing the book from your apartment. The article did me little good. I assume there was other material you kept?"

I remained silent.

"I'm trying to be pleasant here," he said, irritation showing in his voice.

"Excuse us if we don't share your pleasantness," said Sabrina. "Being held at gunpoint twice has something to do with it."

"And I apologize for that, as well." He knew we weren't going to make this easy, so he moved on. "Anyway, I've always wondered if the treasure was still in Fordlandia, but I had nothing to go on. I knew the painting contained a clue, but of course, your phone was locked and I never did see it. So I had my men watch you. When they discovered that you had booked a trip to Miami, I knew where you were going. So we decided it was time we came too. Was the painting as illuminating as we hoped?"

"No," I answered.

Mario waited for more, got nothing, shrugged, and continued. "I'm here to see if we can team up. Somehow, Ms. Worth must have riled the wrong people, because it seems that everyone she came into contact with is in their sights. If they are not here yet, they will be soon."

"They're here, at least in Brazil. We were followed," I said.

Mario showed a flicker of concern.

"I know I'm not a part of this whole affair, but mind if I ask a question?" asked Emil. "If someone is trying to kill you, it seems to me that it has to be someone who knows about the treasure—not just knows about it, but knows where it is. I mean, if he's in the same boat as all of you and is looking for it, it would go against his best interests to kill you. After all, none of you have killed each other."

He had our attention.

"So if he knows what it is and where it is, why hasn't he come before now? Or, if he already found it, what use would he have in killing you?"

As much as I hated Mario Guidry for his actions against us, I didn't want to see anyone else die from this. It was time for me to share a little more information.

"There are two aspects to the treasure," I said. "From everything we've uncovered so far, we believe part of it is gold." Mario nodded in agreement. That much of it he must have uncovered or deduced. "We assume it was gold stolen from some of the managers here who were smuggling gold out of the country. The second part of the treasure we are guessing at, based on some other clues we found. We're not going to tell you what it is, except to say that we think the killers are Russians. The items—if we are right—are important enough for these Russians to kill for. And again, if our assumptions are right, they know they're here. But, like Emil said, if they knew these items were here, why didn't they come sooner?"

"That just confirms my visit to you," said Mario. "In light of the danger we are all in, I suggest we join forces. If there is that much gold—and I would think there is by the use of the word 'treasure', there should be plenty for all."

"It doesn't belong to us," said Sabrina. "It belongs to the Brazilian government or the people of Fordlandia."

"Squatters, all of them. They have no more right to the treasure than we do."

Technically, he probably wasn't wrong. Morally, it was a different story. I didn't need to ask Sabrina for her opinion.

"We wish you well on your search—not too well, of course—but there is no way we can join forces with you," I said. "Frankly, I don't trust you. I believe you when you say you are not killers, but I don't like your tactics and I don't like you. No, we'll do it on our own."

"So be it," said Mario, standing. His goons were on their feet in a second, ready to go into action if called upon. But Mario wasn't ready to fight. He motioned his men outside.

"You're making a mistake," he said quietly. Then he turned and walked out.

"Are we making a mistake?" I asked, suddenly second-guessing myself.

"Absolutely not," answered Sabrina.

"As I said,  I'm not part of all this," said Emil, "from my perspective, you made the right choice."

I felt better.

Emil continued. "I don't think sharing a B&B with those clowns would be smart. If you don't mind sleeping on the couch and the floor, you're welcome to stay here."

Sabrina said to him with relief in her eyes, "Thank you."

"I just hope we haven't put you in danger," I said.

"My choice," he replied, putting the topic to rest.

*****

The night was uneventful. Uncomfortable, but uneventful. We left word with Paulo and Luis that we'd be staying at least one night. From our trip down, they were also aware of the danger, so they moored the boat away from the dock, making it harder for someone to sneak up on them.

The next morning there was no sign of Mario and his men. They were around someplace probably trying to come up with their own hunches. Or, they were watching to see what we would do, but we had no control over that. After they had gone that night, Emil spread the word around the town that it would be to everyone's advantage not to help them. It wouldn't be long before Mario would become a pariah in Fordlandia.

Meanwhile, it was time for us to get started on our search. We began by taking a walk around the town. We had seen a lot of pictures of it online from its heyday. The difference was stark. We saw the remains of the paved roads, the picket fences, and the fire hydrants—middle America plunked into the center of the Amazon. How could anyone really think that just by making things look familiar to the American workers, it would appease them? And the total disregard for the lifestyle and culture of the locals was arrogance at its worst.

It was easy to understand Emil's advice to his friends that the town couldn't be restored or turned into a resort. Simply stated, it was just a crumbling factory town alongside a river. Other than its unique history, what possible draw could it have? The millions of dollars that would have to be poured into the town just to bring it to the point of preparation for a resort would be a complete waste. If they were restoring it to what Fordlandia once looked like, what would be the sense in that? You could find the same sights walking down the main street in a small town in Ohio.

No, the town had long since died. Everything was overgrown. Windows in the abandoned buildings were gone.

The houses still standing all had sagging roofs, and in many cases the whole house had collapsed.

There were exceptions. The houses the squatters had taken over were in relatively decent shape, ranging from the just barely livable to a few places like Emil's—fixed up with care.

As Emil led us around, Sabrina was reveling in the experience. Her eyes were bright and almost dancing as she took notes and pictures. I could see a book coming out of this. She was in heaven. She was getting to experience the adventure and excitement that she wrote about in her books. For Sabrina, this was living. I, on the other hand, hadn't yet decided exactly what it was.

The morning was sunny and warm, more like an early summer's day in New England than a day in the tropics. Hmm, maybe Henry Ford was onto something. A day like this one could feel like home. It almost made us forget the danger we faced. Almost.

"I want you to meet someone," announced Emil as we approached one of the larger houses. It was midway between fixed up and falling down. Dozens of chickens roamed the yard. There was no doubt that the egg supply for the town originated there.

"Eva is somewhere on the north side of ninety and has lived in Fordlandia practically her whole life. Her father was one of the first native workers hired by Henry Ford, and he brought his whole family. Eva was around ten at the time. After Ford left, her family stayed, and she's been here ever since. I did some calculations. If your relative and his friends arrived here around 1930 or a little after, Eva would have been in her early teens. She might have some memories of them. It's a shot in the dark, but her mind is still pretty good for her age, so you never know."

Eva turned out to be a hoot. Funny and talkative—not that I could understand a word of it; Emil translated—Eva loved having the company. She had a large, round body, but a wizened face—like a mummy's head attached to a pumpkin.

For about twenty minutes she regaled us with stories of her chickens and goats. When Emil was able to guide her to the early days of Fordlandia, her tone changed slightly, as she reached back into her memory. We let Emil ask the first few questions, such as what life was like there in the beginning.

With Emil as the translator, she said, "I didn't like leaving my home to come here, but my father said we would have a good life with lots of money. It wasn't a good life. It was a life I didn't understand. The Americans were mean. I don't think they liked their life here either. They made us eat American food. I was sick much of the time. My body was not used to the food. It tasted awful."

Emil asked her about life there after the first couple of years.

She smiled and looked at me when she spoke.

"The Americans were stupid."

She had to look at me when she said that?

"My father always talked about how the Americans didn't know what they were doing. He tried to tell them, as many of my people did, that the trees would get sick and die. But they were ignored. My people got angry, and then the Americans got angry. There was much conflict. Many fights. My father often told me to stay inside the house. He was afraid, but he was also afraid to leave to go back to our home. When the

Americans finally left, we stayed. He said life would be easier after the Americans. He was right."

Emil looked at me, indicating that it was my turn. He informed Eva that I had some questions. At first she was wary, but Emil assured her that we weren't from any government and wouldn't tell her she must leave. Once he paved the way, the worry disappeared and she was back to her jovial self.

"Eva, I'm sure you don't remember, but maybe three years after you came here, four American men arrived on a boat."

"Americans were always arriving" she said through Emil, "and it was always by boat."

"These men weren't workers. They delivered alcohol to the island, then came here for a few days or a week."

She shook her head.

I tried again. "I think one of them killed another."

Her eyes perked up, so I took it a step further.

"Their names were Tony, Bruce, Mikey, and John. I think John ended up stay..." I stopped. Her eyes had narrowed and she began to shake. There was anger there, a tremendous amount of anger.

"Mikey," she said, almost spitting his name. "I remember Mikey. An evil man. A very evil man!"

I looked at Sabrina. Mikey? Wasn't Mikey the "good" one of the bunch? The literate one? The one who wasn't cut out for a life of crime? Could she have confused him with one of the others? After all, it was his book that helped fill in the gaps.

"Were we wrong about Mikey?" asked Sabrina. "Is there more to this than we thought?"

"Are you sure his name was Mikey?" I asked through Emil. "My great-grandfather was one of those men. He never said anything bad about Mikey."

She responded with a short comment. Emil hesitated a moment, then said, "she says he had two faces. Not quite sure … oh, I get it. He was two-faced." He said something to Eva, who nodded, then said something else.

"Eva says she watched him with his friends. He acted one way with them, but different when he was away from them."

"It was over eighty years ago," said Sabrina. "Why is it you remember him so clearly?"

"Because he was the most evil man I have ever met," she stated simply.

# Chapter 33

We waited for more.

"I remember the four men you speak of. Not the names of the other three until you said them, but I remember them. There was another. He was from another country."

"Vlad?" I said to Sabrina.

"Most likely."

"They were looking for the gold."

"You knew of the gold?" I asked.

"Everyone knew of the gold. The men from the company—the big men—had it. They took it from our country and sent it somewhere. They became very rich stealing from our country. Meanwhile, we all stayed poor. Many fights were started because of the gold."

"And the four men?" asked Sabrina.

"They asked many questions, especially one of them. I think he was the leader. He was always fighting with the man from the other country. But when they weren't around, Mikey asked questions. If he didn't get the answers he wanted, he beat people."

"Did he beat your father?" I asked.

"Yes." She stopped before saying anything else. There was more.

"Did he do something else?" asked Sabrina.

A tear rolled down her ancient face.

"Yes."

"To you?" asked Sabrina gently, touching Eva's hand. We

all knew where this was going.

"Yes." We'd heard enough. There was no sense in subjecting her to anything further on that subject.

We gave her a few minutes to compose herself. Then I said, "I'm sorry we brought back all those memories."

She gave a wan smile. "It was a long time ago. It is part of life."

An amazing woman.

"Can I ask you another question about something different?"

She nodded.

"Did you ever hear from them something about eggs?"

Emil translated. She chuckled. The memories of the last few minutes tucked away.

"The eggs. I had forgotten about the eggs. The man from the other country and one of the four were very interested in eggs. They found them with the gold."

"Do you know what happened to them?"

"Not for sure. But I am guessing Mikey took them back to America."

Eva was getting tired.

"Can we ask you one more question?"

"Yes, then I must rest."

Sabrina pulled out her cell and brought up the picture. "Does this house look familiar?"

"Yes, I remember the gravestone. It was there for many years, but fell down in a storm a long time ago." She said something else to Emil, hopefully directions. They were.

"She told me where to look," he said. "It's not far from here."

*****

"So what's the deal with eggs?" asked Emil on our quest to dig up some gold.

"That's the other half of the equation," I answered. As we walked, we gave him the story of the eggs and the Russians. Along the way, he enlisted the aid of two men with shovels.

"Have you actually seen these Russians?" he asked.

"No," I replied, "but we know they exist. I have bullets in the side of my house to prove it, and we almost died getting here."

"I'm not questioning whether the men exist, just whether or not they are Russians."

"Based on Vlad, and the fact that he was working for another Russian, as well as Russia being the source of the eggs, we just assumed," said Sabrina.

"Also the fact that the Russian mob is known for its viciousness—at least in the movies they are," I added. Sounded kind of lame.

"Seems farfetched to me," said Emil. "Sort of like protectors of the Holy Grail being passed down from one generation to the next."

When he put it that way …

"So what are you thinking?" asked Sabrina.

"Something more modern. Closer to home."

"But who?" I asked. "Almost everyone who has come in contact with this case has been affected by these guys."

"Almost?"

"Us, Mario's men, Izzy, Russ Simpson …"

"How about the Flynns?" said Sabrina. "Izzy went to see them early on, but they gave no indication of having been threatened."

Our conversation was brought to an abrupt halt by the appearance of Mario and his men from inside a factory building we were passing.

"Shovels. That's a good sign," he said, sidling up to us. "Look," he said before we could respond, "I'm not going anywhere. I'll just keep following you. Let's just call a truce. If we find the gold, we can discuss the options then. If we don't, we'll all at least have a little more protection against those you call the Russians."

There was really nothing we could do. He was right. He wasn't about to let us out of his sight, so the show of force might dissuade the other guys.

"Fine, but don't try to screw us."

"I won't. My word is good."

Two minutes later Emil stopped.

"This is it," he announced.

It didn't look much like the painting. The scene in the painting was stark—one tree, one house, and the gravestone. In real life, eighty-five years later, the house was gone—well, almost. The foundation remained, but the walls were essentially gone, and what was left of the roof lay in the foundation. The gravestone was gone, and the one tree had become a dozen. If we hadn't been told by Eva that this was the place, we would have walked right by it.

"Where to start?" I asked.

"Do you think the mark would still be visible on the tree?" said Sabrina.

"Maybe. Let's start there."

Sabrina showed Mario and his men, as well as the two shovelers, the picture of the painting so they could see the tree.

"The famous painting," said Mario. "You were right, not much of a clue."

With many pairs of eyes, it didn't take long. It was one of Mario's men who found it. Much of the bark had grown around it, but there was no doubt about it, it was the tree in the painting. I suddenly had shivers down my spine. This was the very tree drawn by John. Eighty-five years ago, John stood in in this exact spot. All around him was the bustle of a town in all its short-lived glory. Now it was dead quiet. Could he have ever imagined that it would take so long for someone to return to the site? If he had known that, would he have bothered? Very surreal.

"Where do we dig?" asked Mario, breaking the silence.

"I guess we find the headstone. X marks the spot," I said.

The grass was about a foot high and there were various species of vegetation mixed in. Emil said something to one of the locals, who pulled out a machete from his belt and went to work on the area around the tree, hopefully making our search a bit easier. When he was done I took one of the shovels and carefully tapped the ground, hoping to hear the clank of metal hitting concrete.

Nobody said a word as I worked. At first I concentrated on the area indicated in the painting, but as time went by, my search area increased. Ten minutes passed with no clank. Then Emil asked the other local for his shovel and proceeded to tap the ground. Another ten minutes passed. Finally, Emil leaned on his shovel and held up his hand for me to stop.

"We're being too gentle."

"I didn't want to break the headstone," I said. "Not sure why."

"I can understand why," he answered. "Historically, this has great meaning for you. Having the headstone intact is important. But I just thought about what Eva said. She indicated that the headstone fell down a long time ago. So it's possible that it has years of dirt covering it. We need to be more aggressive. The shovels have to go deeper."

"Makes sense." I went back to my first search zone and pounded the shovel harder into the ground, in much the same way I would break up winter ice up north.

Within minutes I had success. When the clank came, I knew I had struck pay dirt—then again, maybe I just hit a rock.

Emil's local helpers took over, digging a wide hole to start and slowly going deeper once they had room to work. They uncovered the headstone almost immediately. They picked it up reverently and set it down at my feet. I knelt down and brushed it off, using my fingers to remove the dirt from the grooves of the RIP. The grooves weren't deep to begin with—John hadn't put a lot of work into it. The RIP was almost gone altogether. Once it was wiped off, I moved it away from the dig site.

I had to give John credit. He wasn't lazy. He dug his hole deep. A box about two-feet long, two feet deep, and a foot wide was settled about three feet from the surface. Once the box was cleared of dirt, the two shovelers reached in to pull the box out. Nothing. It wouldn't budge.

"If that's full of gold," said Mario, "it's going to take more than two people to get it out."

It became a group effort. Using branches as levers and group muscle, we tried to extract it from its resting place. Unfortunately, the box was made of a thin metal, and it hadn't stood the test of time. As we moved the box, it began to crumble.

"We'll have to open it in the hole," I said.

I jumped down and, with a fair amount of ease, ripped the top off the box. I stood there staring. Finally, somebody had told the truth. It was packed tightly with gold bars. The bars were dirty, but there was no doubt that they were real.

We had all been holding our collective breath. I could hear the exhales.

"Well that's impressive," said Emil dryly.

"Kinda," I echoed.

We took turns in the hole passing out the bars. When we were done, we had a nice pile. One of the locals had gone for a wagon. I jumped back into the hole for a last look around. No eggs. I looked up at Sabrina. She didn't seem all that disappointed. She reached a hand in to help me up.

"Hey," she whispered. "Don't look so sad. We just solved an amazing mystery. We'll save the eggs for another day."

Then it hit me just how much she was right. What we had just accomplished *was* nothing short of amazing. However, the joy was short-lived.

The local with the wagon arrived a few minutes later. It was like a garden wagon, but slightly bigger—probably something they had used in the factory. Once it was stacked high with the gold, we began our journey back to Emil's house to figure out what to do with it.

Up to that point, we had been very aware of Mario and his

men, but for a few minutes our attention was elsewhere. It was the moment Mario was waiting for. Unnoticed by the rest of us, they had fallen back a few steps and had fanned out behind us.

"New plan," announced Mario, stopping us dead in our tracks. I turned. All three had their guns out. "We're taking the gold down to the dock. You can help us fill our boat."

I was totally disgusted with myself. "You've got to be shitting me."

"Afraid not. I gave you the chance to split the gold, but you got all noble on me. So now you get nothing."

"I thought you didn't kill people," said Sabrina. She seemed very calm. But again, she was dealing with an element she had a lot of experience with.

"I lied." Seeing the doubt in her face, he said, "You are more than welcome to test it out."

We didn't need to. At that moment all hell broke loose.

# Chapter 34

The first bullet took out the man to Mario's left. One moment he was pointing his gun at us and the next he was crumpled on the ground, half his face blown away. Nothing registered at first and no one moved. But when the second shot came and the goon to Mario's right went down, we all dove for cover. I landed on top of Sabrina behind the wagon.

In retrospect, I guess we knew this was how it was going to end. It began with violence, so of course it would have to end that way. For the longest time we thought the showdown was going to be with Mario. But when the realization hit that there was a third party involved—more dangerous by far than Mario—it became clear that they were going to be a force to reckon with. We had seen the results of their handiwork in the States, and their vicious attack on the river showed them to be dangerous and determined. The question was why? We still didn't know who they were, what they wanted, or where they came from. Mario's motivations were clear; he wanted the treasure. These people were different. Killing seemed to be their only goal.

But it was all moot now. Who cared what anyone's reasons were. All we were trying to do was to stay alive. Another shot rang out, and the bullet hit the wagon. More specifically, it clipped the corner of a bar of gold, showering us with little chunks of gold.

"I've got to move," said Sabrina from under me. I lifted my body enough for her to move, but not high enough to make myself a target. She squirmed a bit and finally broke free. Lying next to me, there was just enough cover from the wagon to keep us from being exposed to the shooter, or shooters.

"You okay?" I whispered to her.

"Ask me again if we live through this."

"Everyone okay?" I said in a louder voice.

"Okay here," announced Emil. I looked around. He was hiding behind a substantial rock with one of the locals. I could see the other local behind a crumbling house foundation. I couldn't see Mario.

"How about you, Mario?"

"I'm okay." I couldn't see him, but he was close by.

"I have an idea," I said. "Why don't you take a walk down the road. Then we can see where the shots are coming from."

"Fuck you."

"Just an idea."

"Nice that you can maintain your sense of humor," whispered Sabrina.

"Are you kidding? I'm scared to death. It's either that or I faint from fear. Besides, who said I was joking?"

Another shot came and hit the dirt in front of the wagon, pebbles exploding in my face. I reached up and, one by one, lifted down a few of the gold bars and stacked them in front of us under the wagon.

"Just a little extra protection," I explained.

Sabrina just nodded. She was busy trying to extract her revolver from her pants. Finally free, she checked to see that it was loaded.

"Good idea," I said, and grabbed my own. After all this time, I still wasn't used to it. We were in a bad spot and I wasn't sure how much help it was going to be, but it provided a little comfort.

Another shot, followed immediately by the roar of Emil's shotgun. I heard a scream from across the road.

"You got one," I exclaimed.

"I'm sure I just winged him," said Emil. "I think I'm too far for the shotgun to be very effective."

It wasn't. The shooter, angry now, let out a barrage of bullets from his automatic weapon toward Emil's hiding place. I could see Emil crouched behind the rock, covering his face. Sabrina nudged me and pointed. Five feet behind us was a ditch on the side of the road. It would offer much more protection than the wagon. I nodded. She counted down on her fingers from three. As she hit 'one', we rolled. As we rolled, two other shooters began their assault, the ground exploding around us.. We fell into the ditch and I asked Sabrina if she was okay.

"I am. You?"

"Yes." Not the total truth. I was bleeding from my upper arm and it hurt like the devil. I was either grazed by a bullet or by a rock kicked up by a bullet. I knew there wasn't a slug in me, but it didn't stop it from hurting.

The rain of bullets stopped.

"Give it up," called out a voice directly across the road from us, somewhere in the trees.

Well, that put to rest one theory. There was nothing Russian about that voice. It was as American as mine.

We all stayed silent. I looked back at Emil. He looked okay, but he must've been wondering at that point why in the world he got involved with us.

"Is that gold in the wagon?" the same person called out.

Silence.

"Let me put it a different way. I *know* you've got gold in the wagon. I'll make a deal with you. Walk away and leave the gold and you'll live."

"Keep him talking," whispered Sabrina. "I'll see if I can get a bead on him." She found a space between two small rocks at the top of the ditch and took aim into the woods on the other side of the road.

"If we try to walk away, you'll kill us," I called out.

"You have my word."

"Yeah, right."

"We don't have anything against you."

"Then why have you been trying to kill us?"

"Strictly business."

"What do you mean, 'strictly business'?"

"We were hired for a job. Simple as that. We were promised a lot of money. You give us the gold, that'll pay us a lot more than we would have gotten. In other words, give us the gold, we don't need you anymore. You can walk away."

"There are no eggs here." I figured his reaction would tell me something.

"No what?" Well, I got my answer. They knew nothing about the eggs, so they weren't there to retrieve them.

"Who's paying you?" I asked, trying a different tack.

"An interested party."

"Not good enough."

"I really don't think you are in a position to demand answers."

"I have some time on my hands."

"If ..." Sabrina's gun went off. I rolled away a couple of feet. I would have liked to think it was the force of the blast that sent me rolling, but of course, that was impossible. It was just the natural reaction to having an explosion go off six inches from my ear. Hanging around with her, I was going to need a hearing aid mighty soon.

I rolled back, my ear ringing.

"Hit anything?" I asked.

"The speaker let out an 'umph' when I hit him. You didn't hear it?"

"My right ear was otherwise engaged."

I heard a muffled "shit" come from the woods. I couldn't tell if he was muffled or if my ear made it muffled. Either way, Sabrina had hit him. Sadly, it wasn't a kill shot.

"That was a mistake," came his voice, less muffled now.

I determined that we had three shooters, which matched up with what we saw on the river. Two of them were hurting and really pissed now.

There was no more talking. For the next fifteen minutes nothing was said from the other side of the road. Everyone seemed okay on our side—except for the two dead guys, of course. I hadn't yet located Mario though. Of little concern at this point.

Every once in a while a bullet would come flying our way, but we were all pretty well hidden.

It was a stand-off. We couldn't go anywhere. Beyond all of our hiding places was a fair amount of open space. If we tried to escape, we'd be mowed down in no time. On the other side of the road they could certainly leave if they wanted. They could always try to eliminate us a later. However, the lure of the gold was too strong. They knew that now would be the best time to get it. Once we reached the town and the boat, things would become more complicated.

No one was going anywhere.

They tried another volley of automatic weapon fire—ammunition must not have been a problem. Bullets spat all around us.

And then we heard different guns go off—guns that had a familiar ring. There were about six shots. We heard two men cry out in pain. It was followed my some moaning. And then a voice called out—a voice we knew—"Senhor Honeycutt, it is okay now."

Paulo!

Sabrina and I stiffly stood up and climbed out of the ditch. I saw Emil and the two locals emerge from their hiding spots. Finally, Mario rose from the ditch—the same ditch we were in, only thirty feet further down.

Sabrina saw the blood on my arm and let out a little gasp.

"You've been hit!"

"No, it's okay. Just a flesh wound." That always sounded brave when they said it in the movies. I thought I did it well.

Paulo emerged from the woods, a big smile on his face.

Sabrina went up to him and gave him a big hug. "You saved our lives."

Paulo turned five shades of red, but loved every second of the hug.

"I think two are dead," he said to me when he had recovered. "One is alive. He will not die."

"That was dangerous for you," I said. "Thank you."

"We heard shots from the boat. Much shooting. We knew it

was trouble for you." He held up his rifle with a smile. "See? It comes in handy again."

We followed him into the woods, where Luis was standing over the one I had been speaking with, judging by his location. He was hurt—probably by Sabrina's bullet—and was sitting against a rock. Blood was running down his arm from a shoulder wound, but he didn't seem to be in any immediate danger.

I was about to ask him a question when I heard the familiar sound of flesh on flesh behind me, and then a grunt. I turned to find Mario lying on the ground, his face bloody and his glasses broken. Standing over him was Sabrina.

"You deserve a lot worse than that," she spoke calmly. Never cross Sabrina.

"I wasn't really going to hurt any of you. I just wanted my share of the gold."

"Your share?" I asked. "What makes you think you have a share in this?"

"My great-grandfather was involved in this, just like yours. I deserve as much as you."

"Which is exactly zero," I replied. "I told you before that we're not keeping any of it. Just because your great-grandfather stole it doesn't mean you have any claim to it. He stole it. It wasn't his in the first place."

"Yes, but the people he stole it from had stolen it themselves."

"Shut-up, Mario. You have no say an any of this."

He stayed on the ground nursing his face. Sabrina was rubbing her knuckles, but had a look of satisfaction in her eyes.

I turned toward the wounded assailant.

"Now you're going to do some talking."

"Fuck off. I'm not saying a word."

"Really? You really want to go that route? Think about it. You're here alone in the middle of the Amazon. No colleagues, no guns, and you're wounded. You screwed up the job you were hoping to get paid for, so you can forget about that. You are totally on your own. The people of Fordlandia don't like you and we don't like you. We can make you disappear. You've tried to kill us numerous times; you killed Sabrina's sister; you killed an innocent man in Nebraska; and you killed a total of four of Mario's men. Everyone who has any connection to this you've either killed or attempted to kill, except the Flynns, and they were probably next on your list."

Lying in the ditch had given me time to think, and I was beginning to make some connections. Something Mario had said about Flynn being the only person who seemed unaffected to that point, as well as some things Mikey had said in his book were beginning to bother me. So I took a chance throwing Flynn's name out there.

But it had the desired effect. He had a momentary look of surprise as I said Flynn's name, then it vanished. But it was enough for me.

"You wouldn't leave me out here," he said. "I know your kind."

"You don't know my kind at all," I answered. "Someone once said to me that to protect yourself, you have to be willing to kill your attacker." I gave a sidelong glance at Sabrina. "Trust me, I would have no trouble killing you. You give us the information we want and I will make sure you get some medical help."

"But you'll turn me over to the police."

"Of course. But at least you'll be alive. And somehow I doubt if prison would be a new experience for you. So it's your choice. And unlike you or Mario over there, I keep my word."

There was silence while he considered his options, but he really had no choice, and he knew it.

"We were hired by Bill Flynn and his wife. He wanted you and your girlfriend gone, her sister gone, Guidry gone, and anyone else who knew too much gone. He didn't tell me why, but he said he wanted the slate completely wiped clean. And he paid us well. The guy had money."

He grimaced. The pain was beginning to set in. "Our instructions were clear. Everyone connected to this thing was supposed to die."

# Chapter 35

Bill and Amanda Flynn. The two who wanted nothing to do with the past, who gave me Mikey's book with a good riddance, and who seemed so relieved when they found out they could finally turn in the stolen art. They were the masterminds behind this? Of all the lies we'd had to sort through, theirs was the most convincing.

One of the locals brought a bandage and some antiseptic and Emil worked on the man's arm while he talked. By now, most of the population of Fordlandia—a couple of dozen or so—was observing the scene.

He didn't have a lot of information that was useful, but he was able to fill in a little of Bill Flynn's history. He had been working on and off for Flynn for a few years, "taking care of things that needed taking care of." Although Flynn had never seen the inside of a jail cell, he was well-known to law enforcement and had been suspected of running drugs for years. Foley, the wounded man, confirmed that all those suspicions were true. Foley said that Flynn came from a long line of crooks dating back to the beginning of the 20$^{th}$ century.

"Did he say why he needed you?" I asked.

"Naw, that wasn't how it was done. He just gave me an assignment and I did it. No explanations." Then he added, "I think this one had something to do with his father. The old man died about six months ago and Flynn was real distracted about something right after his death. When this chick showed up at his door asking questions about something, that's when he called me. I was supposed to kill her and you and Guidry. It was supposed to be an easy job. But then your girlfriend came on the scene and you started to travel around asking questions. He was obsessed that anyone connected with this should die. Was it all about gold?"

He didn't rate an answer, so I ignored it.

Foley had nothing else of consequence to say, so we sat him on the wagon with the gold and made our way to the dock. I was trying to figure out how this was all going to be taken care of logistically, but Emil saved me the trouble.

"I have a fast boat," he said. "I can take Foley to Santarém and turn him over to the police. I know a lot of government officials there—the advantages of coming from a wealthy family. If you want to give me names of whoever they need to contact in the states, I can give them all the information. I can take you too. I'm sure you're anxious to get back and to get word to the authorities up there. I can get you to Santarém in a third of the time it would take Luis and Paulo."

We agreed that it was probably a good idea for us to move quickly, so we took him up on his offer.

"What about the gold?" he asked.

"We don't want to put more responsibility on your shoulders, but do you have any suggestions?"

"There are a lot of organizations here that could use the money. A lot of poverty. I can find out the names of some reputable gold dealers and distribute the cash. I'd give some to the residents here, as well."

"You wouldn't mind doing all that?" asked Sabrina.

"I have a lot of time on my hands. It's the least I can do."

"We want three of the bars to go to Luis and Paulo. After

all, they did save our lives."

"I'll have them meet me in Santarém. By the time they get there I should be able to cash in three of them."

"What about Mario?" asked Sabrina.

"Yes, what about Mario?" said Emil, looking at me.

"He's almost more trouble than he's worth," I answered. "Other than to orchestrate some minor crimes in the U.S., he really hasn't done anything of consequence. He's lost four of his men. My suggestion is that we leave him here and let him find his own way home. I'm sure there will be another boat of tourists coming through here soon. He can catch a ride with them."

"Works for me," said Sabrina. "The less time we have to spend with him the better."

Once all the arrangements were set, we said our goodbyes to Luis and Paulo. They were sad that we weren't going to accompany them home, but they seemed to understand. Emil stood by to translate anything Paulo seemed to miss. We paid them the rest of what we owed them, and then sprang the news on them of the gold bars. Paulo's eyes lit up and he hugged Sabrina—funny how he never hugged me. He then told Luis, who had a typical Luis response, who just nodded his head wisely. Obviously it would take a lot more than that to rattle him.

Mario was upset that he wasn't included in Emil's boat, but once we explained that if he came he would be turned over to the police in Santarém, he wisely chose to wait for the next boat.

Paulo hugged Sabrina a half a dozen more times before we left, but finally we were on our way. We watched Fordlandia grow more distant as we headed upriver. We each tried to say something significant about our time there, but no words came, so we just sat in silence. It was going to be a while before we would be able to accurately describe the uniqueness of what we had just experienced.

When we arrived in Santarém, the police were waiting for us at the dock, courtesy of a phone call Emil made from his satellite phone. There was also an ambulance for Foley and me. Emil had patched up my arm, but we all thought it prudent to have it checked out at the hospital. Meanwhile, Sabrina called Marsh in Boston and laid out the whole situation. She brought up the eggs, Flynn, Foley, and other items we hadn't told him before—either because we withheld it or didn't know it at the time. She told me afterward that he was naturally pissed that this was the first he had heard of much of it. He said he would be waiting for us at the gate at Logan when we arrived in Boston. I was not looking forward to that encounter.

He was not familiar with Flynn, but would put in a call to the Vermont State Police. However, it was decided that nothing would be done until after we arrived. Foley's sketchy information wasn't going to be enough to hold him and might just scare him away. Meanwhile, Marsh was going to see the District Attorney about getting extradition orders to bring Foley to Boston.

Saying goodbye to Emil was hard. He had been the biggest surprise in our quest. I think we were both a bit envious of his total freedom in life. Granted, I think he was bored and lonely at times, and in all honesty, I didn't see him staying in Fordlandia much longer. It was too remote, even for him. However, he would always make the most of his freedom. I had a feeling he would always find himself in interesting places and situations.

We all hugged and we thanked him for everything so many times, he finally told us to get lost. With one last round of hugs, we took a taxi to the airport, preparing to leave Brazil behind.

*****

We flew out of Santarém that night and arrived in Boston late the next afternoon, bedraggled and exhausted. Marsh, as promised, met us at the gate and escorted us back to my house in East Boston. He accompanied us up to my apartment and we filled him in on all that we could until we couldn't keep our eyes open any longer. We planned to meet the next day at his office to plot our course of action. I had a feeling I knew what was coming.

Marsh also told us that he had heard back from the Vermont State Police. Flynn was, in fact, on their radar and had been for quite some time for a variety of activities, but they had nothing tangible to charge him with. He was also told by the D.A. in Boston that despite Foley having killed two men in Brazil, he didn't see any problem getting him back into the states to face charges.

Mo and Seymour—who actually ventured from his apartment—each stopped by to see us while Marsh was there. Both looked relieved to see us back in one piece. We promised to fill them in as soon as we could.

We went to sleep that night wiped out but troubled. We sensed that the next day was going to bring movement of some type. But would it bring closure?

# Chapter 36

We knocked on the Flynns' door. I adjusted the wire attached to my body. This was another first in my life. I seemed to be having a lot of them these days. And I wasted ten years working in that hell hole?

I tried not to glance over my shoulder to confirm the presence of the Vermont State Police and Marsh. I didn't want to look nervous, which I was, or give away the plan, which it would. Sabrina took my hand. She sensed my nervousness. I'm sure she was not particularly calm, but she was better at projecting it.

Amanda Flynn wasn't as good at it as Sabrina. She opened the door and let out a little "ooh," before recovering. Well, that told us all we needed to know. They didn't expect to ever see us again.

"May we come in?" asked Sabrina sweetly.

Okay, so Amanda hadn't actually recovered. She didn't say a word. She was the deer, we were the headlights. Finally, she looked over her shoulder and yelled for Bill. His reaction was almost as good as his wife's. The beer he was holding slipped out of his hand, but he caught it before it hit the ground.

"I thought we were done with you." Did that have a double meaning? "You said we wouldn't see you again."

"I notice you haven't turned in the paintings yet," I answered.

"Are you my mother? We haven't had time to do it. It's none of your business."

"It kinda is. Actually, it's all our business, made more so by your attempts to kill us."

"What?" Flynn drew the word out in a high-pitched voice. "What the fuck?"

"Cut the acting. Foley gave you up."

"Who's Foley?" Flynn was game, but the sweat was beginning to well up on his forehead.

"Just the guy responsible for the deaths of at least a half dozen people. And since he worked for you, it makes the two of you responsible. That's life in prison."

"I don't know the guy. I have no idea what you're talking about."

"I've got to admit," I said, "you're good. You had us fooled. We were actually appreciative of your help. Giving us Mikey's book was a stroke of genius. It put us in the middle of nowhere so Foley could kill us, while at the same time allowing us to dig up the gold. Was the book even real? Did Mikey even write it?"

"It was real. But we had no idea what was in it."

"Uh huh."

"Seriously, I don't know this guy Foley."

"Flynn, it's over. We found the gold, Foley is in the hospital in Brazil and is going to be extradited up here to testify against you, we're still alive and Mario is still alive."

"Mario who..." He started the sentence but didn't seem to have the energy left to finish it. He finally said, "You can't prove any of this. Foley's obviously a crook. He's not credible. Other than him, you have no proof. It's his word against mine."

"And ours. If you tell us where the eggs are, we can try to have them go easier on you."

"That's too funny. Your word against ours. Do you have

any idea how deep in this shit you are? And to anyone listening—yeah, I know you're wearing a wire—I'd watch this guy if I were you. I have no idea where the eggs are, and that's the truth. But you do."

"I do?"

"Mikey was a mean son of a bitch, but he didn't have the eggs. Your great-grandfather did, which means he passed them down to your grandfather, your father, and now you. The only person who can possibly know where they are is you. You've figured out everything else so far, so you must have figured out where the eggs are."

I looked over at Sabrina. This wasn't going as well as we hoped. In fact, it wasn't going well at all. Bill Flynn was calling into question my honesty at a time when he should be cracking under the pressure and admitting his guilt. No wonder the police hadn't been able to make anything on him stick. We were going to have to try a different avenue. But what?

Sabrina took over.

"So you're telling us that you had absolutely nothing to do with Foley and his henchmen? Even though he identified you by name in the middle of the Amazon jungle? Is that what you're saying?"

"Yes, that's what I'm saying. Wow, you're swift."

Uh oh. Obviously Bill Flynn had a short memory. Had he really forgotten that you just didn't do that with Sabrina? Apparently he had.

Sabrina's face clouded over. She took a step toward him. He involuntarily took a step back and tripped over a chair, landing flat on his back. It was all I could do not to laugh. He was done for. He clambered to his feet, trying to retain some sense of pride. It didn't work. The moment he was up, she stuck a finger in his chest. She must have got him in his solar plexus, because he doubled over.

"I write mysteries for a living," she said. "If I wrote someone as stupid as you into a book, no one would believe it. You don't get it, do you? You're finished. They will find the connection between you and Foley. They're not idiots. Your best defense is to say that you did hire Foley, but it was only to follow us, not kill us."

"You do realize they are listening to you."

"So? I just want them to arrest you. I don't care what you confess to and what you don't. I just want you out of circulation. We're tired of looking over our shoulders."

He was cooked and he knew it. He probably knew it the minute we came to the door. He looked over at Amanda, who didn't say anything. One would expect that at this point in the game, she would be weeping, or at least have tears in her eyes. Nope. If anything, she looked defiant. She was definitely as much a part of this as he was.

"Yeah, we hired Foley," Bill finally said. When she heard *we,* Amanda snapped her head up and looked at Bill with venom. Ah, the sudden end of a beautiful marriage.

"What do you mean *we,*" she snarled. I had never actually heard someone snarl something before, but there was no doubt about this one. "This was *you,* you and your fucking family. If your father hadn't shown you Mikey's stuff, none of this ever would have happened."

"You mean the book you gave us?" I asked.

"No, something different. Some of Mikey's papers," said Bill, a little shell-shocked at Amanda's sudden desertion.

"Was the book real?"

"It was real. It just wasn't true. Most of it, anyway. It was a novel based on the events as he chose to relate them."

"So you've known about this for a long time?"

"Nah," said Bill finally. "I didn't know anything about it until about a year ago, right before my father died."

I had to give Marsh and the other police credit, they didn't barge in. Flynn was confessing—confessing knowing full well that he was being taped. They must have figured that since we were on a roll, there was no reason to interrupt.

"What I said before was true. Mikey was kind of dismissed in our family. As far as we all knew, he wrote this book that sucked, and that was about it. His real papers he must have packed into a box. I don't think his son—my grandfather—knew anything about it. My father discovered the papers a few years ago, but didn't tell me about them. I think he was going to look for the treasure himself, prick that he was. Then he got himself thrown in prison for murder. Only when he realized he was dying and never getting out did he finally tell me. He died a month later. The papers made it clear where the treasure was. Well, not the exact location, but I knew it was in Fordlandia. I was just preparing to go down there when your sister looked me up. So I asked Foley to keep an eye on her. I didn't know he killed her."

Wow, that was lame. But, if he wanted to stick to that story, we were okay with it. We just wanted Mikey's story. The police could get the murder confession from him later. As it turned out, however, that wasn't necessary. There's nothing like a scorned wife to set the record straight. She had heard *we* one-time too many.

"I had nothing to do with any of this," she said, almost shouting it. "Whoever is out there listening, Bill ordered Foley to kill the woman. I shoulda called the police, but he's my husband. I couldn't turn him in."

She was smart. She knew she was facing jail time. To go in as an accessory would be better than going in for first-degree murder. Bill wasn't having any of it, though.

"You bitch! You're the one who suggested it." He turned to me. "Don't believe her."

I decided that it would be a good time for the police to make an appearance, and they didn't disappoint. Marsh and a half a dozen state cops came through the door, read them their rights, and cuffed them. I asked Marsh if they could wait before transporting them to see if we could get more of the story.

"You two have been a pain in the ass from the beginning, withholding information from me, but you did come through in the end." He turned to the Flynns. "They're going to ask some questions. You have rights. You don't have to answer them."

But answer them they did. Fueled mostly from her contempt for Bill—or for other conniving reasons—Amanda was happy to talk. This meant that Bill had to defend himself and implicate Amanda. So between them, we got the story.

They did, in fact, contract with Foley to kill Izzy. From his father and Mikey's real writings, Bill already knew most of the story. He knew about the gold and that John had hidden it somewhere in Fordlandia. He even knew about the painting; Mikey had described it, not that it helped much. They knew Izzy had talked to Mario, so he had to be eliminated as well. But Mario escaped the first attempt on his life and went into hiding. When they found out that there was another party involved, they came after us, missing me in front of my house. Russ Simpson became a casualty of war when they found out he had the painting. Once they had the painting they—or Bill alone, if you believed Amanda—prepared to go to Brazil. Meanwhile, Foley tracked us to Miami and waited around the airport, not believing that Miami was our real destination. They still had the kill order and made the attempt on the river. Once that failed, Bill—or Bill and Amanda, if you believed Bill—instructed them to wait and see if we found the treasure before killing us.

"So Mikey wasn't the innocent bumpkin he led us to believe in the book," I said.

"Hell, no," answered Bill. "He was a crazy-ass loon. My father said he was the most evil man he had ever met. That's why we all thought his book sucked, because we knew it was garbage."

"Why didn't Mikey go back for the treasure?" Sabrina asked.

"At first, or so the story goes, he was too busy building up his business—drugs, prostitution, the usual—to be bothered. Plus, things were still too hot down there for him to show his face. He did try ransoming some of the paintings from the museum, but that blew up in his face."

"But he obviously didn't die, like my great-grandfather thought," I said.

"Nah. He tried to ransom the paintings because his business was falling apart. He had pissed off too many people. He did get shot—probably where the rumor started—but he escaped to Vermont. The bullet lodged in his leg and he developed gangrene. Lost his leg. From then on he wasn't in the best of health. I think he finally lost interest in the treasure."

"And what about the eggs?"

"Those fucking eggs. I don't even know what they were. He just kept talking about the eggs in his writings. Something real valuable."

"Did Tony bring them back?"

"Hell, no. Mikey did. Tony was a nothing. He made him sound big in his book, but in reality, Tony was a two-bit thug. He never amounted to anything and got himself killed a few years later. You want the eggs? You find 'em. He gave 'em to your great-grandfather. Things were getting hot for him, so he gave 'em to Bruce to hold. He had no idea Bruce was going to take off with them. So your great-grandfather was as much of a crook as mine."

"Yeah, but the nice thing is, it stopped with him, unlike your family."

"Why did Mikey even write the novel? It may not have been true, but it had a lot of truth to it. He named Fordlandia. Wasn't he afraid someone might see it as true and go after the treasure?"

"He was dying. He wrote the book in 1958 and died in 1960. He was in bad health. I don't think he cared. He wanted to write a novel and his life was the only thing he could write about. So he turned it into his novel."

The cops were getting restless to move.

"One last question," I asked. "Did you kill my father?"

"Your father?"

"In Northampton."

"Honeycutt. Northampton." His eyes lit up. "The college

professor who was screwing his student? That was your father?"

I nodded.

"Sorry pal. He did that to himself. I didn't even know he existed."

I believed him. My father was just a victim of the Honeycutt curse.

"But he knew about Mikey and the book. How?"

"You can find anything online these days. Maybe he just followed the people involved and came upon the book. You'd have to ask him."

I jumped at him, intending to beat the snot out of him, but he was saved by Marsh, who restrained me.

"Forget about him, Honeycutt. He's not worth it."

The police took away their catch. Marsh stayed behind and talked to us by our car. The crowd of neighbors who had come out in force when they saw the police cars were still there. A couple of them pointed and I heard someone say "Sabrina." Sabrina was getting fidgety. Definitely time to go.

"Well, we had our moments," Marsh was saying, "but it all worked out in the end."

"Hey, in the Flynn's basement are some paintings stolen from the Brooklyn Museum back in 1933. They'd probably be happy to get them back."

"One would think. Still going to look for the eggs?"

Sabrina turned to me. "Are we?"

"Don't need to."

She raised an eyebrow.

"I know where they are."

# Chapter 37

We were back in Fairfield at the home of Harry and Edna Simpson. We knocked and waited for Harry to shuffle his way to the door. He opened it, took one look at me, then at Sabrina, and his face broke into a wide smile.

"Miss Spencer! How nice to see you again."

Invisible again.

"Edna, come quick. Miss Spencer is back."

Come quick? Yeah, right. However, Edna must have been working out. At the mention of Sabrina's name, she set all kinds of records making it to the door.

"Sabrina!" She put her hand over her mouth. "I'm sorry, you don't mind me calling you Sabrina, do you?"

"As long as I can call you Edna."

Edna giggled, turned red, then excused herself as she headed for the bathroom.

Nothing was said until she returned, at which time Sabrina said, "You remember Del?"

Edna gave me a quick glance, nodded, then turned her attention back to the real star. "I was so sorry to hear all about your story. That must have been terrible. Imagine my surprise when that famous reporter came to my house. I guess she heard in the local newspaper that I had met you. That was okay that I talked about you, wasn't it?"

It wasn't, but Sabrina was gracious. "Just fine, Edna."

"I was sorry to hear about your nephew," I said. Leave it to me to bring up the dark topic.

"No loss," said Harry.

"Harry!"

"Sorry, Edna, but it's true."

"You were right," I said. "He wasn't a good person, but he didn't deserve to die. I'm afraid it was because of us that he died. For that I feel bad."

"Did you find the painting you were looking for?" Evidently it was time to move on from Russ.

"We did, and it helped us solve the mystery, except for one last thing."

"Do you need to go down to the basement again?"

"We do, if you don't mind. Won't take long. I know exactly where to go."

"Be our guest."

After a few more niceties, we descended into the fifty years of clutter they called a basement.

"Now are you going to tell me?" All I had told Sabrina was that I was pretty sure the eggs were in the basement. Why I wanted to keep it a surprise, I'm not sure. Maybe I was just proud of my deduction and wanted to present the grand reveal. Who knows, but to give her credit, she played along. Although, if it wasn't there, I was going to look pretty foolish. But looking foolish in front of Sabrina didn't bother me.

"When we were down here before, what did we see?"

"Dust."

"Besides that." We reached the corner with the Simpson Gallery items. "What is out of place here?"

She looked at the labeled boxes—the two opened *Paintings* boxes, the *Sculptures* box, *Records* box and *Christmas Decorations* box. And then I saw the light go on in her head.

"Of course," she said, "Christmas decorations."

"You've just gone out of business and you are storing the items not picked up by people. What possible use would you have to save Christmas decorations? If Bruce felt it was safe enough to hide the painting there, why not the eggs? This Simpson guy must have been someone he knew—from his childhood, maybe?"

I reached in and pulled out the box. It was about two feet long, two feet deep, and two feet wide.

"Drumroll, please."

The tape had long since disintegrated, so I just opened the lid. Tinsel. Well, that was a little disheartening. I pulled away the tinsel to reveal Christmas ornaments—brightly painted bulbs of all shapes and sizes. Carefully, one by one we lifted them out of the box. At the very bottom were three items individually wrapped in paper. I looked over at Sabrina. I was having trouble breathing. No wonder, I was holding my breath.

I picked up the first one. It was heavy. Definitely not a Christmas bulb. I unwrapped it. A Faberge Egg! There was no doubt about it. It was gold, with an ornate design along the top and a ring of jewels around the middle. It sat in a small, square, jewel-encrusted base.

"Oh ... my ... God!" said Sabrina.

We opened the other two. Equally as ornate, but very different from each other. We knew we were in the presence of a great historic find—not to mention a fortune. Before we flew out, I had seen online that one of the eggs from the same collection had recently been found at a flea market and had sold for a reported thirty million dollars.

We just sat and stared at them. Finally, Sabrina said, "I

wonder why Simpson didn't sell them."

"Two guesses. First, if he and Bruce were indeed friends, he probably felt a certain loyalty to him. Bruce may have also stressed the danger that came with the painting and the eggs. Second, it was the height of the depression. If you couldn't eat them, eggs were of little use. Who had the money to buy them? Especially, who would he know who could buy them?"

"Technically, that was three guesses."

I gave her a playful tap. "What do we do with them?" I asked.

"They're not really ours, but since we found them, I guess it's up to us to figure that out. I'd rather see them go to a museum than a private collector."

"I agree. Neither of us needs the money. In truth though, we did find them in Harry and Edna's house, so they kind of belong to them."

"I think we can convince them to do the right thing," said Sabrina. I was sure she could convince them to do anything. "No matter what they do, they'll end up rich."

We wrapped them back up in the paper and put them back in the box, sans the other bulbs. Then we took them up to show Edna and Harry. Edna made another trip to the bathroom while Harry sat in a chair fanning himself. They informed us immediately that they trusted Sabrina to do the right thing. Meaning they didn't trust me? This invisible thing was getting old.

*****

Needless to say, the art world was set on its ear. Bestselling mystery author Sabrina Spencer and friend solved not one, but two mysteries. The Brooklyn Museum was getting back its stolen paintings and the world now knew the fate of three of the missing Faberge Eggs. Harry and Edna became quite wealthy overnight and were the toast of Fairfield and beyond.

Sabrina's publisher offered her a seven figure advance for the true-life account of our adventures. She insisted that it be co-written by me—we knew who would do the actual writing part of it—and that half the advance would be mine. I decided I didn't have to look for another job. My invisibility was ending, as well.

Sabrina and I moved into my father's house, but I couldn't bear the thought of leaving my apartment in East Boston, so I contacted the owners and convinced them to let me buy the building. Offering them above market value helped clinch the deal. I kept my apartment as our city retreat. Sabrina had developed a nice relationship with Mo, so I had a feeling we would be spending a fair amount of time there. Since I now owned the building and didn't need the money, I informed Mo and Seymour that they could live there rent-free. Seymour actually smiled. Scary.

*****

We were lying in bed in our new house about a month after the announcement of the finding of the eggs and the resulting furor. It was still my father's furniture (except for the bed and the couch in the den, both of which we replaced immediately), as we hadn't had time to shop for anything. Somehow we hadn't been discovered there by the media. Some of the neighbors knew who we were, but being a neighborhood of academics, they had little use for reporters tramping all over their yards, so they kept quiet.

Sabrina had just turned down her 52nd interview request and was quickly developing a reputation as the new J.D. Salinger.

"I guess I failed," she said.

"Failed what?"

"My 'trust' class. You did great in your class. You discovered the secret of self-defense. I didn't learn to trust at all. If anything, I want to back ever further away from people."

"Maybe my teacher was better than yours."

"You were great. I just didn't want to embrace it."

"It's going to take time. And it doesn't mean that when you learn it you will suddenly want to do interviews. You may never want to, but that has nothing to do with trust. Look at the sincere people you encountered—people who weren't out for themselves: The Simpsons, Emil, Luis and Paulo, even all the people on the flight to Miami. Those people were protecting you. They weren't doing it for what they could gain. They were honestly moved by your story and saw those photographers for the parasites they were. They came to your aid honestly."

"They did, and I appreciate all of the 'real' people we met. But I'm just not..."

"...Ready yet," I finished. "I understand. Despite my progress, I don't feel I'm ready yet either in my training. We just have to accept every little step we can."

She leaned over and kissed me and we made love slowly and tenderly. There was no clinging on her part, no holding on for dear life. It was love and it was trust. She may not have seen it, and maybe she never would, but as far as I was concerned, she had come a long way.

Afterward, with Sabrina sleeping in my arms, I thought about my family. I finally felt that I knew them. I didn't like any of them, but I knew them. In every case, lies and bad decisions had destroyed them. And not just my family. Sabrina's family, Bill Flynn's family, and even Mario's family, were all affected by the greedy actions of a group of men 85 years earlier.

I'll never know what my father was trying to tell me on his deathbed, but it had become moot. I was never going to follow in the footsteps of my ancestors. And the proof of that was the woman lying by my side.

The End

# AUTHOR'S NOTE

Several real historic places and events are referenced in **All Lies**. 1) Fordlandia is a real town and a fascinating footnote in American history. I have tried to be as accurate as possible in my brief retelling of the story of Fordlandia, but in the effort to tell a good fictional story, some of the facts may have become a little smudged; 2) The Brooklyn Museum heist was also a real event, and is still considered an unsolved mystery to this day. the *New York Times* article referenced in **All Lies** was the exact article published in 1933 after the heist; 3) The story of the stolen Faberge Eggs is also true, including the tidbit about one being recently uncovered at a flea market and subsequently sold for more than $30 million. 4) The first entry in Ray Worth's log was taken verbatim from my father's log (a bombardier on a B-24). One other entry was paraphrased from his navigator's log.

# ABOUT THE AUTHOR

Andrew Cunningham is the author of the Amazon bestselling thriller **Wisdom Spring** and the mystery **All Lies**, as well as the post-apocalyptic *Eden Rising Trilogy*: **Eden Rising**, **Eden Lost**, and **Eden's Legacy** (due December 2015). He is currently working on a disaster novel set on Cape Cod. As A.R. Cunningham, he has written the *Arthur MacArthur* series of mysteries for children. Born in England, Andrew was a long-time resident of Cape Cod. He now lives with his wife, Charlotte, in Florida. Please visit his website at *arcnovels.com*, and his Facebook page at *Author Andrew Cunningham*.

Made in the USA
Charleston, SC
07 February 2015